THE CHUPACABRA
AND
THE BAT RASTARD

MARK D. TROLLINGER

TABLE OF CONTENTS

Published by Myths and Malts Productions Chandler, AZ

The book is a work of fiction. The author drew the characters, incidents, and dialogue from his imagination and did not construe them as real. Some events from the original cryptid sightings have been retold, modernized, and at times, fictionalized.

This book includes the use of trademarks for realism. Product names, logos, brands, and other trademarks featured or referred to within this manuscript are the property of their respective trademark holders.

These trademark holders are not affiliated with the author or any of the author's representatives. They do not sponsor or endorse the contents, materials, or processes discussed within this book.

Drink responsibly and do not drink and drive

If you or a loved one need help with an alcohol problem, please reach out to SAMHSA's National Helpline: 1-800-662-HELP (4357).

The author will donate 15% of the sales from this book to the San Antonio Zoological Society. I will make donations quarterly. See the *Field Notes* section at the back of the book for more details.

Cover by Nyssa Iniguez

Library of Congress Control Number: 2023905658

First Edition, first printing

Printed in the United States of America

ISBN: 979-8-9880828-0-4

also by Mark Trollinger

Texans Investigating Mysterious Entities Series:

The Chupacabra and the Bat Rastard

Champ and a Bit of Sunshine

The Red Ghost and a Chocolate Bunny

The Loveland Frog and the Narrow Path

Tegan Stone and the Gibson County Beust

The Ringdocus and a Guy on a Buffalo

Other Books:

Corrè

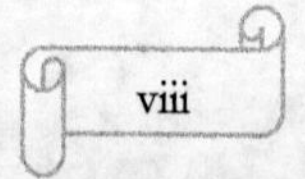

"The team was more like Scooby Doo and less like X-files, but enjoyable, nonetheless. I read this on vacation, so it was perfect fun and light reading." - Matt Stoessner

"*The Chupacabra & the Bat Rastard* by Mark Trollinger is a beguiling story that is beautifully written with a unique culture..." - Reviewed by Romuald Dzemo for *Readers' Favorite*

"If you like reading about urban legends and monsters, give it a look!!!" - Charles Verner

"Whether you love craft beer or not, I'm pretty sure you will love this book! It intrigued me more and more on every page, just read it and you will see!" - Deveo Young

"It wasn't boring. I promise. I enjoyed it!" - Beverly Longoria

"I liked it. It had a lot of details in the story, but it made it feel real." - Gaby Lopez

"Cryptozoology and local beer! I am so ready for this book!" - John Randall

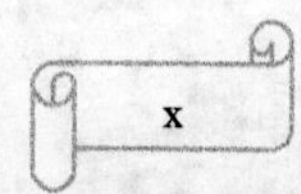

x

DEDICATION

To my lovely wife Susana, Jorge and Karmina, and Lydia for listening to me talk about the chupacabra for years. To my mother for being a role model and showing me to always pursue your dreams. To my college and high school friends who have written books and made me wonder why not me? And to World of Beer (Tempe, AZ) and JP Watts for expanding my world… of beer. Thanks to James Clark for the WhaleSlayer and Charles Verner for the Old Bat Rastard.

Thank you. Without your support and patience, I would have never achieved this.

ACKNOWLEDGMENTS

I started the idea for this story back in 2012. I was getting into craft beer and enjoyed learning more about it. Sitting in my apartment, I remembered that my ex-wife used to love to read mysteries. She liked Aaron Elkins and the Gideon Oliver series where he was a forensic anthropologist and his stories incorporated actual forensic science into solving the crimes. There was also Carolyn Hart and the Death on Demand series with Annie Laurance who owned the Death on Demand bookstore. Her stories incorporated mystery books and authors into the plot. Lilian Jackson Braun and the Cat Who series that incorporated a cat as a lead character in solving the crimes.

I thought why not apply that concept to things I like? I like craft beer and it is growing at an explosive rate across the country currently. I also like cryptozoology and the paranormal. At least on television. I liked MTV's Fear, Ghost Hunters, Chip Coffey, Destination Truth, Fact or Faked, and my current favorite shows: Ghost Adventures, Dead Files, Mountain Monsters, and Ghost Brothers.

I love to watch those shows on TV, but the few instances of real life unexplained situations that have happened to me - like growing up in a house where I always heard faint music and once someone whispered my name, to an odd night at the Stanley Hotel, the time a friend and I saw a boy's face in the schoolhouse's window at Bodega Bay only to realize years later after watching a news show on a television no one lives there, the unexplained face that appeared in a photo taken during a behind the scenes tour of The Winchester Mystery House, to being downstairs at Sun Devil Liquor in Tempe, AZ and feeling a hand on my shoulder. So much so I thought it was my friend coming up from behind, so I stepped aside… only to see him then coming down the stairs. The real-life unexplained events have left me uneasy, unlike the countless hours of shows I watch on television. Still, all those shows I enjoy are some of the more popular on television. Last year I wrote an idea for a television show that a TV executive had interest in, but the television channels already had a full slate of paranormal shows already, so it didn't get off the ground.

Why not combine two areas that are both seeing expansion in growth: craft beer and cryptozoology? With that, the idea for Carson Quinn was born. A cryptozoologist who enjoyed beer, but only his familiar, the traditional beer. His story was like some of my friends who only enjoyed the beers from the big companies. My Dad loved beer and drank a lot, but that was before craft beer. He drank Red, White, and Blue, Wiedemann, and Hamm's.

My first beers were in college when I purchased some Keystone and Keystone Light off a friend on my floor. From there it was Jack Daniels and Flaming Dr. Peppers, but when I drank a beer, it was a Natural Light. My Dad and I both liked beer, but only once did we have a beer together. That is something I envision a lot of fathers and sons do, and I feel I missed out on that rite of passage. It was at my cousin's wedding, and it was a Bud Light. I was still drinking Natural Light and Miller Lite until 2012, when I discovered Stone's Russian Imperial Stout. I remember thinking $6 for a beer?! But it was so good I returned days later and had one or two more. A few weeks later, World of Beer (WOB) in Tempe, AZ opened. I liked them on Facebook before they opened and before I even knew what it was, but the people were friendly, and I enjoyed the beer. The staff there, especially JP Watts, helped expand my beer knowledge.

Sadly, the Arizona WOBs closed. During its time, I spent countless hours there racking up loyalty points (which, thanks to awful laws in Arizona, did not allow customers to receive rewards like in other states). I even worked on my dissertation along the way in the bank vault. Thinking of the world of beer and the world of cryptozoology, I envisioned a ten-book series where the crew of investigators traveled the country, explored the local monsters, and drank the local beers.

So with that, I set out to write the tale of a group of adventures who not only get to the bottom of cryptozoology mysteries but get to the bottom of local pint glasses. I have spent several years writing research papers for my master's degrees and an on-hold Ph.D. Getting back to creative writing has been a challenging work in progress. I tried to incorporate research into my story.

When I started it was present time, but by the time I finished it was more than a year later. I used a calendar, and I tracked the date in the story so that it would flow with the storyline and real-life events. I used Google maps to zoom into the exact locations so I could see what was around the area. I used Yelp to access businesses and pull up their menu so it would match what a person could order there. When I named a bar or brewery, I used Untappd and scrolled back through sometimes hundreds of user activity to see what was on tap that exact day the story was taking place. The same occurred with local events, such as baseball games, basketball games, and concerts. I tried to make it as realistic as possible, yet it was a story of fantasy. Near the book's ending, I found myself challenged with how far to drift from reality into fantasy, and yet still make the story enjoyable. As I write more, including future adventures with these main characters, I hope to improve my creative writing and tell even more interesting stories. I hope you come along with me for the journey.

So here we begin a tale by weaving together some things I like: urban legends, craft beer, and a sprinkling of pop culture.

Hopefully, it comes out okay.

ACCOLADES

The Chupacabra and the Bat Rastard won Third Place in the category of Fiction > Supernatural - Supernatural Creatures & Beings at The BookFest Awards Spring 2022

PROLOGUE

MONDAY, JUNE 8, 2015

The night air hung thick with humidity in the southeastern San Antonio community of Elmendorf. Just after 3 a.m., the last quarter moon rested high above the sleepy town, providing a peaceful illumination over the farms below. While chickens roosted in their coops, cows laid across the terrain in a calm state of sleep. A lone goat wandered about in the stilly night, navigating between slumbering cattle as it grazed near a small pond.

A snap of a branch in the brush and bramble near the edge of the farm broke the silence of the night. The goat halted its grazing and raised its head toward the distant woods. The animal searched the dark landscape for the source of the noise. It continued to pause with raised ears as it sniffed the early morning air. The goat's nose picked up an unfamiliar, alarming scent. Startled, yet uncertain of what lurked nearby, it changed direction and bounded off through the lower pasture and to the safety of the old wooden barn.

From the shadows of the bordering woods, a dark, crouched figure emerged and slunk forward into the meadow. Under the soft light of the moon, the quiet, unseen figure moved in shadow toward the unsuspecting animals. If man or beast attempted to catch a glance of the creature, its only distinguishable feature was a glowing pair of red eyes in the darkness.

An unfamiliar scent traveled the night wind and caused a stir among the cattle; their senses alerted them to the strange invader. An old bull stood and faced the woods with a lowered head and arched back. He let out a series of snorts and pawed the ground with his front feet. The bull's alerts awakened the rest of the herd. A combined chorus of moos and bellows filled the air as the group expected danger and stirred into a chaotic, yet cohesive group.

The mysterious animal remained unseen, but the livestock sensed something dangerous nearby. Increased fear motivated the cattle to move, but in the commotion, some of the younger calves fell behind as the lead steer guided the herd toward the barn. The stalking figure needed only a small gap in the pack to charge the lagging animals.

Once within range of a young bovine, the dark creature used its paw to slap the rear of the animal and knock it off balance before it dragged it down to the dusty ground. A high-pitched bawl alerted the mother and others to the distressed calf's separation from the group, but the herd continued to move.

In a flash, the beast sprang from the darkness toward the small calf. Claws dug into the calf's hide and moonlight shone on sharp teeth from drooling, rabid jaws. A powerful bite to the neck ended the animal's cries for help.

CHAPTER 1

THE RANCH

WEDNESDAY, JUNE 10, 2015

A storm neared. Despite the best effort of the comfortable king-size foam mattress purchased three months ago, Fred Dalton laid awake plagued by uhtceare. Two days ago, a young calf from a local herd was dead, and the culprit remained unknown. Although Fred hoped this was an isolated issue, he empathized. Rising feed and machinery costs made life on the farm more difficult, and a loss of livestock would affect an already strained paycheck. A strain that Fred knew all too well. A similar loss to his ranch would put his family in a tough financial position. The recent attack was close to his ranch and since then, Fred's herd appeared to be on high alert. The impending storm would push them over the edge.

Fred was still tired from the night before. A sleepless night worrying about his herd and the unpaid bills only added to his exhaustion. He briefly fantasized about catching a few more minutes of sleep, but it was 3:25 a.m. and it was time to get up. He had to check on the herd and start the morning chores, despite the rain. Maybe he could steal a few minutes? Five short minutes later, the alarm clock returned to life as Clint Black sang *Killin' Time*. Fred blindly slapped the alarm clock's snooze button and silently begged for a few more minutes.

Too soon the clock sounded again as Garth Brooks' *Unanswered Prayers* ended and San Antonio's 92.5 K-BUC transitioned to George Strait's *Amarillo by Morning*.

"Fine!" Fred sighed as he turned the clock off and gingerly sat upright on the edge of the bed.

He lowered his head, ran his fingers through his short, brown hair, and tried to grasp the idea of another day. He paused for a moment, then wearily reached for the well-worn jeans on the floor beside the bed. Getting up in the morning was a more arduous process than he expected at his age. Naturally, working on the ranch was hard work, but he often wondered if all thirty-four-year-olds felt like this each morning. He looked over at his wife, Jess, who lay motionless, still sound asleep.

"Must be nice," he uttered under his breath.

Fred's face responded with a slight wince as he lifted his aching legs and purposefully placed his right foot into the jeans and stood. After stepping into the left pant leg, he arched his back and gave a slight stretch before he slipped each foot into his worn brown Cattleman's boots. He maneuvered through the dark room, navigating around piles of *clean* clothes on the bedroom floor as he made his way into the small walk-in closet. He pulled a long sleeve plaid shirt from a hanger and grabbed his brown leather cowboy hat from atop the shelf.

Putting the hat on first, he then carefully slid each aching arm into the shirt, right first, then left, before he buttoned it and shuffled toward the dark kitchen.

Fred always started the morning with a cup of black coffee before heading out to tend to the herd and start the day's chores. Despite many technological advances, Fred continued to use the trusty percolator he inherited after his father's passing. He had fond memories of learning about ranching life from his father and starting the day brewing coffee before the two of them went out for the day. The sound the coffee made as it splashed against the clear top reminded him of the sound of waves crashing on the beach, and the coffee coming from the old percolator still made the best coffee Fred had ever tasted. His current brew, a blend of Trader Joe's Ultra Dark French Roast and Ultra Dark Sumatra, provided enough of a kick-start to wake him from his sleepy state. The coffee's aroma always made him forget how painful it was to be awake; at least temporarily.

The recent events were troublesome, not only because a neighbor lost a valuable calf, but Fred realized the financial hardship it would cause the family. He thought of himself in a similar position and how it would be difficult. San Antonio rarely experienced much annual rain, except during the rainy months of May and June. Normally, a storm was a welcomed sight, but this storm was blowing hard, a real gully washer. The rainfall would help the drought-stricken area, especially the hayfields Fred grew for the cattle to supplement the time when the pasture grass was scarce. However, this time it was different because of the attack. During the monsoon seasons, the rains in Texas blow up fast with sheets of hard rain, intense winds, and lightning. The cattle already had their ears back and had a heightened awareness of their surroundings.

Fred finished his coffee and sat the empty blue tin cup in the sink. As he made his way to the dimly lit entry room, the wooden screen door banged against the doorframe, a signal of the increased wind outside. Through the porch window, the heavy rain made it difficult to see the trees as they swayed in the gusts. He removed his overcoat from the rack and took his grandfather's old Winchester from beside the doorway before he headed into the elements to check on the cattle.

He lumbered through the newly formed puddles gathering in the dirt driveway, his size twelve boots leaving new indentations as he rushed to the old wooden tractor barn. He pulled back the blue tarp covering his trusty four-by-four and loaded two plastic buckets filled with corn kernels on the back. Fred may have been only five-nine and of average build, but he was country strong. The rain battered down on the barn's tin roof while he gathered the tools needed to repair any damage the property fence may have incurred.

The dirt driveway stretched from the house, between the tractor barn and hay barn, down a small hill, and across a cattle guard. It curved around into a half-mile lane that ran through the center of the sixty-two-acre ranch. The pasture rotation fenced all the cows and chickens into the back twenty acres. The path rose over a slight hill, which cut off the view of the herd until Fred reached the hill's crest.

As he reached the hill's summit, the cattle came into view. Some were up at the bale feeder, some at the feed bunk, and others grazed in the pasture as the rain fell. Others stood under small sheds while a different cluster of cattle held under a grove of trees on the east end of the field. As he passed the mobile chicken houses, some hens ran to greet the vehicle, thinking more food was coming.

Fred stepped off and grabbed one bucket filled with ground corn. As he walked through the gathering crowd of hungry chickens, he plunged his hand into the bucket and broadcast the grain across the wet ground. The chickens pecked at the strewn kernels. Though a small group of chickens came out to greet Fred, the majority stayed back. He understood chickens were good watchdogs that were intelligent and aware of their surroundings. The demeanor and noises coming from the flock showed there was a problem or a recent unwanted visitor in the area. The longer he stayed, the more individual hens cautiously approached. Fred blanketed the immediate area with corn and walked through the rows of mobile chicken houses, liberally tossing food for its residents.

Fred returned to the four-by-four and continued down the dirt road. A short distance past the mobile chicken houses, the first of the herd appeared. The rain lightened as Fred drove closer and found several cattle lying down on the muddy earth. Others looked at the incoming Kioti but offered little interest in inspecting the vehicle.

The next group of cattle Fred encountered stood with their tails tucked between their legs, a sign of being cold or scared. Further back in the pasture near a large pond and bank of trees, Fred observed the herd with tails raised, showing they were alert and exploring a threat.

Fred once again dismounted the vehicle and briskly walked toward the alarmed cattle. A young bull dashed to the top of the dirt bank around the pond. He lowered his head, shook it from side to side, and arched his back as the man approached. Fred stood his ground and kept his eye on the bull. He knew never to turn his back on an aggressive animal.

Closer cattle reacted to the approaching human by observing his movements and then turning away to escape. The motion showed Fred had entered the flight zone; the space around a cow where she felt safe and represented how close a person could get before the animal ran away. As Fred continued to walk toward the pond, the cattle galloped away once he got within two yards. The bull no longer showed aggression but maintained a watchful eye on the intruder.

Nearing the bank of the pond, Fred stopped. His heart suddenly as he noticed the motionless lumps of not one, but two bodies. Both were in the mud along the bank, their heads partially in the water. The dead cows were both Charolais yearlings not yet ready for market, but the future economic loss would be challenging to overcome.

Fred hurriedly returned to his vehicle and retrieved his cell phone from the glove compartment. He called the Bexar County sheriff's department to report the incident and requested an officer investigate. The dispatcher took down the information and said the sheriff would drive out later in the morning to look. However, Fred realized without an incident in progress, there would be little the sheriff could do except file a report.

Half-past nine, the sheriff arrived, and Fred greeted him. Sheriff Barnes was a plump man in his mid-fifties with straight gray hair and a scruffy mustache. His uniform shirt tucked snuggly into his pants as his belly hung over the hidden belt.

He walked with Fred as both men scanned the pasture's landscape. Fred told Sheriff Barnes he fed the cattle between noon and 1 p.m. the previous day and they heard nothing unusual that evening. The animals were fine when he and Jess headed to bed around nine-thirty. Fred wanted to know who, or what, killed his and his neighbor's cattle. A killer at large could be devastating for the economy of the local community.

As Sheriff Barnes explored the scene of the incident, he paused and scratched his head. One of the most puzzling things about the remains was the lack of blood. Fred and the Sheriff found both bodies drained with no visible signs of scattered body parts. The only clue was three small puncture wounds in the neck. In fifteen years as a farmer, Fred had seen nothing like this before, and the sheriff, in all his years of experience, was unfamiliar.

The first suspect in Fred and Sheriff Barnes' minds was a large canine; a carnivore such as a coyote or wolf. That would not be uncommon on a large ranch, but predators rarely leave a carcass intact or drink eleven gallons of blood. There were also mountain lions, but they stayed in the montane regions and rarely visited ranches.

Another recorded eater of cattle in North America was the grizzly bear, although most lived in Montana and Wyoming. Recent reports had surfaced showing an increase in the number of black bears in Texas, but their diet consisted of plants, fruits, nuts, insects, and small mammals. Nothing the size of a yearling calf. There were rumors of a black panther being spotted in Hill County a couple of years ago, but that creature wasn't captured or identified, although some thought it to be a jaguarondi.

With a shake of his head, the sheriff turned toward Fred with a puzzled look.

"I don't know, Boss… aliens?"

The two exchanged a welcomed chuckle as they continued to search the ground for clues. Footprints formed on the soggy ground as they traipsed around, but any prints from the night before were likely washed away by the heavy rain. After another twenty minutes, Sheriff Barnes concluded they found everything there was to find. Which was nothing.

"Best thing you can do is buy a couple trail cameras," suggested the sheriff. "I've seen them used on those Bigfoot shows on Animal Planet. You might get lucky enough to catch something on film before he does any more damage to your herd! Sorry I couldn't be of more help, but I will file this report and we'll go from there."

Sheriff Barnes gave Fred's hand a hardy handshake, wished him well, and returned to the dry interior of his white Ford Explorer. Fred turned and gave another long-distance scan over the pasture before returning to the four-by-four. As he drove back up the road to the barn, the cattle casually returned to eating grass as they were before the rancher interrupted.

Hours later, it was afternoon, but Fred didn't feel like working. He entered the mudroom of the house, removed his soggy boots, overcoat, and hat before joining Jess at the kitchen table. She saw his tired, worried look and asked what was wrong. When he explained, she shared his fears regarding not only the immediate impact on their financial situation, but potential long-term implications if they could not catch the killer. Then what?

Knowing her husband hadn't eaten all day, she offered him a B.L.T., but he declined, instead satisfied to steal a lightly salted potato chip from her plate. As he sat quietly pondering his next move, he remembered the sheriff's suggestion and walked over to the sideboard to get the laptop. Moving a growing stack of past due bills, he returned to the table and searched online websites for reviews on the best trail cameras. He initially narrowed his choices down to Moultrie, Bushnell, and Browning, but then chuckled when he saw the Primos Truth had good reviews and was cheaper. Fred told Jess the truth was what he wanted to find, so it sounded like that's the one he should purchase. He could order it on Amazon, but didn't want to wait five to ten business days for it to arrive.

"When are they going to use those drones to ship products in a couple of hours?" he asked.

Instead, he visited All Seasons Feeders later that afternoon. He called his friend and fellow local rancher, Eric Vega, to ask if he wanted to run into town with him. He figured they could pick up some cameras and talk about the events over a couple of beers. Fred agreed to pick up Eric around 5:00 p.m.

Eric was a young rancher. A lanky, married Puerto Rican man in his mid-twenties who moved into the area last year. He and Fred liked to talk about ranching over a couple of beers. Respecting Fred's ranching experience, Eric looked at him as an informal mentor and was eager to learn more about the insights of the industry.

Arriving at the Vega Ranch, Fred gave a quick two-honk signal, which Eric soon acknowledged with a wave as he emerged onto the front porch. He adjusted his hat as he walked to the truck. K-BUC played in the background as Fred drove down Stuart Road toward Highway 87 East. After twelve miles, they arrived at All Seasons Feeders. Walking around the store, Fred did not see the trail cameras, but according to the website, they were in stock. He asked a store associate and after some searching in all the wrong places, the clerk located two cameras in stock and on sale for under sixty dollars. Fred purchased both.

"Ready for a beer?" he asked, glancing over at his friend. Eric nodded in agreement.

Close to All Seasons, Longbranch Saloon in Adkins. A family-owned business known for tasty food, some of the coldest beer in town, and provided locals with a nice spot where everyone knew everyone else. It was a little country/cowboy spot with darts, billiards, and a large stage area for musical acts. Sitting at a wobbly wooden table in the corner, the duo ordered a bucket of beer and a large pizza. Ten minutes later, the server brought a Miller Lite bucket filled to the top with ice and five Bud Light bottles inserted up to the base of their necks. There wasn't a band that night, but the beer was cold, the pizza hot, and the karaoke bad.

Each man grabbed a bottle, twisted the cap off, and took a couple of long drinks, bringing each down to the halfway point.

Eric said, "Brewed the hard way!" and they both laughed.

Still, it was refreshing on a humid June evening. After the second beer and third poorly sung karaoke-version of a Hank Williams, Jr. song, Fred suggested a game of pool. As they removed and caulked the sticks, Fred told Eric about the day's events.

Being a new rancher, the news concerned Eric. If an experienced rancher like Fred had seen nothing like that before and was uncertain who or what the culprit was, Eric knew he couldn't handle the situation if a similar event happened to his herd. Just starting out, his ranch was in a worse financial position because of startup costs and limited cattle sales. A loss of one or two heads and it could signal an end to his ranch. He hated it had happened to his friend, but Fred could absorb the loss a little more than a newbie like Eric. The trail cameras would help to identify the thing behind the killing, and he hoped that would be a limited incident. He wanted to help in any way he could to end this situation without further incidents.

Eric took the final Bud Light and signaled the server for another bucket. "What's next?" he asked Fred as he placed the triangle rack on the pool table and set up all fifteen balls within the triangle in random order.

"Dunno… hang the trail cameras and see what turns up?"

With that, Fred broke the balls, and a stripe fell into the corner pocket. Eric hit three solids in a row, and a couple of turns later called the eight ball for a quick victory. Grabbing the delivered bucket of beer, they returned to the table to each have another slice of the now room-temperature pizza. The simplicity of a pepperoni and cheese pizza always hit the spot for Fred and, ranking the past pizzas he had, he placed this near the top.

As they finished the last bites of the pizza pie, a patron attempted a drunken version of Billy Currington's *I'm Pretty Good at Drinking Beer*. From the sound of it, Fred and Eric surmised he was an *expert* at drinking beer. After listening in wonder for a few seconds, they realized it was an excellent opportunity to down the remaining beer and head for the truck. Eric offered to stop by in the morning and help Fred install the cameras and assist with whatever else he needed. Fred agreed, dropped a five on the table for the tip, and both men exited to the parking lot.

Early the next morning, Eric pulled into Fred's ranch in his 1979 Chevy Scottsdale truck. The truck's better days were past, but it belonged to Eric's late uncle. Plus, the upkeep and maintenance of the old vehicle was much simpler than today's trucks with their complex computer systems. Fred heard Eric's tires grind against the few sparsely covered areas of gravel on the driveway and walked out to greet him. Fred read the trail camera manual the night before and was ready to install them. He determined the installation locations, hoping to identify the unknown assailant.

Walking to the tractor barn, Fred and Eric each grabbed a couple of plastic buckets to put in the back of the 4x4 and made the drive to the back pasture, hoping not to see a repeat of the day before. Fortunately, there were no fresh developments. The friends exchanged a sigh of relief and exited the vehicle.

Fred placed a camera on a tree close to a fence that overlooked the pond where he discovered the bodies. He wanted to save the second camera to mount on the back side of the hay barn. It was closer toward the house, but it overlooked the pasture and might give a long-range view of the ranch and woods past the edge of the property. After installing both cameras, the men returned to the utility vehicle.

"Not much else to do but wait," said Fred.

He invited Eric to watch the game and have a beer, but Eric declined. Fred thanked him for the help and Eric headed back to complete work on his own ranch and look over his herd. Fred grabbed a bottle of Budweiser, the half-empty bag of chips, located a comfortable spot on the sofa, and turned on the San Antonio Silver Stars vs. Atlanta Dream basketball game.

He dragged the ottoman closer and prepared for some deep couch sitting. His favorite player on the Silver Stars was Danielle Adams, a recruit from the 2011 Texas A&M National Championship team. She reminded him of Charles Barkley with her ability to run the court, block, and rebound - plus she could hit the three. Another of his favorite players, Shoni Schimmel, was playing for the home team, Atlanta. Fred considered her an incredible athlete. One of the best ball-handlers in the league with an ability to make a highlight reel pass any time in the game. She reminded Fred of Steve Nash in his prime.

It amazed him that few men watched or attended the WNBA games as much as he did. He considered the WNBA his guilty pleasure because most of his friends mocked his interest in the game. They didn't understand how a rugged Texas rancher could be interested in women's basketball, but he didn't care. He enjoyed it and attempted to recruit new fans to the game every chance he had. The women played hard on every play, the games were exciting, and the atmosphere was always electric in person. Plus, there wasn't the constant flopping that occurred in the men's game. That, and the lack of defense, were aspects of the NBA that Fred hated.

After the game, Fred walked to the window and looked out toward the barns. He wondered what was out there in the woods looking back at him. Not much to do now as eventide approached, but wait. Soon it would be nightfall and the unfolding mystery would be to wonder what morning would bring.

He returned to the living room, and Jess joined her husband on the couch. She grabbed the remote and turned the television to *Property Brothers* on HGTV. Leaning against him, she put her head on his shoulder; her long dirty blonde hair draped down his back. Watching the show in comfort, she soon got drowsy, but was able to comment favorably on the open concept of the proposed remodeling design. The couple fell asleep on the couch following the third episode.

A couple of hours passed before Fred awoke. Jess was sleeping on his arm and House Hunters International played on the television. He thought maybe they should be like the couple in the episode and move to Puerto Peñasco to get away from this ranching life and its financial troubles. Besides, the beach looked wonderful. A couple of margaritas, a cigar, and the ocean might just be the ticket. He allowed himself to enjoy the fantasy for a few seconds before he scooted forward, put his hand under Jess' head, and attentively lowered her to the couch. At only 5'1", she could sleep comfortably on the couch. Besides, Fred's curiosity was getting the better of him and he had a gnawing feeling about going out to check on the cattle.

Grabbing his small flashlight, Fred snatched his hat in passing the coat rack and walked out the front door. It was 12:15 a.m. and completely dark. The darkness felt heavy, oppressive, almost supernatural. He recalled that according to the movie *Midnight in the Garden of Good and Evil,* he was not only right in the middle of dead time, but the half hour after midnight was for evil. It was something evil he was looking for and he wondered if the time to find it might be approaching.

He slowly walked from the driveway toward the barn. Two things amazed him about living well outside the city: how silent it was at night and how bright the stars were. He took a few pronounced footsteps toward the barn while he soaked up the moment and looked up at the night sky. As he got closer, a noise came from the tractor barn and caused him to pivot to shine his light in the direction where it appeared to originate.

His light illuminated a couple of stacked bales of hay, a small pile of hay on the barn's dirt floor because of busted twine, a knocked over tin watering can, and a fifty-pound bag of yellow corn. As he walked at an increased pace toward the noise, he discovered its source was a couple of guinea hens that were in the barn. Relieved, he walked on. The rest of his walk around the two barns and dirt road was quiet and uneventful. He walked up the dirt road toward the pond where the deadly incident took place a couple of days prior.

The light from the flashlight ebbed and flowed across the pasture as Fred's arms swayed while walking. As he reached the top of the small hill, it startled him to see an animal walking along the dirt wall around the pond. The creature was dark and mostly hidden in the shadows, but he could see it hunched low with its head down and plodding in the manner that a cat stalks a bird.

Fred had seen nothing like it. The animal looked like a medium-sized dog, but didn't appear to be a canine. The creature seemed to have no hair or short, light brown hair that made it appear hairless. As the light shone upon the strange creature, its eyes glowed red in the darkness. It had a hunched back and appeared to have bluish-gray spikey fur covering the spine. The creature stopped, raised its head to look at Fred, and Fred back at it. It held a penetrating glare for a moment with large, pointed ears, then turned and ran back toward the woods.

Fred froze momentarily but decided, perhaps unwisely, to give chase, even though being on foot, there was no way he could keep up with the creature. Fred suddenly realized his cardio days were well behind him and pulled up out of breath, bent over with his hands on his knees, and his eyes steady on the horizon where the creature was last seen. Who would believe him? Hopefully, the trail camera picked up some shots of the animal. One thing was certain, if he had not been there at that moment, he would have awoken to at least one more missing cow.

Fred walked over to the fencepost overlooking the pond where he had earlier mounted the first trail camera. He opened the unit, removed the SD card, and walked back toward the barn to inspect the other camera. After Fred removed both cards, he went back to the house. Too excited to sleep, he inserted the cards into the laptop and downloaded the photos.

The camera from near the barn didn't contain footage other than a couple of photos of some guineas and a distant cow that wandered into view from the barn. As Fred looked at the captured images, he realized the location was too far to pick up anything off in the distant woods. Unless the animal was close to the camera, it wouldn't snap the photo.

The second camera had many more pictures, but most were of cattle. Then he found it. Actually *them*. Three images of the unknown beast he encountered near the pond. The only issue was the quality of the photos. They were a little overexposed, blurry, and lacked sharp detail of the animal. But the culprit was on film. Fred was eager to show Eric his proof and solve the mystery of what type of animal was stalking his herd.

Early Thursday morning, Fred and Eric met for breakfast at Baldy's Classic American Diner. Fred ordered the *Big Nasty*, a fried chicken breast stuffed between two home-baked biscuits and topped with sausage gravy served in a skillet with fried potato hash browns with onions and green peppers, and all on top of two eggs over-easy. Eric went with an enchilada omelet topped with sour cream and avocado. He ordered a side of bacon and toast, and both men ordered coffee.

"I saw it last night!"

"Saw what?"

"The creature killing the cattle in the area!"

"What was it?" Eric asked with an excited tone.

"I don't know. But I got these from the camera," he said as he removed the photos from inside his jacket.

Eric stared at the somewhat blurry, somewhat dark photos of the animal.

"Coyote?" he said with uncertainty.

"No," responded Fred. "This animal looked hairless and had a hunched back with some patches of fur along the spine!"

Eric studied the photos but couldn't identify what he saw. "Then what the hell is it? A wolf? A mountain lion? I can't tell if it is a canine or something else!"

"Don't know. Never seen a wild dog attack and drain an animal of its entirety of blood like that," revealed Fred.

"Me neither… and I don't know that the sheriff will be much help." Eric paused and continued to look at the photo. "I met a guy. A few years back, but I have heard nothing from him since." Eric took a bite of his omelet and a swig of lukewarm coffee. "This guy was up in Austin," Eric continued. "Said to be an expert in cryptozoology."

Fred looked puzzled at his friend. "What the hell is cryptozoology?"

"You know, hidden animals…. bigfoot and shit," Eric replied.

Fred looked skeptical.

"C'mon, those things don't exist. If there was a bigfoot, don't you think we would have discovered one by now? At least a body, a pile of shit, or something."

"I don't know, buddy. We've seen nothing like what's in those photos, but there he is."

Fred looked at his friend with an awkward pause, but he couldn't deny Eric's words. He had never seen an animal like that until the night before and see it he did. And not just in those blurry photos. He came face-to-face with it.

"You're right. Maybe alternative experts are what I need to help track this monster. Do you know who this guy is?"

Eric picked up his cellphone and started looking through the contacts.

"It's Carter, I think. Met him once at a dive bar before a Longhorns football game. He worked at a middle school. I think a teacher. Somehow, we started talking about mythical creatures."

Eric continued to scroll through his phone, but stopped when he found his target.

"*Carson*. That's it. Carson Quinn. Here's his number here if you want it."

He asked the server for a pen and scribbled the number on a napkin. Fred looked down with a stare of uncertainty at the number, then up at Eric.

"What the hell can it hurt? I'll call and see if we can get him down here."

CHAPTER 2

GIDDY UP

FRIDAY, JUNE 12, 2015

A lush field of bluebonnets overlooked a crowded, cracked, and weathered blacktop driveway of a South Austin classic, Giddy Ups Saloon; a bar known to be a little divey and a lot of a that is a still-open piece of old Austin. There was a small stage inside with live music throughout the week, a dartboard, shuffleboard, a small dance floor, and a patio in the back. Since the remodeling and re-opening last year, patrons packed the saloon nearly every night.

Past the jukebox blaring 80s and 90s country music, the pool tables with worn green felt covering, glowing neon beer signs, and dense clouds of cigarette smoke sat a wooden table. At that table sat a gloomy, lonely man with a scruffy beard and tired brown eyes that made him appear older than his actual mid-thirties. The man had been in that same spot since early afternoon, which was not an uncommon occurrence. He was one of the many regulars who frequented the saloon and often greeted strangers with what some described as a small-town gaze.

The past couple of years had been difficult for the man. Once extroverted and optimistic, he was now quiet and dejected. Carson reached the end of his Lone Star and pushed the empty bottle into the center of the table with four others and motioned to the server for another. Lone Star, an American adjunct lager, was a staple of Texas and a prominent feature in one of the man's favorite movies, *Urban Cowboy*. He felt like a cowboy when he drank it, although he found it somewhat odd considering Pabst Brewing Company owned it and the label showed Brewed in Los Angeles.

The man pulled the brim of his dark brown straw cowboy hat down and wondered how much time had to pass before he could no longer consider himself between jobs. In March 2011, the Round Rock Independent School District principals met with employees to talk about job cuts after a $60 million budget shortfall. The announcement affected two hundred eighty employees, two hundred thirty-four of them probationary classroom teachers like Carson Quinn. The most substantial cuts eliminated over fifty positions at district middle schools. Carson was part of that demographic as well. In the months following the cuts, the district found new placements for about one hundred previously laid-off employees. All displaced teachers had to reapply and interview for new opportunities, but Carson was not one of the fortunate ones.

Carson talked to the bartenders and, at times, some of the other patrons, although he found most of them to be ultracrepidarians. Still, sometimes it was nice to have someone to talk to, even if they didn't know what they were talking about. Tonight he didn't talk. He sat hunched over at the table, lost in-between memory and pensively pondering the future while he drank his Lone Star and listened to the sounds of the Sam Bentley Band on the stage.

The band's drums, two guitars, and the lonesome cry of the steel guitar provided the perfect slow downbeat honky-tonk music of heartbreak. The band played *Excuse Me (I Think I've Got a Heartache)*, and Carson realized he was feeling the same emotion. It wasn't because of a woman, but the turn of life events he had experienced over the past few years. After the teaching job, he tried his hand at a couple of entry-level jobs in customer service and retail to keep up with the mountain of student loan payments and regular monthly bills, but none of those jobs interested him enough to display the type of work ethic managers were interested in retaining. Other than teaching, the only other job he ever enjoyed was more of a hobby, and one many people considered unusual: cryptozoology.

He enjoyed being outdoors, and he loved animals, but he did not spend most of his time in the woods hunting deer or looking for wild turkeys. Instead, he searched for legendary creatures. These were animals that many people called urban legends and were ignored by modern scientists. Carson was different. He felt – no, he *knew* existed.

He had been a middle school science teacher at Walsh Middle School, and he considered his hobby to be science as well, even if many considered it a fringe science. To him, he used the same scientific methodologies in the field as he did in the classroom: being objective, open-minded, using comparative analysis, and collecting data. And a lot of existing data in the field provided evidence to support the existence of these mythical creatures.

He used to enjoy his time searching for and attempting to prove these animals existed, even if when talking about them others viewed him like the crazy-haired guy from *Ancient Aliens*. He couldn't help but get excited speaking about cryptids and his search for the unknown. It was more than a hobby. It was his passion.

Sam Bentley sang a cover of *Amarillo by Morning*, causing Carson to drift away into nostalgia not only about his days as a monster hunter, but of growing up and hearing that song on the radio in 1996 while riding through Knoxville on vacation with his grandparents. Young and the entire world before him then, he now wondered how he got to where he was today. More importantly, could he get back? He exhaled as he sunk his head down and stared at the bottle in front of him.

In his daydream-state, he was oblivious to the other patrons. As if the universe reached out to intervene, a man walked past, stopped, and returned to stand in front of the table. He paused, squinting his brown eyes to analyze the inebriated man in the brown straw hat.

"Carson?" inquired a tall, athletic Black man in his early thirties.

The befuddled man raised his head and tried to make out the figure in front of him, wincing as the lights from the bar shone behind the man's head, concealing his identity.

"Carson Quinn, is that you? If it is, you look like shit," replied the man.

Carson rubbed his eyes. He recognized the voice. A ghost from his past, Tyson Carr, worked in the IT Department and taught an occasional computer science class at the University of Texas at Austin. Years ago, they were college roommates and remained in contact for a few years afterward, but then time got away, and they hadn't spoken in over five years. Carson and Tyson were close friends back then and together used to search for those legendary animals about which Carson was just reminiscing. With Carson's science background and Tyson's technological skills, they were an impressive team.

"Ty?"

His cloudy mind tried to comprehend the man before him. He stared blankly for a minute, then reluctantly invited his old friend to sit with him. Tyson turned and glanced over his shoulder.

"For a minute. I'm here with some coworkers for happy hour. This isn't normally my place. They serve little of the type of beer I drink."

He took notice of the island of bottles in front of Carson.

"I see you're still drinking that swill we drank in college," Tyson badgered.

Carson scooted over and allowed his friend to sit down. He attempted to smile. His glazed eyes and scruffy beard showed how rough the past couple days, or years for that matter, had been.

"Been a few years. How the hell have you been?"

Carson glared at the man's hands.

"And what the hell are you drinking?" Carson asked with a slow and detectable slurred diction as he squinted at the unfamiliar label on the bottle in his friend's hand.

Tyson chuckled, "It's a local brewery called Austin Beerworks. I like to support the small, hometown guys when I can. Small, independent companies provide jobs and support the local community. Plus, I like the variety. Those Lone Stars are the same every time and mass produced for a wide audience. They brew craft beer in smaller batches using traditional ingredients," Ty replied.

"Small guys? I know nothing about that. Beer is beer, and I like this beer," asserted Carson.

Unfazed, Ty continued. "What's cool is the brewer can also try innovative brewing methods or different ingredients to alter the recipe. With each batch, the creativity and passion of its maker and the complexity of its ingredients come through."

He sat his empty bottle on the table and raised his glass.

"This one is called Peacemaker, and it's a light session pale ale."

Carson stared at his friend with a puzzled expression. "What is a *session beer*, or a *pale ale*?" he asked, his head swimming with unfamiliar words.

Tyson defined a session beer as low alcohol content, under five percent alcohol by volume, allowing someone to have multiple beers within a reasonable time or session without reaching inappropriate levels of intoxication.

"Lone Star's around four percent, so technically, you're drinking one now." He added, "One difference between a pale

ale and a lager is they brewed ale with top-fermenting yeast, while lagers use bottom-fermenting yeast."

"If I had to choose, I'd rather be the top," Carson teased.

Ty stared at his friend as if he were still a teenager.

"Yeah… Well, another difference is the temperature at which fermentation occurs. You're a scientist. You know how important temperature is because chemical reactions happen more slowly at lower temperatures."

Carson sat up a little taller in his seat. Although the beer was unfamiliar to him, the science behind Ty's answer pierced the drunken cloud in Carson's mind and piqued his interest. But he was still confused.

"Tell you what. You're empty. I got your next beer."

Carson raised a finger to draw the server's attention.

"Another Lone Star?" Carson asked.

"No, not this time. My choice," replied Ty.

"I don't know. I'm not much on trying new things these days," resisted Carson.

"It looks like you're not much into showering or shaving either. Besides, it's important to shift your paradigm a little. We get old when we become stagnant and stop learning new things."

Ty motioned for the server to come over to the table. Dot Ross was working Carson's section, which was also a regular occurrence. Dot, a short, young college girl with jet-black hair and a tattoo sleeve on both arms, was Carson's favorite. Perhaps it was the tight sleeveless tank top, the short, cutoff denim jean shorts, or her thick Appalachian accent from her native West Virginia. Carson thought it was probably a little of all those things, but whatever the reason, she was his favorite, and he always tried to sit in her section.

Dot hurried toward the table, glancing around to see if anyone else immediately needed a drink

"Hey, boys," she greeted them with a flirtatious smile.

"Hello. Can you bring my friend a Guns & Oil Maverick Lager?" asked Ty. "This one's on me." Turning back toward Carson, he added, "This beer is comparable to what you are drinking now. Similar in alcohol content at four-point-six percent."

Dot opened the bottle and poured it into a pint glass before handing it to Carson. He stared at the glass, uncertain about this unknown beer, but returned to his position that beer was beer - especially after the number he had already consumed. How bad could it be? Plus, Ty was buying. Although he loved Lone Star, he knew the best beer was a free beer. He inspected the beer in the odd vessel and took a sip.

"Tastes the same to me. Maybe a little lighter." Carson said. "And..." he began as he pulled the menu close to his face and his drunk-heavy eyes scanned the beer section, "looks to be a couple of dollars more than the Lone Star. I think I will stick with Lone Star... What's with the fancy glass?" questioned Carson.

"The glass alters the aroma, appearance, and the taste of the beer," reassured Tyson. "If you want some more science, scientific studies show the shape of glassware impacts head development and retention. It impacts the volatile compounds that evaporate from beer to create its aroma. Things like hop oils, all kinds of yeast fermentation byproducts like alcohol, fusels and fruity esters, spices, or other additions." He paused while Carson drank more of the Maverick.

"I mean, don't get me wrong, it's fine, but it's more expensive and tastes the same as what I already got," said Carson. Ty scrutinized his closed-minded friend sardonically. Carson finished the remaining beer and sat the empty glass on the table.

"You driving tonight?" Ty asked.

"Nope," replied Carson. "Calling an Uber at the end of the night."

"Smart man. Here, let's try something a little different. Move your scale a bit," he suggested.

When Dot returned to check on the table, Tyson ordered a Pearl Snap, another beer from Austin Beerworks. When it arrived, Dot brought a different glass; this one taller and thinner. As she poured the beer, Ty spoke, sensing the confusion in his friend's face, without looking at him.

"That's a pilsner glass. The tall, slender shape helps to showcase color, clarity, and carbonation. It also promotes head retention and enhances the volatiles I mentioned earlier. What you had before was a lager. An American adjunct lager. A pilsner is also a lager, but specific to the Plzeň Region of Germany."

"Sounds complicated," Carson replied, shaking his head.

Ty explained, "It's not complicated. You have two types of beer - ales and lagers. Lagers come from all over and have various colors and flavors. Pilsner beer is simply a lager from that area of Germany. You'll notice this one is also light, but with a bright, hoppy character. It's about five percent, clear straw color, and has a head that dissipates quickly. You should smell just a little maltiness and some grassy, citrus scents from the hops. It's a classic pilsner, and the refreshing taste makes it a great drink for our hot summer days. I think that's one of the better beers produced in Austin."

Carson took a sip, but this time Ty saw a light in his friend's eyes as if a door somewhere deep in his mind disengaged from its locked casing. The beer surprised Carson as the pleasant bitterness caught him off guard.

"I kinda dig the bitterness," he said.

"That's the hops," added Ty. "It's a good gateway beer to other craft brews and a good lawnmower beer after being out in the blistering sun."

Ty read his watch and stood up. "I had better return to my coworkers," he said as he jerked a thumb toward the area behind him where his other friends were sitting. "Great running into you. We gotta get together again and kick back."

Carson agreed and said with sincerity and a little more clarity, "I enjoyed seeing you again, and I appreciate the lesson. Maybe you could introduce me to some more of your fancy beers sometime?" Carson said openly.

"For sure. I'd enjoy that! Catch ya on the back side, Brother," Ty said with a firm handshake. The two men exchanged numbers, and Ty disappeared into the crowd of people.

Dot returned to check on Carson and collect the various empty bottles and glasses from the table.

"Who's your friend?" she asked in her heavy Appalachian drawl. "Every time I've seen you, you're alone."

Carson, still groggy from the multiple beers, was surprised to feel an unfamiliar, almost upbeat reflection of the recent chance encounter.

"My old college roommate. Just happened to bump into each other tonight after several years. Crazy! It was fun and brought back a lot of memories."

"Ready for some wings? Another beer?" asked Dot.

Carson paused and scanned the room to assess the situation. The band was on intermission, but he figured he would stick around a little longer.

"I could go for a dozen wings," he ordered. "And, uh… what other local beers do you have, Dot? Your choice."

She flashed a dimpled smile before leaving to disappear behind the bar. Moments later, she returned, presenting Carson with another local beer, Austin Amber from Independence Brewing Company.

He stared at the glass. This beer was a darker beer, causing him to give the glass another suspicious glare. At least the ones Ty had him try were like what he was familiar with, but this?

Dot encouraged, "'T'aint gonna bite! Ya fixin' ta just look at it or ya gonna drink it?!"

"I don't know about dark beers, Dot. I've never had one before."

Dot chuckled as she replied, "I figured as much, but that ain't a dark beer. It's an amber. There's much darker beers out there."

Carson stared at the glass and noted the color and the thin, white head. Dot suggested he smell it first, saying the sense of smell creates anticipation of taste.

"Normally you just drink beer," he said. "I never stop and smell the Lone Star, but whatever. I guess I'm learning something new."

He raised the glass and inhaled. His eyes contracted, and he looked puzzled, but intrigued. It smelled of yeast - or bread? Maybe biscuits? He also thought it smelled kind of malty, like butterscotch or caramel. Maybe creamed corn. Visions of many flavors raced through his mind, fighting their way through the clouds in his head.

"Hmm, that's interesting."

Carson pulled back and examined the glass curiously and again focused on the color and appearance. The level of carbonation was modest. Glancing over at Dot, he raised the glass in a toast.

"Bottoms up I guess."

He took a slow sip and was surprised that the taste followed what he smelled. Malt up front, then hints of sweet crackers, and then just a little bitter finish. He remembered Ty saying those were hops. He imagined hazelnuts, leather, and a brown sugar sweetness. The whole sensory appeal of using his nose and eyes before tasting it allowed him to enjoy the drink on a different level than he had experienced before. He could see what Ty was talking about when he mentioned not only the appeal of the beer and the volatiles, but also the creativity of the brewer. From working in science, he knew slight adjustments to the recipe created drastically different results, and that interested him. Another smile crossed his face as Dot placed the order of wings in front of him and the smell of the seasoning hit him.

"How did you learn all those things about beer? I mean, I know you work in a bar, but Ty said it's not the type of beer y'all typically sell," inquired Carson.

He guttled the wings, distracting Dot as she told him about a group of friends who also worked in various bars around town. They got together on their days off and drank beer. With the increased number of breweries, not only around Texas but also just in Austin, the friends sought unknown places to try new beers and support the local beer culture scene.

"Beer culture scene?" interrupted Carson.

"Yessir!" she exclaimed. "And if I had my druthers, I'd stick to craft. Tastes better on account the brewers focus on the quality rather than focusing' on marketing' and stock prices. Plus, there's more alcohol in them. Two or three beers packs a wallop like five or six of yours, and you ain't fixin' to go to the bathroom all the time. Ya don't Bull Moose or shotgun them. You casually drink them and enjoy the experience. Some say craft beer's got more health benefits and more nutrients than red wine."

"Yeah, but those beers are more expensive than the beer I'm used to," replied Carson.

"You had what, six Lone Stars? That's four bucks each - twenty-four dollars for a six-pack and they ain't got no flavor. Same beers will be two or three good craft beers - and even if they're five or six dollars, still comes out cheaper. Folks sell growlers for five bucks on some days."

"What the hell is a growler?" asked Carson.

"It's a vessel for carryin' beer. Some breweries don't have bottles or cans. They only have beer on tap, and ya can't take it home unless you've got a growler. You can sometimes find a sixty-four-ounce growler for five dollars, and that's over five beers for five bucks. Lone Star can't beat that!"

Carson finished the final wing and licked his fingers clean before reaching for the napkin. "Well, between you and Ty, I am interested in learning more. Maybe expand my horizons?"

Dot smiled, "Might could!"

Carson returned the smile, stood up, dropped the cash down on the table to cover the bill and tip. He hugged Dot and thanked her for spending some time explaining the Austin beer scene. As the band played the final number of the night, Carson waited outside for his Uber to show up and take him home for the evening.

For the first time in a long time, he had an enjoyable night.

CHAPTER 3

MAN IN THE MIRROR

FRIDAY, JUNE 12, 2015

The Uber ride home was quiet. The driver attempted to talk, but Carson was not interested in conversing. He was tired from the drinking, the bar food, and all that talk from Ty about craft beer. It was nice to see a familiar face for a while, but Carson was glad that Ty was gone now. Carson didn't like people seeing him like this. Especially people who knew him before. He recalled earlier in the evening when Ty approached. He wasn't even sure it was his old friend, and he said if it was him, he looked like shit. Carson hung his head in reflection. Ty wasn't wrong. Carson not only looked like it, but he also felt like shit.

How many consecutive days had he been to Giddy Ups now? Six? Seven? he wondered but couldn't recall. Whatever the number, it was enough to make a person wonder how a man without a regular job could afford to drink beer and eat wings so frequently. It was quite easy - skip a few payments on the credit card, pay the electric bill a few days late, and always fight with the cell phone company to turn the service back on. Then the money that was supposed to go to paying those bills could be used to forget those problems as well as others that maybe had not yet presented themselves.

Now he was home. He didn't have to worry about being on the roads and he didn't have to worry about anyone else seeing him and wondering what awful life events caused him to let himself go so much. He didn't want to think about those things; it was late. Since it was late and he was home alone, might as well pour a little bourbon nightcap and see what was on the television. Not like he had to be anywhere in the morning.

His hands were slightly shaking as he picked up the glass and stumbled into the living room. He was aware of his poor motor skills as he made his way through the cluttered living room and plopped into the overstuffed recliner. The room was dark, which is how he liked it, and usually kept it. The only light was coming from the kitchen, which he didn't turn off when he left the room.

Maybe a zombie movie? he thought.

Right now, he felt and moved like a zombie with his limited ability to walk. He scrolled through the channels but found nothing that looked remotely interesting. He wondered how he had all these channels and still couldn't find anything on television. At least it wasn't like when he was a kid and the television channels signed off at night. He could watch infomercials or a shopping network if he got desperate enough.

His mind drifted to earlier in the night and he wondered why he had to run into Ty? He took a sip of his drink, feeling a combination of depression, anger, and hopelessness. The conversation was kinda interesting, but his life was comfortable now. A bit shitty, but comfortable. He had his routine, as depressing as it was, and here comes Mr. Tyson Carr, like a blast from the past, with an attempt to ruin it and make things uncertain again.

He took another sip from the glass and thought about their experiences. He scowled as he tried to remember the past. There was something about Ty he didn't like, right? They probably had some fight back in college, or maybe after college. Why did they stop talking? He couldn't remember.

Perhaps another sip would bring it back. Jog his memory about the events of the past. He remembered he had an old photo album inside the nightstand across the room. It had a door that he hadn't opened in years from what he could recall. As life drifted further out of control, he felt it was best to leave Pandora's Box closed. But something was different tonight. It felt as though he were living in a repeating loop, like Groundhog Day, but with more depression and alcohol. That is, until Ty showed up as an inciting event, attempting to introduce chaos into his shitty, comfortable life. Ty is the abnormality in this otherwise consistent world. Why?

"Time to walk down memory lane," he muttered as he wobbled to stand up. After making it to his feet, he stumbled and placed a hand on the arm of the chair to right himself. Looking down at his glass, he noticed it was already empty.

"Better fill 'er up before I look at those photos. Strolling through years of memories might conjure up a powerful thirst."

He ran his fingers through his hair and took a deep breath and sighed as he prepared to pour another drink. Once the room stopped spinning, he would pour it. His hands were quivering as he raised the bottle, despite its lighter weight. A slow cascade of brown liquor flowed into his glass as he tilted it.

He didn't screw the cap back on the bottle. He sat it on the counter and started his temulent wobble back to the chair.

"I gotta whiz first," he said crudely, talking aloud to himself, and he shuffled to the bathroom, using his hand against the wall to balance.

In the bathroom, he noticed the scale sitting on the floor.

"Might as well check out and see how the old bod is doing," he groaned, looking down at the gray metal device.

He gingerly stepped on and attempted to maintain his balance. The red numbers displayed a rotating line while calculating, then stopped. He gasped at the large red number staring back at him.

He stared at the scale but couldn't make out the numbers. He blinked and tried to refocus his vision. The number remained the same as he stepped off and back on.

"Jesus!"

It was obvious his days of drinking and consuming greasy, fried bar food as his only source of nutrients were having a negative effect on his health.

"Who asked you anyway?" he shot back in an irritated tone at the still object as he kicked at it with his right foot, causing him to stumble.

"Damn thing must be broken," he decided as he turned toward the sink and bent over, uncertain if he was going to puke from the evening's beverages.

He braced himself with both arms, bent over, and waited. His hair fell in front of his face, but nothing happened. He took a couple of deep breaths and raised his head. Still bracing the counter with one arm, he used his left hand to brush his hair back. He took a long gaze in the mirror but didn't recognize the face looking back at him. It was a disheveled man who appeared to be older than him. Who the hell was in his house and looking back at him?

"That thing must be fucked up too," he concluded as he returned to the living room, barely lifting his feet, and moving more in a shuffle.

He made it to the opposite end of the living room and opened the door to the nightstand. He got down on one knee to see inside, but there it was, a green photo album just like he remembered.

"See, the old noodle still works like a charm," he said as he put his hand on top of the nightstand and carefully stood by pushing his weight down until he was standing. At least somewhat standing. He stared at the chair, which now appeared to be an impossible distance away. He grabbed the glass of bourbon from the top of the nightstand and made his way back to the chair. Dropping into the chair quickly, some bourbon splashed on his shirt.

"Damn it! That's expensive shit too!" he growled.

He placed the photo album on his lap, and the drink on the floor where he could still grab it.

"Now, let's see what we have here. Let's see what the hell ol' Tyson Carr did back in the day," he said eagerly.

The binder of the album creaked as he languidly opened it. It was the first time in several years it had moved. The pages were stuck together with static cling as he pried the first page from the adjoining second.

He looked at the images as if he were looking back at someone else's life. He stared at each photo and tried to recall the day the photo was taken. Images of track meets, parties with friends, sporting events, and pictures of him and Ty back in the dorm. He was much younger then, and judging from the man he saw in the mirror, maybe a little more time had passed than he recalled. In all the photos, Carson was smiling. A fresh, clean-shaved face, shorter hair and well-groomed. He half-smiled briefly at the images as some memories trickled back to him. The moment passed quickly.

He continued to stare at the book and cautiously turn page after page, looking back at his happier days. Days when he enjoyed college life with friends, especially Ty. There were a couple of photos of them going out on one of their cryptid expeditions. Who took that photo? Maybe an old girlfriend? Yes, that had to be it. What was her name? Sallie. No, Charlie. Samara? No… Sa- Damn it! The name was on the tip of his tongue. He thought about it but couldn't recall. That seemed to happen more frequently lately. He didn't discover anything that suggested he and Ty were anything but the best of friends. So why would he come into life now and disrupt a good thing? Well, a mediocre thing, or was it even that? He looked up and distantly stared at the wall, sighed loudly, and closed the book. A heavy wave of sadness rushed over him as he saw those good times and realized his life today was far from that. It was like looking at the photo album of a stranger.

"Forget this thing," he expressed as he flung the book to the floor, exchanging it for his drink. He mumbled into the glass as he prepared for another drink, "Glory days will pass you by."

He paused and stared into the abyss of the rocks glass for several seconds.

"Quicker than a wink from a young girl's eye," he concluded as he finished the drink.

He staggered back down the hall and into his bedroom. It was already dark in there - and fresh, thanks to the air conditioner. He hadn't made the bed in days, so it was easy to fall in and bury himself under the covers. He didn't see the point of making the bed when he was just going to sleep the next day and mess it up again. He crashed onto the mattress and rolled over onto his back, looking up at the ceiling fan.

He was exhausted, as he was most nights. He didn't understand how he could always be so tired, yet also have incredible insomnia. His body was begging for sleep, but his mind would not grant it. Images ran through his mind, constantly running through his mind: bills, work, or lack thereof, his appearance, his health, and how he was tired from always thinking about being tired. It never ended. And he was tired. Tired of dealing with it and all the aches and pains his body was feeling.

He thought about the happy young man in the photo album, the crabby townie man in the dark corners of Giddy Ups, and the weary old man in the bathroom mirror. Those were all the same person? How could that be? Impossible. It had to end, some way, somehow. But how? That was the question. He couldn't even wrap his mind around the problem and the steps needed to correct the descent into darkness.

That made him chuckle. He used to be a problem solver. People brought their problems to him to solve because they trusted him, and he had a logical, analytical mind that relied on the Scientific Method to explain issues others couldn't grasp. Now he was the one who could not understand. But it was nice seeing Ty… no, no, that was too much to deal with, he thought as he pulled the blankets closer to his head. Too many new things and he couldn't possibly do that because every time he tried before to change, he failed. When he failed, he not only returned to his normal routine, but sometimes the realization of another failure made it worse. No matter what, all roads led to failure, and he was tired of trying.

He could not sleep now with all these images racing through his mind. So rapid, like a blur. A blurry movie of his past life, a life that he barely recognized now. The images began slowing down as they crept into more recent events. His mind raced through images, trying to solve the puzzle. How could he get back to the old Carson and stop this sad, lonely life from bringing him down further?

Dozens of pictures in his head, then they stopped at just one visual: the medicine cabinet. He remembered the medicine cabinet. Behind the mirror where the old man stared at him. They said mirrors are gateways into other dimensions. Maybe this dimension had the answers to his problems?

Yes, he had a bottle of Valium that his doctor prescribed for his anxiety. A few of those and another bourbon or two would do the trick. It would be so easy. So peaceful. Who would notice? No one, he thought as he contemplated the walk into the bathroom. He wouldn't have to worry after that. Everything would be gone: the pain, the depression, the loneliness. A calmness fell over him, and a peaceful smile graced his face. Yes, that's what he would do.

But he didn't move. He just lay there thinking about it, smiling, and feeling a warm glow, too tired, and too drunk to stand up. With his mind in a calmer state, his body took over, claiming what it desperately needed until finally, he slept.

CHAPTER 4

ACE OF BASE
(OR I SAW THE SIGN)
SATURDAY, JUNE 13, 2015

It was early afternoon when Carson finally awoke on Saturday. His head rang with an all too familiar hangover. The morning after was getting increasingly more difficult to handle. Waking up in the afternoon usually depressed him even more because he felt as if he had wasted the day. A day that he had nothing to do in the first place, but he thought there was always the possibility this day would be different. But it never was.

What if it were? Maybe today he would leave the house, take in some fresh air, and do something. He thought about the prior evening's events. It was a day that was the same as every day before it in recent weeks, yet it was different. An unexpected anomaly occurred. A long-lost friend resurfaced. Carson wasn't looking for him, but there he was, and that chance event brought a few moments of happiness, or at least nostalgia, and that was something he hadn't often contemplated. Was it a chance event? There was a time when he didn't believe in chance. Everything happened for a reason and things like good luck, chance, or accident did not exist.

He struggled to recall distant knowledge that once was very present in his daily life. He thought back to physics and its general principles. There are no uncaused effects. An effect or an event that has no cause is self-created since it does not depend on anything for its creation. There is no such thing as chance - chance is not an entity which causes things to happen. Nothing happens by accident. Causality is the Law of Identity applied over time. The Law of Identity is one of those elementary ideas that is so universal it's difficult to describe it in words. The Law of Identity is one of those elementary ideas that is so universal it's difficult to describe it in words. It is the fact that whatever exists does so in a particular way. Everything that exists has an identity. He recalled the book The Celestine Prophecy, which followed an enormous shift in consciousness for the main character as he came to understand nothing happens by coincidence. Even small things that seemed to be innocent accidents, such as running into Ty at a place Carson was a regular, were not without meaning. No one is here by accident. Everyone who crosses our path has a message for us. Otherwise, they would have taken another way, or left earlier, or stayed later. The fact that these people are here means that they are in our lives.

That was the message of the book, and now Carson pondered how it applied to him. What was the purpose of running into Ty and what was the message he brought? As he drove through the streets of South Austin, he continued to dwell on that incident. He remembered daydreaming about life and how simple it was growing up. He remembered thinking about things he enjoyed in life, and his time in college was one of those. Fun times with his roommate talking about science, hunting for creatures most people did not believe in, and a youthful determination to prove them wrong.

That roommate during those good times was Ty, and even though he was drunkenly unaware of his surroundings at that moment, it was as if the universe heard him and sent Ty out of nowhere into his life. Maybe Ty is a spirit guide? Or a spirit guide that took the form of his old roommate? He tried to solve the problem as he continued to drive. In research, there are assumptions, and if one assumed Ty was a spirit guide, what was the message he wanted Carson to receive?

He said I looked like shit, which the bathroom mirror later confirmed, he thought. He said craft beer is better than the stuff I have been drinking. More than that, he spoke about socializing and having fun. Things Dot also substantiated, he continued, as his analytical mind struggled to resurrect itself. So what does it all mean?

He zoned out while driving and paid little attention to where he was going. Almost as if the universe had him on autopilot. He stopped along the side of the road. He didn't know why or even realize he had done so in his disconnected state. When he looked up, he was across the street from an Austin brewery, South Austin Brewery, to be exact. He had driven down St. Elmo Road many times and never realized there was a brewery there. Here it was, and here he was. He stopped on the street right in front of it.

This had to be another sign from the universe. First Ty and now this. A nervous feeling ran down his body. This was it. Ty talked about craft beer and how different it was. The few beers he tried last night while Ty introduced them seemed to be enjoyable. He was interested in the topic yesterday and allowed himself the fantasy of a life where he was craic with friends and always having fun. Later, he realized it was a crazy pipe dream. Or was it? He was here. All he had to do was walk inside. What would happen then? He wouldn't know his pale ale from his saison or whatever other crazy words Ty used to talk about things that, to Carson, were simply just beer earlier in the day.

He remained in his car, staring at the gray aluminum building. On the precipice of opening the door and walking inside. He imagined inside there were cool vibes, a river of beer flowing with ecstasy, and cool, interesting people who would embrace him and welcome him into their niche community.

The longer he sat in the car and thought about those things, the more nervous he became. Sure, yesterday it was all fun and games discussing beer with Ty and Dot, but here he would be on his own trying to order things he didn't understand. He would surely mess up, and those people would not embrace him, but recognize him for a fool. They would laugh at him, and it would be embarrassing. He didn't want to be embarrassed. His life was already in disarray. He couldn't handle another failure. The universe must be wrong with its messages of old college roommates and shiny aluminum beer houses. He wouldn't succumb and become a fool. He was too smart for that.

He looked in the rear-view mirror to check himself out. His hair was a mess. He looked down at his outfit, a gray t-shirt with black letters that read "Sorry I'm late. I didn't want to come". The shirt summarized his mood, and he realized he didn't want to come here, and it was time to leave. The universe would have to do without him in whatever part of the puzzle it was trying to place him. He imagined the photos of him from that album at home fading out of existence, like Marty McFly in 1955 playing guitar on stage. That's okay. Those days were long gone. People grow up, they move on. That Carson Quinn was likely dead and buried, and this shell of himself is the sad remnants of what he was now. He glanced up and caught his reflection in the rear-view mirror and stared dolefully.

Feeling a need for comfort and familiarity, he put the car in drive and headed to Giddy Ups. At least there, people knew him and welcomed him. He had a regular table and a regular waitress that accepted him and whatever flaws he had. That is where he belonged, and that was where he would return to spend the rest of the evening.

CHAPTER 5

ARE YOU READY FOR SOME FOOTBALL?

SUNDAY, JUNE 14, 2015

The morning after this time was much smoother than the previous nights. Carson had not spent the entire day and night drinking at Giddy Ups. Instead, he had a couple of beers and returned home sober. Perhaps because he was thinking about Ty and the universe's message or possibly because Dot was not working, and he didn't find Brad the Bartender to be as exciting. Either way, he could drive home on his own and spend little money. Not to mention, he could get to bed and enjoy a good night's sleep for the first time this week - possibly this month.

Things were looking up today. He didn't have a hangover. Not even the slightest sign of a headache. Like Ice Cube said, *I don't know, but today seems kinda odd...* He found himself at home and thinking about the coming months. He realized that football training camps would start soon and summer camp for the NFL started soon after. Weeks later, college football would be in full swing. He enjoyed football, both college and professional.

In Texas, sports were almost a religion. They assigned every baby in Austin a shirt with the burnt orange of the Texas Longhorns, or at least Carson thought they should. As they got older, the ritual became tailgating with the massive drinks and barbeque warm-up for the college football game on Saturdays. Sundays were for the Cowboys.

He thought about the upcoming seasons and contemplated taking in some games with Ty. Football would be an excellent way to catch up, and if memory served him, Ty also liked football. Of course he did. What guy didn't like football? That's it. He would call Ty and ask him if he wanted to catch a game. Ty had given him his phone number, and they were old friends, even though it had been years since they hung out, so surely, he would say yes. Right?

Or would he? Maybe he wouldn't want to hang out? The talk the other day was one of those gestures people do when they unexpectedly run into someone. Speak with good intentions, without meaning to follow through. They hadn't seen each other in about five years. What would be the chances that either of them would call and attempt to reconnect? Yes, the other night was just a safe conversation.

The more Carson thought about it, he realized Ty was just being polite. He saw Carson and couldn't just ignore him, even though Carson didn't see him at first. There was the chance he would look up and notice Ty walking past his table. Ty didn't want to come off as a dick, so why wouldn't he say hello and be polite for a few minutes? He already had an out in saying he was with his coworkers. That must be what it was. Just a moment that was nice when it happened, but it was gone.

He realized if he called him, it would be awkward as Ty would be in an uncomfortable position of having to say no or make up some lame excuse when he had no expectations of hearing from Carson again. If he called, he would take being polite and move it into a weird space. He always did that. Move things into awkward places. He should learn from his past mistakes. He knew better than to do that, and this time, he would let it be. It is what it is. An unexpected happy moment that was fleeting and has since passed. Maybe understanding that and enjoying those small moments of happiness was the key to turning around this bad mood and shaking the funk?

CHAPTER 6

SOME ASSEMBLY REQUIRED

MONDAY, JUNE 15, 2015

Carson reflected on the events and the difficulties of the past few days. Despite the difficulties in attempting to alter his mindset, he still had a somewhat positive feeling about his encounter with Ty at Giddy Ups and getting a brief introduction to craft beer. He still liked his Lone Star, but was more than curious about trying new beers in the craft world. He was interested in the social aspect that Dot described. Maybe getting out and trying some of these new beers would be the thing he needed to break out of his funk.

As he thought about the weekend, his phone rang. It was Ty following up after their reconnection.

"Hey, man! It was awesome seeing you the other night. Whatcha got going on tonight?" inquired Ty.

"Hey, buddy!" Carson answered in a surprisingly optimistic tone. "I had fun catching up. I don't think anything. Probably just hanging around the house watching the Astros on television."

"Man, bump that! They play like six months out of the year. You can watch them another time. Come with me instead." Carson felt hesitant but intrigued.

"Well… I guess that's true... what you got going on?"

"Some friends and I usually get together once a week and try a new brewery. Want to join us?" invited Ty.

There was a long, silent pause as Carson said nothing for a moment. Then he thought about the movie Yes, Man, where Jim Carrey played a recluse who didn't have fun or hang out with people until he stumbled upon a motivational speaker who challenged him to say "yes" to every presented opportunity. It was one of Carson's favorite movies.

"You still there?" Ty asked, breaking the silence.

"Yeah. Yes, I'm here… um, sure. Sounds wonderful. Just tell me where and when, and I'll be there," Carson said cautiously.

"We are going to meet about 7:00 p.m. at Black Star Co-op on Easy Wind Drive here in Austin," replied Ty. "I have two other friends coming tonight - Kareem and Tegan. You'll like them. They're cool people and they love trying new beers too."

Carson paused again until he heard the voice of John Michael Higgins in his head.

"Yes, man! Yes, man! Yes, man!"

"Um… Yes, sounds good," Carson said. "I'll see you guys there."

After ending the call, Carson reflected on the conversation. He had said yes, but was now fighting the urge not to go. It had been years since he hung out with Ty, except for those few moments the other night. Ty would get over the minor disappointment if Carson failed to show up. He doubted it was that important, especially since he said he had other friends coming with him. And those friends didn't even know him, so they wouldn't care. Reconnecting with Ty would be one thing, but now meeting strangers? He thought it was all too much.

But the more he thought about it, he felt a new, odd fascination with the universe and the messages he felt it was sending him. In his younger days, he often felt a little nervous about searching for cryptids, but pursuing the unknown was a powerful pull. He felt this opportunity was similar and perhaps he should give in and decide to trust his gut's surprising request to take the chance. As he reconciled the options and went through with the meeting, the first image that popped into his mind was that of WWE Superstar Daniel Bryan, one foot on the top rope and one foot on the middle rope thrusting both hands in air, index fingers pointed up as Bryan and fifty-thousand fans in attendance chanted *Yes! Yes! Yes!*

What the hell could it hurt? he concluded.

His brief stop in front of South Austin Brewery was a solo mission, and he wasn't ready. This time there would be at least one person he knew, and who knows, meeting Ty's friends could be entertaining. In the past, he had always trusted Ty's judgment, and he said they were nice people.

He took the time to get ready and at least clean up a bit. A shower, a shave that at least addressed the scruff, but kept a thin chinstrap beard with a connecting mustache and soul patch, and a splash of aftershave. He changed into a fresh pair of jeans, a Spawn orb t-shirt, and an Astros baseball cap. He studied himself in the mirror, and this time he liked the reflection staring back at him.

Thirty-seven minutes later, Carson pulled into a parking lot behind the bar's patio area.

The weather was humid, but the temperature was not excessive. A man, two women, and two dogs relaxed on the back patio, enjoying a round of drinks. Beer for the humans, water for the dogs. Not seeing his friend, Carson made his way inside. An audible "wow!" escaped his lips as he walked inside.

He was used to dark, loud bars overcrowded with people who had been there for most of the afternoon, jukeboxes, and shenanigans that resembled a prelude to something seen on the reality show *Cops*. But this place was different. For starters, the exterior was a blue building with clean lines. Not an old barn-like structure with faded red paint from twenty-five years ago or old white concrete like another one of his local hangouts.

As he opened the giant wooden door, he stared in wonderment. A wooden bar separated the patrons from the staff and behind them, a red wall with an aluminum backsplash containing over twenty tap handles. Above it, a chalkboard spanned the length of the taps and announced the list of beers. Bright colored walls of orange and green surrounded tables in an open room.

The front window allowed full light into the bar during the day but gave a beautiful view at night. One wall was made of glass and separated the main room from brew tanks. Carson stared in amazement while looking at the tanks and the colorful walls. While looking around, he heard Ty call out to him. He snapped back to reality and noticed his friend and two others sitting at the end of the table.

Carson made his way to the table and Ty stood to greet him. Extending a hand to his reacquired friend, Ty bypassed it and went in for a hug.

"C'mon, man. We hug," said Ty.

He turned and introduced Tegan Stone, a white woman in her early thirties with a bright smile and deep red hair just past shoulder length, that swept across her face, covering one of her green eyes. She was seated, but her feet barely reached the bottom of the barstool, revealing she was short. She appeared to work out, and by the tone of her arms, Carson suspected CrossFit.

He was drawn to her smile. It was a warm smile that brought a sparkle to her eyes. Ty introduced her as a psychologist who specialized in behavioral and cognitive psychology. Carson assumed she was successful at her job because her smile alone connected with him and reduced the level of anxiety he was feeling. It was a smile so genuine he felt comfortable and trust in her.

The other man at the table was Kareem Ortiz, an athletic Mexican man in his early to mid-thirties with a tight haircut that revealed a salt-n-pepper tint. He had the build of a long-distance runner and looking at him, Carson was surprised he wasn't only a water drinker. Carson was aware of his recent display of the stereotypical belly most people assume signified a beer drinker, but Kareem was solidly built.

Carson appraised him and returned a smile with an almost jealous admiration, wishing he had a similar physique. Kareem gave a confident, bright-eyed smile that reflected a man happy and energized about life and its opportunities. Ty introduced him as a physical therapist. Carson could tell Kareem was supportive and compassionate, knowledgeable, positive, yet realistic, and humble.

"Guys, this is my old college friend, Carson," introduced Ty.

Tegan smiled and Kareem gave a solid handshake that made Carson realize he did more in the gym than just running on the treadmill. Carson pulled up a stool next to Kareem and across from Tegan. He took a deep breath, knowing he was on display, and got nervous now that it was his turn to speak.

"Hey, guys," he said with a raised hand, acknowledging the fiends as he sat down to join them. "Thanks for the invite, Ty."

He was worried Ty's other friends would not accept him. He didn't have a job or a fancy title to go with this introduction. What if they wrote him off as a loser? His thoughts were quickly put at ease as they brought him into the conversation.

"So, what do you like to drink?" inquired Tegan in a silvery voice.

"I am trying to wean him off the Lone Star," interrupted Ty.

"Yes, guilty as charged!" said Carson, raising his right hand. "I drink the popular, big label beers. I am a craft beer virgin. Well, near virgin, thanks to Ty the other night!" shared Carson.

"Just the tip, buddy. Just the tip," Ty added sarcastically as the table erupted with laughter.

"Hey, don't let Ty give you a hard time," added Kareem as he tapped his right hand on top of Carson's left hand resting on the table, then retracted it. "We all started there, and there is nothing wrong with the popular beer brands. Even now, sometimes… rarely…" he said with a slight head tilt. "But sometimes, I still have one. Some are quite nice, and they are comfortable. But what I like is craft beer brings something different, yet still familiar. Look around. The look of the bar, the large tanks, and, with Black Star, there is an added feature of it being a member-owned co-op. It shows the care that the brew master puts into making each batch and the value he places on member feedback. This place has tasting panels and member-owner beer-design meetings that give the brewers input into what customers want to drink, and they brew beer to meet those wants."

Carson was immediately put at ease with Kareem's acceptance and showing his support for Carson against Ty's rantings.

Ty spoke up, "You don't see the big beer guys asking people what they want and changing their recipe or product line based on that information."

Carson reviewed the menu with a confused reaction upon seeing the wide selection of beers on the page. He shook his head in disbelief.

"I don't know, guys. There're so many choices. Ty showed me some at Giddy Ups, but he picked them. I'm a little overwhelmed looking at it myself and seeing the choices. I'm used to seeing only Bud, Miller, Coors, and Lone Star," replied Carson.

"Don't worry about it. Yes, there are a lot of choices. That's one of the cool things about microbreweries," said Tegan. "There are over three thousand active microbreweries in the United States, each making sometimes dozens of different styles of beer per year. And that number, both breweries and the number of beers, is increasing each year," she added.

"I heard there are festivals where you can meet cool people and even some brewers," spoke Carson.

"Oh man! We have to take him to a festival!" said an excited Kareem.

"Not to mention a Jester King bottle release!" added Tegan, her eyes expanding as widely as her bright smile.

A young lady entered the room, her hips swayed as she approached the table.

"Have you decided what you all want?" asked Hannah, a tall blonde that resembled a professional football cheerleader.

Ty ordered first.

"Do you still have the El Vulcano cask?" he asked.

Hannah affirmatively nodded her head.

"Let me start with a pint of that."

Kareem ordered next while Tegan and Carson continued to review the menu.

"I'll have the Conceit." He leaned in toward Carson and added, "I love IPAs the most, but sour beers are so hot right now."

Carson listened to him and then turned to Tegan.

"You better go next. I'm still confused!"

Tegan ordered the Waterloo.

"Easily one of my favorite styles of beer is a Berliner Weisse," she said.

"I don't even know what you guys have said! Is that English? Am I going to need Rosetta Stone to order beer from now on?" quipped Carson with a soft chuckle.

Hannah recommended a flight so that he could sample a variety of styles and beers.

"A flight?" asked Carson. "Another new term for me. Oh man!"

Hannah smiled. "A flight is a sample," added Hannah. "You get four 4-ounce tasters so you can try a few different beers and decide what you like. Sometimes people just come in for a flight and a burger," she added.

"That sounds like a plan!" Carson replied while still looking over the menu. "Okay, here goes!" he said with a deep breath. "Waterloo, Moebius, Epsilon, and I guess," he paused as he continued to search the menu, "um... Brimstone Barrel-Aged Crotchety Dockhand. Man, that's quite the name on that one!"

Hannah clarified, "that last one is two dollars more because it is a special barrel-aged beer from 2013. Is that okay?"

"Yeah, sure. What the hell - let's go for it!" said Carson.

"How about some food?" Hannah suggested.

"Not just yet. Let's have some drinks first, then we'll order food," spoke Ty. "This place has some excellent food," he added in a softer tone as she headed behind the bar to get the drinks.

"You picked that last one based on the name?" asked Kareem.

"Yes, it was different, and it drew me to it," admitted Carson. "That's part of marketing. A lot of beers have crazy names, and I must admit, it works on me too," responded Kareem.

Soon Hannah returned with the pints for Kareem, Tegan, and Ty. She sat a wooden paddle down in front of Carson.

"What the heck? Am I in the fraternity again?" joked Carson.

Hannah explained, "Think of a flight of steps as a series between levels. A flight of beer is the same thing. The beer is arranged on the paddle in a particular order. We typically start with the lighter brews instead of the bolder, darker brews. Drinking the beer this way ensures that you'll be able to enjoy each beer's distinct flavors and nuances without being overwhelmed by the previous sample. So, from left to right, we have Waterloo, Moebius, Epsilon, and finally, the Dockhand."

Carson chimed in, "Dot said the other day there were darker brews. Seems like I just found three of them!"

"Looks good to me!" reacted Ty.

Carson examined the samples and felt an excited anticipation to try them. He wasn't sure what the terms meant, but he was open to taking the road less traveled; at least for him.

"Tegan, we both have the Waterloo. You mentioned it was your favorite style of beer. I forget what you called it… can you tell me more about it?" requested Carson.

"Oh man, it is so refreshing! Especially on hot summer days," she said with glowing eyes and that incredible smile. "It is sour, tart, and typically low in alcohol. Something interesting about it is that it is only brewed in Berlin and dates to the Middle Ages," explained Tegan.

"Wow! That old? And why just Berlin?" asked Carson.

"It is protected by law, an appellation d'origine contrôlée, if you will. Like Trappist beers in Belgium or how French wine Bordeaux only comes from that region, or true champagne comes from that region? You get the idea," said Tegan.

Ty spoke up.

"Carson is a science geek." He added, "It ferments with both yeast and lactic-acid bacteria. The bacterial strain used in Berliner Weisse is called Lactobacillus delbrückii, named after Max Delbrück, a noted biochemist and 1969 Nobel Laureate in medicine. And it's named after him because he isolated the lactobacillus bacteria while he was head of the Institut für Gärungsgewerbe in Berlin during the 1930s," said Ty.

"Those foreign phrases are more captivating when Tegan says them," Carson said to Ty. Tegan smiled, and the guys chuckled as Carson regrouped. "So Ty said you guys hang out every Monday?" asked Carson, "How'd you all meet?"

"Hmm, that's a good one," reflected Ty, as he interrupted his sip and pulled the glass away from his lips.

"I think for us it was early last year, wasn't it?" asked Kareem. "The release of Kentucky Streetwalker at Naughty Brewing?"

"Yeah, that's right!" Ty remembered. "We were both there waiting in line and started talking," he said.

"That was a damn excellent beer," recalled Kareem.

"I think I still have a bottle in the cellar," said Ty.

"And I Think She Hung the Moon with the Belgian candy sugar, the Mexican piloncillo sugar cones, sweet pecan smoke, and the hibiscus was excellent as well," said Kareem.

"For me and Ty, it was a little longer. I first met him at the 2013 Austin Specialty Beer Festival when some friends I was with also knew him. But later we met up again when one of those same friends had a bottle share," said Tegan.

"2013? Wow, it *has* been a couple of years, hasn't it?" replied Ty.

They shared their stories and enjoyed the memories. Tegan and Ty also shared laughs. Her personality and smile shone through, and Carson understood why the guys enjoyed hanging around Tegan. As the stories continued, she smiled with her dimpled grin as she chortled in amusement. Carson watched the others and joined in the laughter with a nervous titter at the inside jokes he didn't grasp. Instead of feeling jealous at the stories they shared from different time periods of Ty's life, it surprised him to feel intrigue in learning more about his former best friend.

Kareem also enjoyed the reflection and laughed with Ty and Tegan. His laugh was more of a restrained chuckle. Looking at Tegan, in Carson's mind, her smile reminded him of the innocent smile and laughter of a small child but one holding a beer.

"This is an English pale ale, but also somewhat sour," said Kareem, taking a sip from the Conceit. "It's tart and fruity, a soured mash and single-hopped with Amarillo hops. It's a nice sour, but not tart or sweet."

It was another new word that confused Carson for a moment until Ty explained that the mash was created by combining crushed malt with hot water. It's a step in the brewing process to convert complex starches into simple sugars so fermentation can more easily occur. He explained further that a sour mash involves using Lactobacillus delbrückii bacteria.

"They made this beer in Austin, but it is a collaboration with Beavertown Brewing from London," said Kareem.

Taking his first taste of a sour beer, Carson drew his head back and furrowed his brow, but not negatively. More like surprised. It was tart, with a hint of peach. Or was that apricot? No doubt it was a refreshing drink with a little pucker, but not like Warhead sour.

"Wow! I could see drinking a couple of these on a hot summer day," stated Carson.

"See? That's what I said!" replied Tegan. "It is so smooth and light. I could drink these all day, and just under four percent, I could have a few. Not to mention, if you've had a variety of beers, a sour is a great palette cleanser."

Carson called over to Ty, "How's your Volcano or whatever you called it?"

"That's El Vulcano, but technically, you are correct. This is a rye beer, so that means malted rye is used instead of some portion of barley malt. A cask is the vessel it comes in. You're familiar with a keg."

"Remember them well from college," stated Carson.

"When beer is first put into the keg at the brewery, it has just completed fermentation and possibly some aging. For some beers, a filtering process is used to extract most of the yeast and protein particles, making for a clear beer," continued Ty.

"Once the beer is inside the keg, carbon dioxide is pumped in, and all the air is pumped out. Because of pressurization, the carbon dioxide will slowly mix with the beer itself, creating carbonation."

"When a keg is tapped, more CO_2 is pumped into the already pressurized container so that beer will be pumped through the line into the glass. It not only carbonates the beer, but it also keeps the beer's shelf life nice and long. Just like food, beer can spoil if put in contact with oxygen for a prolonged period. Follow me?"

"That's intense, but it makes sense," Carson responded favorably.

Ty continued, "Casks are much older than kegs. Twenty-five-hundred years ago, casks were often made of clay or even wood. Today, it is usually steel or aluminum. But when beer fills these containers, it is neither filtered nor pasteurized, which is the way beer has been served since its creation. By not filtering the beer, even though it may look completely clear, yeast remains floating in suspension, and this is where the difference begins. Yeast works by eating simple sugars such as maltose, glucose, and fructose, and their byproducts are alcohol and CO_2. With yeast still in the solution, more sugars can be added to the beer to give the yeast something to eat. Once the cask is closed off, the yeast does its thing. When CO_2 is created, it has nowhere to go since it is in an enclosed area, forcing it into the beer, creating natural carbonation. Once the beer is ready to be served, it can either be poured directly from the cask or pumped from a beer engine. The carbonation level of the beer is going to be much less than that of a kegged beer, which makes the beer itself much smoother and easier to drink. Because oxygen is pumped inside of the cask instead of CO_2, the shelf life of an opened cask is only about three days, and the serving temperature is typically warmer than a kegged beer, but the characters the beer can pick up from its location make for a truly remarkable drink."

After the lengthy explanation, Carson waited for a second. "So, how does it taste?"

Ty smelled the glass and took a small sip.

"It smells… fragrant."

Thinking about the initial taste, he said, "I think the rye masks the hops a little. But there are still some hops, and it has a smooth finish. It's an excellent variation of the regular Vulcan, which is a fantastic beer itself. I like it."

"Okay, I am going to move on to beer number two!" Carson said with optimism. "Lighter to darker like Hannah said, so that makes this one the Moebius." He paused and asked, "Isn't that a vampire or something from Marvel Comics?"

Kareem replied, "No, that's Morbius. But it is over ten percent, so it packs a bite!" he said with a laugh.

Ty added, "The guys who created this bar are math fans. Hence, the beers are classified as rational and irrational. It could be named for the Möbius strip or the Möbius function. But likely it's named after German mathematician and astronomer August Ferdinand Möbius, who handled both things."

Hannah dropped by again to check in with the group. Seeing where Carson was on the flight, she said, "Mobius is one of the most time-intensive beers we make, and the most complex in ingredients and flavors we produce. It's aged for six weeks in Balcones Brimstone whiskey barrels."

"That's the same barrels used in the Dockhand?" asked Carson.

"Yes, but instead of six weeks, that Dockhand has been aged in the barrel much longer. That version has been aged since 2013."

Carson noticed this beer had a smooth feeling in his mouth and he detected bourbon, but also a hint of coffee, dark roasted malts, dark Belgian candy sugar, and possibly even a little licorice. He was surprised that he liked it as well.

"I'm getting a little hungry. Who's with me?" asked Carson.

Like elementary children, eager hands shot up, making it unanimous.

"You'll have to forgive these two," replied Ty. "Tegan has a legendary appetite, and Kareem is a foodie. They are both always hungry."

"So, do you guys go somewhere every week?" inquired Carson.

Tegan answered, saying their weekly meetings were still somewhat new, but that was the goal.

"I take it this is your first time here?" asked Kareem

"Yes, I typically only go to one place and drink the same beer, so this is all new to me. Both the beer and the brewery concept," Carson replied.

"And we are kind of crazy. Crazy in general, but also crazy about the beer," said Tegan. "Hopefully we don't appear weird. I know you and Ty were friends before and sometimes that can be awkward meeting other friends you don't know," she said.

"No. No, it's cool. It's kind of nice. To be honest, I have been down for a while. A lack of interest in doing things, distancing myself from the few friends I had, eating poorly, and having horrible sleeping habits. Overall, just kind of being a loner. It sucks because I used to be fun," said Carson. "You *think* you were fun," added Ty. "I've known you a long time, my man!"

"No, I'm fairly certain I was. After running into Ty the other night, I went home and found an old photo album from when we were in college. I looked fun. You were in the photos too and you didn't seem to mind hanging around me," Carson said to Ty with a smile.

"Carson, you shared you've been feeling down. Can I ask how you felt looking at the album?" asked Tegan.

Carson paused and glanced down at his drink and attempted to collect himself as the uncomfortable feelings surfaced. It wasn't often, or ever, that he allowed himself to be that open to a stranger. But he released a deep sigh, comforted because she was a therapist. After a moment, he raised his head and answered her question.

"Truthfully? Sad. I felt sad. The night I ran into Ty at Giddy Ups, I heard a song playing, and was daydreaming about growing up when things were easier… and happier. No stress back then. No bills to worry about, no concerns about a job, about health issues. The things most of us worry about today. I didn't even notice Ty walk up. If he hadn't noticed me, and looking like I did, I am surprised he noticed, I would likely still be there in the dark corners pondering life. But it was wonderful reconnecting, and I thought this could be a second chance," said Carson.

"It is important to take those chances. As Ty said, I am a behavioral and cognitive psychologist, so I work with people struggling with the same thing. It is scary to take chances, but there is also a reward. Do you write in a journal?" she asked.

"No, I have done little writing. At least since college," he said.

"I recommend it. You can write about things that are happening and I suggest including things that were positive things that happened, no matter how small. For example, you made the bed, you ate a healthy breakfast, took a walk, reconnected with Ty, or made new friends like you are doing now. Many times we see small things and take them for granted, but when you look back over the journal and you see win after win after win, that builds confidence. Plus, you are learning new beers and breweries. It would be a handy place to record them, so you know later what you liked and didn't," she suggested.

"That sounds like something I could do," he said positively.

"Whenever I get down, I just go back and read my eBay feedback. 'Great buyer', 'fast shipper', 'highly recommended'. 'Would use again'. Perks me up every time," said Ty.

After a chuckle from everyone, Ty continued. "Just kidding, but you're a scientist. You know the importance of documentation and building supporting evidence," reminded Ty.

"I would suggest you also give that photo album a second look. You just said you were happy and smiling in the photos. Look at it for the positives rather than dwelling on the negative aspects or thinking that those days are over. You can get back to those feelings," she said.

"I certainly hope so," Carson replied.

"Can I ask you something else?" asked Tegan.

"Sure."

"Have you ever had thoughts about hurting yourself?" she asked. Carson briefly locked eyes with her, then glanced down at his beer again.

"Well… to tell you the truth, yes. That same night, yes. But I know that's not the thing to do, and I didn't attempt anything," he said. "But it was in my head."

"I will give you my number and if you ever feel like that again, please call me. I am glad to talk to you and listen," she said.

"Me too," said Kareem. "Plus, now that you met us, I am sure you love us and will want to do things together all the time. There will be no time for those Debbie-downer thoughts," he said, placing his hand on Carson's shoulder.

Hannah returned once more, ready to take the food order. It was a pleasant break from the heavy conversation.

Kareem said, "I am all over this Doughnut Double!" He read the ingredients to the group, "Two 44 Farms ground brisket patties, several slices of American cheese, sauteed onions, and aioli on a jalapeño glazed doughnut!"

Carson starred in shocked silence as he remembered his initial impression of Kareem and how healthy he appeared.

Kareem noticed Carson's gaze.

"Oh don't worry, hunny. I will burn it off at the gym tomorrow, but tonight I am relaxing."

Not to be outdone by Kareem, Tegan reviewed the menu.

"Put me down for a burger, too," she said as she tossed the menu on the table in front of her. "I will have the root beer burger, root beer caramelized onions, pickled jalapeño, gruyere & cheddar cheese, bacon, and beer mustard. Just sounds good!"

"Wow, impressive," said Carson.

"I have an appetite with the best of them," she said. "Sometimes I'm a bottomless pit."

"That's why she hangs around with us," said Ty. He was the third to choose a burger as he ordered the rainbow chard kimchi burger topped with a fried egg, cheddar cheese, and sriracha aioli.

"I will not be the one to disrupt the burger trend. Make it a chili pequin burger for me," said Carson as he ordered the 44 Farms ground beef brisket burger, topped with chili dust, avocado, jalapeño, lettuce, tomato, onion, and chili aioli.

Ty spoke, "Another cool thing about this place is not only the beer, but the food is local. All those burgers use beef from 44 Farms. It's locally sourced beef. That keeps ingredients fresh, nearly farm-to-table, and it helps the local farmers."

While Hannah was still at the table, Tegan, Ty, and Kareem ordered another drink. All three ordered an Elba, a four percent pale wheat ale garnished with a cucumber. Carson moved on to the twelve percent Epsilon, a peated Scotch ale aged in Balcones Brimstone whiskey barrels.

"Man, they love these Brimstone barrels. That's three of my four beers in them!"

But this one caught Carson's attention. It was dark, but twenty and a half IBU. Not as bitter as the over sixty-six IBUs on the Moebius. Earlier he learned from Kareem that IBU stood for International Bittering Units, and the higher the number, the more apparent hop bitterness in the beer.

He told Carson it was chemistry measuring how much isohumulone acid was in a finished product. Isohumulone was an acid in hops that gives it the bitter taste. Different hops contain different amounts. It isn't flavor, just bitterness. Flavor comes from other aspects of hops. The isohumulone is all the same except for concentration, so dilution also affects the beer's bitterness.

Epsilon had a smooth but thick mouthfeel and a sweet, nutty taste. Carson could taste the peat heavy with minimal bourbon. It was well-aged, like a nice cognac, and Carson understood what both Ty and Dot mentioned the other day about these beers being sipped and enjoyed. No shotgunning this bad boy! There was a hint of grape musk, or perhaps prunes, but not overwhelming. Just enough to make it interesting and a little mysterious. The combination of flavors was complex, and Carson noticed that as it had been sitting and coming closer to room temperature, the bourbon notes increased. This was one that he could enjoy.

The last beer was the Brimstone Barrel-Aged Crotchety Dockhand, a stout. Ty told Carson that Dockhand was a popular beer with a lot of variations. Besides the Crotchety Dockhand, there was a Recalcitrant Dockhand, a Rebellious Dockhand, a Cantankerous Dockhand, and an Insubordinate Dockhand listed on the brewery's website. The menu described this version as being inspired by the old grouch of a man that enjoys roasted coffee with his morning oatmeal. Carson thought that somewhat sounded like him, at least before meeting back up with Ty the other day, and now his other friends. Kareem and Tegan seemed cool, and Carson was surprised that it was another fun evening. Now it was about to get even better as Hannah approached with the burgers, their scent arriving at the table a few seconds prior than she did.

"How are you, hun?" asked Hannah with a wink.

"Doing great and loving these beers!" replied Carson.

"Can I get you another one?" she asked.

"You know what? I really loved that Epsilon. Can I get a pint of that? It can warm up while I finish this Dockhand."

"That's how you do it!" she said. "You learn fast!"

The words of encouragement made Carson feel happy, and a smile crossed his face.

Hannah walked away but returned with a short glass of beer - a beautiful reddish amber, light tan head that lingered.

"Is this beer rational or irrational?" asked Carson.

"It is in the Infinite Series, a subset of the Irrational Series," responded Hannah. He returned to the Dockhand to finish it up. That had less alcohol, but a higher IBU, making it have more of a dark and roasty taste with the added morning flavors of coffee, oats, and molasses. Looking at the empty flight paddle, the beer impressed Carson with both the taste and the complex characteristics. He enjoyed all the beer, but Epsilon was his favorite, followed by the Moebius, the Dockhand, and the Waterloo. He did like the Waterloo, but he enjoyed the darker beers more than he expected. He looked eagerly at the Epsilon, then turned hungrily toward the burger. Great beer, great food, and great friends. All surprising discoveries.

Carson grabbed the burger with two hands and took a huge bite. With a full mouth, he mumbled, "Sweet mother of Jesus, that's good!"

As she chewed her own burger, Tegan said, "You're right. So fresh!"

Carson looked around at the table, the brewery, and the other patrons enjoying beer and food at their tables, and back at his new friends. He took it all in and was enjoying the night.

Can this night get any better? he thought internally.

He squirmed a little as he felt the cellphone in his pocket vibrate. A muffled song played while the phone was in his pocket. He was having such a good time he momentarily forgot about the phone. Usually it was in his hands, busy surfing the internet, but tonight he hadn't looked at it once since arriving at the brewery. He removed it from his pocket and looked at the unknown number, attempting to recall if he knew it.

"What's up?" asked Ty.

"Hmm, I don't think I know this number. Someone in San Antonio," responded Carson.

After another ring, Ty said, "Either answer the damn thing or turn that ringer off. What is that? Justin Bieber?"

"No, smartass! It's Tom Petty!" sassed Carson as he clicked the answer button and an unknown voice on the other end spoke.

"Hello? Carson? This is Fred Dalton in Elmendorf. I got your number from Eric Vega."

"Eric Vega?" Carson searched his mind and concluded, "I don't think I know an Eric Vega. Are you sure you have the right number?"

"This is the number he gave me. He said he met you a couple of years ago in a bar before a Longhorns game. Said you were a science teacher."

Carson said, "Well, I *was* a science teacher."

Fred continued, "He also said you were into mysterious animals and things maybe not everyone believes in."

Carson listened quietly.

"Thing is," added Fred, "I need someone with your expertise down here. Something killed a couple of my cattle last night. Other ranchers in the area have experienced the same thing."

Carson paused for a moment and reflected on his past adventures, but that seemed like a long time ago.

"Yeah, well, the thing is, I don't really do that anymore either," a dejected Carson replied.

Fred reassured, "Well, I don't know anyone who does, so you are kind of my only hope."

"I don't know…" pondered Carson.

"I can pay. Not much, but some. Finances are tight now, but if I don't stop this creature, I will be out of business," confessed Fred.

Intrigued, Carson asked, "Creature? How do you know it's a creature?"

"I've seen him! And I got some photos on my trail camera!" Fred said excitedly. "Can you get down here closer to this weekend and have a look? The local sheriff has been out, but it isn't something that fits his skill set, but you have experience with this sort of thing."

That *Yes, Man* voice returned to Carson's head. He had a good time researching in the past, and he needed money, even if it was a one-time, small paycheck.

"Let me check my calendar and get back to you. What's a good number?" He asked Tegan for a pen and transcribed Fred's number on the back of a Black Star napkin.

As he pressed the End Call button, Ty asked if everything was okay. Carson had a distant, uncertain look on his face, but filled his friends in on the details of the call.

"What type of creature?" asked Ty.

"I don't know. He didn't say. He just said it was a mystery and something law enforcement couldn't help with."

"Hey!" said Ty, slapping Carson on the shoulder. "That sounds like our old times, buddy!" reflected Ty.

As the two looked across the table at each other, Kareem interrupted.

"Road trip! Let's all go down and have a look. We'll see what this *creature* is all about, then try local San Antonio beers!"

"Are you guys sure?" asked Carson.

Ty nodded his head, Kareem concurred, and Tegan said, "Hell yeah! I'm in! Make the call!"

Carson hit redial and told Fred he and some friends would be down Thursday.

"Thanks, Carson. See you Thursday," and hung up the phone.

CHAPTER 7

SECOND THOUGHTS

TUESDAY, JUNE 16, 2015

Carson awoke after 9:00 a.m. and realized what he agreed to last night. Still in bed, he thought about the call from Fred and wondered what he was thinking. Maybe those beers were stronger than he was expecting, and he wasn't in his right mind. He stared at the spinning ceiling fan as thoughts ran through his mind. It was crazy enough to agree to meet new people and try new beers, but to agree to drive down to San Antonio and investigate some insane story about a creature running around killing livestock?

But to drag new people into the situation with him? What the hell was he thinking? It had been several years since he searched for any animal. When he did, it was a jackalope. Not a threat to kill anyone if it was out there. Besides, he never found the damned thing. Was it that they didn't exist, or was he not good at finding them? In college, if he failed, no one cared. But now he roped others into his crazy pursuits.

This time, an unknown creature threatened an entire community. Fred and other ranchers might lose their life savings, their house, their farm, and whatever else. These people were desperate for answers, and if the truth turned out he was not good at searching for these types of creatures, it would be a colossal failure. Tegan and Kareem were nice, but they just met him. If he took them to San Antonio and failed, it would make him look like an idiot. What would they think then? And how would it look on Ty? It would piss him off and he would regret running into Carson that night at Giddy Ups. Carson realized Ty had to sell his friends on meeting him and vouched for his worthiness. How would failure make Ty look in his friends' eyes?

He thought more about it and decided the only logical thing to do was to call Fred back and call the whole thing off. This was something much too big for him. Sure, Ty had experience and would be helpful, but it had been many years since he searched for hidden animals. At least Carson assumed it had been. And Tegan and Kareem had no experience. He figured they were only viewing this only as a road trip with some potential for adventure, but how would they hold up if they were in the woods? The woods could be scary during the day, but at night they take on a whole different persona. What if they freak out then? And what if they found this creature? The shit might hit the fan once things went down. Not only for Tegan and Kareem, but likely for him as well. It had been a long time since he felt that adrenaline rush. How would he react? Yes - best to call it off and save everyone the trouble.

He continued to look at the ceiling fan and work through the problem. But what if they could help? How cool would that be? To help multiple people in a small community. People were asking for help, and if they were to receive that help, they would be grateful. And talk about a win. If they pulled this off, it would be a huge confidence boost. He thought about his assembled team: his science background, Ty's technology skills, Tegan brought psychology, and Kareem was strong, patient, compassionate, and humble. He would be cool under pressure. Considering the make-shift team had no experience working together, they appeared to complement each other's skills well and might help increase the chance of success.

It might help take his mind off things. Tegan told him yesterday, specific methods of thinking could trigger health problems, including depression. Embarking on this project was a whole different realm than he had been operating in, so it might be a pleasant distraction. It would take his mind off his fears and worries. Plus, the journal was a good idea. Documentation in a journal might be useful, not only to alter his thinking and help remind him of the minor victories and positive experiences each day, but to document evidence of their investigation. If there were an unknown creature in the woods of Elmendorf, the journal would prove solid scientific evidence of their discovery.

A discovery of that magnitude would bring tremendous opportunities to get back into work. Not only a job, but meaningful work he enjoyed. At least he knew he used to enjoy it, and he thought he would enjoy it again. Being outdoors, searching for clues, proving those who doubted him wrong… those were things he wanted to do. Maybe he could do it after all?

He decided not to call Fred and cancel.

Not just yet at least.

CHAPTER 8

CUPPA JOE

WEDNESDAY, JUNE 17, 2015

arly Wednesday morning, Carson found himself awake at 7 a.m. without the aid of an alarm clock. Only the chirping of birds outside. As he awoke, he opened one eye and winced with the other as a ray of sunshine broke through an opened blind and fell across his face. Instead of being irritated, he felt rested. He got up, and instead of dreading the day from the edge of the bed, he tidied the room. He couldn't recall the last time he made his bed.

Afterward, he reviewed the room and evaluated his surroundings. He walked over to the blinds and opened them to let in some sun. It was a positive change from the darkness that usually lived in the room, but now he saw the room was a mess. Without thinking, he began tidying things up and turned to his phone for some added music to aid in the cleanup. It didn't take long to transform the dingy and cluttered room into something presentable. Now for the other rooms in the house. It was more than an hour of work, but the house looked and smelled wonderful. Carson was proud of his work.

Write that down in the journal, he thought to himself.

Not that he had a journal yet, but he planned on taking Tegan's suggestion to heart. He glanced at his phone, impressed it was still early. On a normal day, he wouldn't even be out of bed yet, but today he already accomplished more in a couple of hours than he did all yesterday, or the day before - or any day.

Full of energy, he put on his shoes and went for a walk. It was less than one mile from his house to Coffee Cup Cove. The exercise and fresh air might do him good, he thought. Plus, he could hang out and people watch. It used to be one of his favorite activities. He left the house and began walking to the coffee shop.

Mindful of his surroundings, it astonished him to see the neighborhood. The trees were bright and full of leaves swaying in the gentle morning breeze. The sky was a beautiful blue, and he noticed the clouds were different colors. Everything was more vibrant than he remembered, and he smiled. A squirrel scampered up a nearby tree as he walked a little too close. Neighborhood dogs barked as he passed by their houses, and the birds chirped as if they were happy to see him. He wondered if this was how Snow White felt when she opened the window in the morning.

Twenty minutes later, he arrived at the coffee shop after a leisurely stroll and felt relaxed. He walked up to the window and placed an order for a medium hot breve, then found a table outside near the sidewalk. How uplifting it would be to relax outside and watch the world pass by. It sounded pleasant and peaceful to him. Moments later, a young man in the window called his name. He smiled and signaled an acknowledgement to the man, picked up his drink, and returned to the table to enjoy it.

He sipped the hot coffee and thought again about tomorrow's trip to San Antonio. Yesterday he almost called it off, but today it sounded like something exciting. A gateway to a new life of adventure.

That's why people sleep on big decisions, he thought.

He made his mind up. They were going to go to San Antonio to investigate the sightings.

The ring of his cellphone interrupted his thoughts. He reviewed the screen, surprised to see the name on the caller ID. It was Tegan. He wondered if she had misdialed.

"Hello?" he answered.

"Hey, Carson. It's Tegan… from the brewery yesterday?"

"Uh, yeah. I remember. How are you?" he asked.

"Oh, I'm good. I wanted to check in on you. See how you were doing. Are you ready for tomorrow?" she asked.

"Yes, I am ready. I was thinking about it. I got up this morning and went for a walk. Now I am at a coffee house enjoying the beautiful weather. It's been a long time since I was up and outside enjoying things," he admitted.

"I am glad you are outside. The sun and fresh air does a body good. Plus, a little morning caffeine never hurt, am I right?" she laughed again with that laugh that made Carson smile.

"I think the trip will be great. I look forward to getting to know you and Kareem more and see what all this fuss is about some creature down there," he said. "But what do you think? I know you and Kareem haven't been on a trip like this before."

"Yes, but it's exciting. Who knows what we will find?" Tegan replied optimistically. "I am excited to see what's going on down there. It sounds like a mystery, but one that needs solving to help those people, and my job involves helping others. I can't imagine losing your only source of income because of something unknown."

"Yes, it must be tough. Helping them is my main reason for going through with it. I was on the fence about canceling last night, but helping those people overruled my concerns," Carson answered.

"Putting the needs of others ahead of your own. That's progress. We won't know what we will find until we get there, but at least we can try," she said. "Hey, I will let you get back to your coffee. Hit me up any time you want to talk or need someone to listen."

"Thanks, I appreciate you checking in on me."

"If you haven't yet, take another look at the photo album as you get out and take an interest in the world around you. Bet you see those photos in a different light," suggested Tegan.

Carson enjoyed the walk home as much as he did the walk to the coffee shop. He passed people in their front yard or getting into their car to head to work. Most smiled and waved at him. He returned the gesture. He made it home to his familiar chair, but this time with the curtains open and raised windows to let some fresh air into the house.

The photo album was on the floor next to the chair. After he stared at it, he picked it up and thumbed through the pages. They weren't stuck together as much as they were the other day. The images staring back at him were the same as the night after Giddy Ups, but he understood what they were, Glimpses of frozen happy moments in his life. He understood that time was fleeting, and even the most comfortable times would pass.

He used to take pictures to capture himself in those happy times and to record what he considered a full life. These were not memorials to past events that were to be forgotten, but reminders of what happiness looked like: hanging out with friends, taking on adventures into the unknown, and celebrating minor achievements in life. These photos were a roadmap of happiness that he could use to follow the route back. Hanging out with friends and taking on fresh adventures happened in the past, yes, but they also were happening in the future. Tomorrow. And he couldn't wait to begin the journey.

CHAPTER 9

WAELZBRO

THURSDAY, JUNE 18, 2015

Carson woke up early, anticipating his new friends' arrival. It wasn't typical for him to wake up at 5:00 a.m., although sometimes he dragged himself home not long before that time. But today was different. He walked into the bathroom, sat his phone on the counter, and hit play on his music library app. Reaching into the shower, he turned on the water, and, after a few minutes, stepped inside as Hey, Soul Sister played. Squirting an ample amount of body wash onto a blue mesh sponge, the friction between the sponge and his wet body caused the lather to build, allowing the aroma of the cedarwood to reach his nostrils and bring him to life.

He took a deep breath and smiled. His toes tapped in the sudsy water, and he sang along with members of Train, hitting the high notes in the song. Or at least, he attempted to hit them.

He turned his back to the shower head, letting the water fall over his head, then stepped forward and applied shampoo. After massaging it into his hair, he turned around and grabbed the wooden handle of an exfoliating loofah back scrubber that he discovered doubled as a microphone as the phone's media player moved to Bon Jovi's Living on a Prayer.

Stepping out of the shower, he dried off with a towel and continued to sing and dance with the radio. A feeling he had not experienced in a long time. Wrapping the towel around his waist, he turned on the water in the sink and removed a can of shaving cream from the underneath cabinet. He took the razor from a cabinet drawer, wet his face, and applied the shaving cream to the areas he wanted to shave. Still keeping his beard and mustache, he trimmed and touched them up, giving each some maintenance. The mint from the shaving cream caused his face to tingle, making him feel alive and inspired like the old Zestfully clean commercials from the early 1980s.

Returning to the bedroom to get dressed, he grabbed a comfortable pair of jeans and a blue Nirvana t-shirt. Sitting on his bed, he put on his socks, then stood to step into the jeans. He looked down at his watch and slipped a foot into his brown loafers just as he heard a car pull up in the driveway.

At 6:45 a.m. Tegan's 2015 white diamond Buick Verano pulled into the driveway of Carson's 1973 avocado green single-family home on Deadwood Drive. Two quick honks of the horn signaled their arrival. Carson bolted out of the house with a grin, eager to begin the adventure. He locked up and slightly jogged to the car.

Tyson sat in the passenger seat and Kareem was in the back, ready for the drive down to San Antonio. Carson opened the rear driver's side door and Tyson held up a medium-sized white bag.

"Sausage Egg & Cheese McMuffin or McGriddle?" asked Ty.

Carson muttered, "McGriddle".

Tyson added, "We picked up Dazzle Coffee on the way. We've got a Zebra Mocha, a Caramel Macchiato, or a Snickers Mocha. Tegan already laid claim to the coconut latte."

Carson selected the Snickers. With breakfast served, the quartet began the ninety-minute drive down I-35 to Elmendorf.

It surprised and impressed Carson to discover Tegan's car had Wi-Fi. Now he could use Hotels.com to book a hotel for the weekend. Searching the local area, he found a Red Roof Inn off I-10 East for the cheap price of forty-six-dollars per night.

"Free breakfast, free parking, and free Wi-Fi? What more do we need?" he stated.

Tegan suggested, "Carson, if you and Ty don't mind sharing a bed, we could just get one room."

Ty spoke up, quoting Phil from the Hangover.

"Guys, we are not sharing beds. What are we, twelve years old?"

The passengers laughed at the line, and Carson changed the search to include two rooms. He and Ty could share one room and Kareem and Tegan in the other. With a couple of clicks on the mobile app, the reservations were confirmed.

Carson said, "I suggest we go to Fred's place first."

"We might as well. He's a rancher, so 8:30 isn't too early for him. But it is too early to drink," quipped Ty.

Kareem added, "Hopefully, we will have some time for that! There are a few craft beer spots in San Antonio I've been wanting to check out!"

Carson looked over at Kareem and asked, "How do you keep track of it? There are so many beers. I'm just learning and already feel lost. How do you know what you want to try and what you have already had? And how do you remember the ones you liked and the ones to avoid?"

Almost simultaneously, the other three passengers said, "Untappd!"

"What is Untappd?" inquired Carson.

Ty spoke, "It is FourSquare for beer. Download it on your phone and check in beers as you drink them. You can type in tasting notes, select the location, and even take photos of your beer so you can remember them later."

"And you can make friends and see what others are drinking," added Tegan. "That way, you can receive an alert if there is a rare or new beer in the area."

Kareem stated, "I like to use it for tracking whales too, especially if I am traveling!"

"Whales?" asked Carson.

"Yep, there be whales! You may hear them called whales or white whales. It's like Moby Dick, and just like Captain Ahab, it's all about searching for a beer so limited and rare it's almost mythical."

Tyson spoke up, "In the words of Herman Melville, *such a portentous and mysterious monster roused all my curiosity.*"

Kareem continued, "As you have learned by now, production and distribution limits craft beers. So beer drinkers and collectors from other places where that beer is not available may go to great lengths to acquire beers. There are online beer retailers such as CraftShack or Inside the Cellar that have a limited inventory that rotates frequently. There are online communities such as BeerAdvocate and RateBeer.com that list what people have and want, and they also have online forums where members can list what they are in search of and what they have for trade. Facebook also has communities dedicated to trading."

Carson looked surprised. "I thought shipping beer would be illegal. Isn't that like bootlegging?"

"Shipping beer to any state is filled with… gray areas," said Tyson. "It is a federal offense to ship via the postal service. UPS and FedEx will not ship beer."

Tegan added, "But… they will ship other liquids such as olive oil or marinade or even other things like yeast samples, wink wink."

"Hmm…sounds complicated," said Carson. "So, just download Untappd and start from there?"

"Yes," said Tyson. "You will need to create an account name and use your email address. Add me as a friend. TechieTyson."

Kareem spoke up, "KareemTheDream for mine."

Tegan said, "AustinTegan."

"I might as well use the Wi-Fi and download it now, then we can search the area for mysterious beasts!" said Carson.

"Mysterious beasts, indeed!" said Kareem.

At precisely 8:23 a.m., the group pulled into the driveway of Fred and Jess Dalton. Fred was standing on the enclosed front porch, drinking his morning coffee, and awaiting his visitors. As his guests emerged one by one from the car, Fred opened the door and walked out to greet them.

"Good morning!" he spoke in an inviting tone.

"Hello, I'm Carson. You called about some trouble?" Carson asked as he stepped forward, extended a hand, and exchanged a handshake with Fred. "I hope you don't mind, but I brought some friends along."

"No, I don't mind. I called because something got in with my cattle the other night, and a neighbor's a couple of nights before that. I caught the sumbitch on film!"

"You did what?!" Carson exclaimed. "Can we see it? What was it?"

"I don't know what the hell it was. At first, I thought it looked like a hairless wolf or coyote, but then I wasn't sure it was a canine at all. I saw it with my own two eyes and have it on the trail camera."

Kareem asked, "And it killed some of your cattle? Times are tough. That must be difficult!"

Fred replied, "Yeah, this farm's all we've got. We must find out what that thing is and stop it. Not just for my farm, but for everyone in the area!"

"Have you seen it since that night?" asked Tegan.

"No, ma'am," he said, tipping the brim of his hat toward Tegan. "It's been a quiet couple of nights, but I am nervous it's ready to strike again. It may have had its fill for a while, but it could be hungry again by now."

"Did it eat the calf?" asked Ty.

"No, just drank the blood. Didn't eat the meat. That's the weird part! Damndest thing I ever seen."

Carson looked over the group and said, "What do you say we take a look at those photos?"

Excitement was in the air. Ty and Carson were familiar with the feeling from their college experiences. The cattle felt it, and Kareem and Tegan felt an uneasy, excited nervousness that was an equal amount of anticipation and despair. Fred opened his phone and showed it to the group, hoping for an answer.

"I have a few photos of the creature, but I went back and reviewed some video footage from the trail camera. We can see the trail camera videos on here." Fred pulled up a web browser and located a link in his favorites.

The group drew in close to watch as the grainy video played. It showed darkness and cattle, but then something else. An animal unlike anything they had seen before. It stood upright on slender hind legs, like a kangaroo, but dropped to all fours and dashed out of camera range. In that instance, it somewhat resembled a canine, but it had a unique shape, like how a slender man would look if he were crouched down, ready to leap. But this animal had a head that differed from any canine they knew.

"What the?!" Tegan said in disbelief.

"That's some shit!" said Carson. "Can you show us where this was shot?"

"Of course," stated Fred.

Fred told the group the photos came from the camera by the old fence post. The one by the barn didn't turn up much. Despite the lack of photo evidence, Carson wanted to visit the barn location as well to see what the surrounding area looked like and if any evidence could be located.

Walking the grounds, the group noticed little by the tractor barn except some overturned bags of corn and the broken bale of hay.

"We keep small bales of hay here," said Fred. "The hay barn across the drive is where we keep the large round bales we feed to the cattle in the winter months."

As they walked past and headed toward the pasture to the other camera, Kareem noticed a small patch of dark fur sticking to a splintery side of one of the fence posts.

"Do you have a dog?" asked Kareem.

Fred shook his head no.

"I wish I had a baggie," stated Kareem. "Carson, get that McDonald's bag and a napkin. We can pick it up and put it in that for now."

Carson handed the bag to Kareem and said, "Whatever it is will smell like McGriddle now!"

Ty spoke up.

"I thought you said the thing in the video was hairless?"

"Yes, mostly hairless, except for a patch of spiky dark fur down its back that resembled a spine or quills," added Fred.

As the group continued down the dirt path, Ty asked, "We saw a blurry image in the video, but how big is this creature?"

"Hard to say," said a puzzled Fred. "It was big, from what I could see. Maybe three feet tall and four feet long? But what we saw in the video standing on its hind legs, I don't know? Four to four and a half feet? He didn't do that when I saw him! The thing that really stood out was the red eyes."

"Jesus! That's what's crazy," said Carson. "The description is like nothing I've ever seen before. Red eyes. Standing on hind legs. Canine teeth. What the hell?"

The group continued to the other camera, walking amongst cattle that paid little attention to the trespassing humans. Fred took his visitors to the site of the camera that picked up a good visual of the creature, and near the spot where he himself had an encounter. Tegan and Kareem looked at the ground as they walked through the pasture.

"I doubt we find anything here. It's been a few days and the footprints are gone. Whatever was here is mixed with the hoofprints of cattle and washed away with rain from the other night," said Tegan quietly to Kareem.

"Yeah, there's nothing here," added Kareem as he ambled and kicked at the ground.

Carson and Ty looked around at the landscape, the cattle, and off into the horizon.

"It's a pretty nice place you have here, Fred," said Ty.

"Thank you. It goes out to those green metal fence posts.

It's got a barbed wire and an electric fence because the barbed wire will not stop a two-thousand-pound bull if he decides he wants through there. The electric fence gives him another reason to reconsider, but it mustn't be too effective against that creature," said Fred.

"The pond and trees must be nice for the cattle," said Tegan.

"Not bad for them. Best we can do. We have a lot of dead trees around the property. Had a drought a few years ago. It was bad for us and we lost a lot of trees. The pond lost a lot of water during that time. It has a natural spring feeding it, so even if she's low, she doesn't run dry. Of course with this heavy rain the past few nights, the pond is doing pretty good," observed Fred.

"Hopefully not too much to wash away the grass for the cattle," commented Carson.

"We have some rolls of hills headed back toward the house. Those are water breaks to slow down the water so it doesn't wash the grass away," replied Fred, pointing to the ground rising taller than the neighboring landscape.

Carson spoke, "I don't think we're gonna find much here. Fred, can we take the photos with us and get you to email me a link to the video of the creature? I think it's best we analyze the photos you have and go from there."

"You mentioned it's been in the area. Maybe we can talk to other ranchers to see if they've had sightings?" added Ty.

"Right!" said Fred. "That's a good idea. See what they've seen. There was an incident down the road a few days before mine, and who knows where it might go next? Maybe I scared him off to somewhere else?"

Taking the photos, the group reviewed the information, set up a local meeting with the neighbors, and learned more about what they were dealing with. Fred and Carson shook hands again, commented that they would each be in touch, and the four individuals returned to their vehicle a little muddier and more confused than when they arrived.

As the car navigated the driveway, Kareem looked at his watch and noted, "It's not even noon. We can't check into the hotel yet. Whatcha say we grab some lunch and a drink?" The car's passengers agreed.

As Kareem looked at his phone and the Yelp mobile app, he suggested, "Southerleigh Fine Food & Brewery isn't too far from the hotel, and it's near the San Antonio Zoo. Maybe we can look at some animals?"

Carson spoke up, "Food and a brewery sounds pretty good to me. That McGriddle is long gone after walking Fred's ranch."

"Done!" added Tegan. "Google me the directions."

Tegan took I-37 leaving Fred's ranch and headed north toward the next stop. Exiting the highway, she briefly got lost on Avenue A and initially got excited seeing a brewery on the corner. As the car pulled into the destination, he old outward appearance impressed the group. An old silo bearing the name of the brewery looked much older than a newly opened craft brewery.

Still checking reviews, Kareem added, "This brewery moved into the old Pearl Brewery building. It just opened a few months ago."

Walking inside, they marveled at the interior of the building, an excellent integration of the old brewery with the new. A tall, slender young man with curly blonde hair with a permanent cowlick approached.

"Hello, I am Timothy. How are you this afternoon?"

"Hungry and thirsty!" said Ty.

"We have twenty-one beers on tap. Twelve of those are house beers and the others guest taps. Our chef focuses on a contemporary take on Texas cross-cultural cuisine, especially Gulf Coast dishes," reported Timothy.

Kareem said, "We're digging that silo on the way in."

Timothy responded, "Can you believe that is a private dining area that seats up to twenty people?"

Ty looked over the drink menu. "You have a rauchbier? I will have a Smoke on the Water."

Kareem ordered the Darwinian IPA, Tegan the Seawall Belgian Wheat.

"I think I am going to stick to flights to learn my way around," said Carson as he continued to study the menu.

Timothy said, "We have a beginner flight of four or an advanced flight of eight, but you select four beers and get two of each."

"I am a beginner, so I will stick with the beginner flight. How about the Dog Ate My Alarm, Putin's Revenge, Darwinian IPA, and Straight Outta Hopton."

"Nice choices," said Timothy. "I will give you a chance to look over the food options."

As Timothy walked away, Carson addressed the team. "So what do you think about the photos?" he asked. "I've gone on hunts looking for creatures for a long time and I haven't seen anything like it. Many times, you don't get photos you can make out. These are pretty good," he said as he flipped through the three photos Fred gave him. "And asking the people in the area for help is good, but how are we going to reach them? We only have a couple of days."

Tegan suggested, "We could contact the local radio station and see if we could get on for a few minutes. Maybe tonight we ask around at the grocery, restaurants, bars, or other stores in the area. Other than that, just go door-to-door and see what turns up?"

"Speaking of turn up, I'm fixin' ta turn up on some shrimp boil with pork jowl & okra, and a side order of Gulf crab spiked mac & cheese!" replied Ty.

Tegan selected the 44 Farms burger with bacon jam, Carson the cornmeal crusted saltwater catfish po'boy, and Kareem the 44 Farms Texas chili dog with hand-cut fries. Timothy returned with the beers, took the order, and disappeared again toward the kitchen. Tegan grabbed her pint of Seawall and breathed deeply.

"Hmm, it has a hint of fennel, I think." She took a sip. "Kind of like a hefe, but with a hint of blueberry instead of banana. Not too strong. Could be a little stronger, but, yeah, coriander and Belgian wheat. It's crisp and maybe a slight biscuit taste on the backend."

Kareem picked up the Darwinian. "Superbly hoppy!" he said after the first sip. "That's a solid IPA, with just a hint of tropical fruit yogurt. The higher IBUs give it a nice bitterness, and maybe there is just a touch of mango?"

Carson looked at Tyson. "What type of beer did you say yours was?"

Tyson replied, "Rauchbier. An old German smoked beer that has a definite unique flavor created by using malted barley dried over an open flame." He took a sip of the Smoke on the Water. "Oh yes," he said as he sat back in his chair with a big, cheerful grin, "Big smokiness, hints of cherry at the start, clean finish. Some rye spiciness. This is going to pair well with that shrimp!"

Carson looked on his phone for some contact information at the radio station. He thought maybe Tegan could go while the guys walked the town looking for people to speak to about any strange creatures in the area. He took a sip from the Darwinian IPA and agreed with Kareem's review. He found he liked the bitter-hoppiness flavor and concluded IPAs were much more flavorful and interesting than Lone Star. The Dog Ate My Alarm was a milk stout with a luxurious chocolate appearance that brought a smile to Carson's face.

It surprised him that the first sip was a little fizzy through the thick head. Even though it was a milk stout, he picked up a good amount of coffee, a delightful mixture of sweet coffee and chocolate. He looked at the menu and noted the beer was brewed with Café de Olla, a traditional Mexican coffee.

Thinking of that ingredient, he thought it would have had a little cinnamon to it, but he loved the opaque dark color with the creamy brown head and chocolate flavor.

"Man, this one is excellent," said Carson.

Carson's call to K-BUC went through as Timothy brought the food. Carson walked away to make the call while the others reviewed their plates with anticipation.

A few minutes later, Carson returned and told Tegan it was all set. She could go down to the station and ask for Jeff. He would put her on the air for the announcement. He also revealed he just talked to the City Hall manager to reserve a conference room for the town hall meeting.

"Now, to dig into this po'boy!" he said with an eager grin.

The portions were massive, which Carson appreciated because the menu price was more expensive than he expected. Kareem's gaze diverted as another server walked by, delivering a pot roast sandwich to a nearby table.

"Damn, that looks good too," said Kareem, distracted by the sight and smell. But he returned to his meal, satisfied with the Texas chili dog. The split bun gave a good appearance to the hot dog topped with chili and onions. "Few things beat the simplicity of a good ol' fashion chili dog," he marveled.

Kareem tasted the chilly and nodded with approval. Ty looked over the shrimp boil, unbuttoned his sleeves, and rolled them up.

"Oh, it's on! On like Donkey Kong!" he exclaimed.

Tegan looked at the thick hamburger and wondered how she could even eat it. The catfish po'boy was also stunning in size and appearance. The mac and cheese was rich, but Carson didn't note any crab included. Maybe it meant flavored? Unphased, Carson moved on to the Straight Outta Hopton, another IPA, but this one was over eleven percent.

"Wow, this one is dank and pungent," said Carson as he re-read the menu and noticed it stated the beer had a 134 IBU. "But it is amazing and has a wonder bitter finish." Another sip and he concluded, "This might be my favorite beer so far!" Tyson looked over Carson's flight.

"You picked some big ones. That last one is eleven percent and you still have Putin at fourteen. Just that flight has more ABV than a full six-pack of Lone Star!"

Carson nodded his head in agreement. "You're right. That Straight Outta Hopton was excellent, and I am looking forward to the final one. Leaving that one for last should allow it ample time to warm."

He took a sip, and a smile crossed his face. "Whoa! Even better!" said Carson. "Rich, bitter chocolate, coffee, maybe a hint of bacon, creamy, yet smooth, and the high ABV is masked. Just from the taste, I wouldn't know how high the ABV is."

He took a last bite of the catfish and looked content. Carson added, "If this were our final stop for the night, I would have a full pint of that one!"

Kareem threw down the napkin and suggested they get the check. "We have a lot of work to do this weekend, so we should get to the hotel and get ready." He gave a wave and Timothy came over with the checks.

"The good thing is the hotel is just down the road," Carson added as he stood up.

"Before we head to the hotel," began Ty, "we should stop by one of San Antonio's greatest attractions, and it is just a few miles away," he said.

"The Alamo?" answered Kareem.

"Nope. Not that one," responded Ty. "I'm talking about Barney Smith's Toilet Seat Art Museum," he said.

"Are you serious?" asked Tegan.

"Of course I am!" responded Ty. "This guy is in his 90s now. A retired plumber-turned-artist who has created a garage museum with over twelve hundred artistically designed toilet seats," Ty described. "These lids chronicle his life and the world around him. Reviews say he has marvelous stories, shows a little talk show video, and can tell you something about any toilet seat you see. Where else can you see that? And how can we possibly pass it up?" inquired Ty.

Carson looked at Ty and turned toward Kareem and Tegan. "I don't honestly know how we could skip that," he said. "And it is just down the street?" he asked.

"Yes, sir. And…it's free," said Ty.

"I'm sold," said Carson.

"Let's go check out these toilet seats!"

Ty pulled out his phone. "Let's just see if he's in," he said. More softly he added, "You have to phone ahead first to check, according to the Yelp comments," he said as the phone rang.

Barney answered the phone and said he would open the museum up for the travelers. He was accommodating and welcomed the opportunity to showcase his work to them.

Less than a four-mile drive down Broadway, they pulled up to the museum with propped open garage doors. Barney Smith greeted the group and happily gave them a tour with an in-depth description of many of his seats. The designs ranged from toilet seats with automobile license plates to seats decorated with everything from Troll dolls to a piece of the Berlin Wall to part of the Challenger space shuttle.

The group walked in awe as they made their way through the garage with the slow-walking Barney, busy telling them stories about several individual pieces.

"Who knew a toilet seat could be so interesting?" said Tegan.

"Not me. I thought he was kidding. I need to get a selfie. No one will believe this one," said Kareem.

Near the end of the museum, they stopped at a room to the far right. In the back corner, a small television was set up with recordings of Barney's TV appearances on the Montel Williams Show, The View, and other news and radio shows. Each member of the group signed the visitor's log and even signed the toilet seat depicting the state of Texas. The detour to the museum took about forty-five minutes. The group left enjoying the stories of Barney, the pride he showed in his craftsmanship, and the passion and energy he displayed. It was well worth the extra time to see this unique museum.

They climbed back into the car as Barney gave them a wave and called out, "Thank you for stopping by," as they drove away.

Eight miles later, the group pulled up to the Red Roof Inn, a terracotta and white-striped building with the American and Texas flags flying out front. Tegan and Ty waited in the car while Carson and Kareem went to the lobby to check in. Quickly returning with keys in hand, the guys walked to the car and began unloading the travel bags.

"Looks like we are side-by-side on the second floor," said Carson. "Room 207 and 208."

Ty examined the pool, and the group walked toward the white iron staircase leading to their room on the second floor of the three-story motel.

"We might have to take a dip in that bad boy later tonight. I hope you boys and girls brought your swim trunks!" said Ty.

Opening the door to room 207, Carson was pleasantly surprised. For the price, he expected a small, dingy room like the roadside motel in Joyride. He was prepared not to answer the door if anyone knocked asking for Candy Cane. But this room was agreeable: two large queen beds, a desk, a nice-sized small refrigerator, and a dresser with a good-sized television. It was not a flat screen, but it was sufficient. Carson sat his duffle bag down.

"If you don't mind, I think I will grab a shower and get ready for this evening," Carson said.

"Go ahead. I am just going to relax and watch some TV for a bit. Too bad we didn't pick up some shower beers on the way!" said Ty.

Carson grabbed a handful of clothes, a small back of toiletries from his duffel back, and disappeared into the bathroom. Turning on the shower, he got undressed as the water warmed. The water pressure impressed him and, sticking a hand in to check the temperature, he found it to his liking. The base of the shower was a white plastic bathtub. As Carson pulled the curtain to the side and stepped in, the plastic tub made a loud creak! Causing Carson to stop immediately and pause. As he fully entered the water stream and pulled the curtain back, the tub continued with the loud noise. He became uncertain with each cautious step. The tub made him question his lunch choices and wondered if a diet and exercise regimen was drastically needed. Then his thoughts turned to empathy for the people staying in room 107.

Fifteen minutes later, Carson reemerged wearing olive green cargo shorts and a navy-blue t-shirt with orange text reading *Bigfoot saw me! But nobody believes him*! Ty looked him over from head to toe, shaking his head.

"I see you are with the guys at BroBible on the defense of cargo shorts. Where's the mandals? You're over twenty-five; you should stop wearing cargo shorts. What's next? The backward ball cap?" Carson shot a look back at Ty.

"Don't hate, bro. They're an American classic. Like blue jeans. Besides, they are comfortable!"

"Yeah, well, maybe they didn't believe Bigfoot saw you because he said he spotted you in cargo shorts and it's 2015!" snarked Ty.

Carson tossed his wet towel at Ty and countered, "Don't ask me to hold any of your shit because you don't have pockets while we are out in the woods!"

Ty took the wet towel and snapped the end at Carson's bare legs, but he nimbly avoided the strike.

"I'm going to get ready, fool."

"I can't wait to see that fashion show," mumbled Carson.

"One thing's for sure, we're not going back in time, Dr. Brown!" quipped Ty.

Ty returned from his shower in a pair of black pants, a solid dark blue dress shirt unbuttoned with the sleeves rolled up, a black belt, and black shoes. Carson just looked on silently.

Tyson crowed, "Trunk club!"

Carson shook his head.

"Maybe we should check on Tegan and Kareem?" suggested Ty.

Carson and Ty knocked on the door to find Tegan already dressed and ready to go. Kareem was still in the bathroom, getting ready.

"What's the delay?" asked Ty.

"You know Kareem," said Tegan. "He's more of a diva than me! He takes forever to get ready!"

Finally, Kareem came out brushing product into his hair. He looked around the group. "What? We are going out. We should look good!" said Kareem as he sprayed a couple pumps of Jimmy Choo Man cologne into the air and walked into the fine mist.

"Tegan, are you ready for the radio station? I think if you drop us around De Leon's Grocery & Market, we can make our way through there, Tejano Taco House, the Elmendorf First Baptist Church, and some neighbors. Maybe something will turn up. We will hold the town hall tomorrow at the Elmendorf City Hall. I already cleared that with the clerk," said Carson.

"Maybe we can create and print some flyers downstairs in the business center to hang up around town?" suggested Tegan.

"Good idea. Let's take Fred's photos with us," added Kareem. "Maybe someone will recognize that animal."

Downstairs in the business center, Carson took a picture of the image in the photos with his smartphone, then emailed them to himself. "I can use Paint to crop it and add an image to our sign," suggested Carson.

He was quite proficient with Paint and in a matter of minutes had the image and his cell phone number. They printed twelve copies to post around area businesses. The town hall was ready for tomorrow evening at 6 p.m. A time they felt would allow most people to get off work and make it to the building. They hoped hitting the radio station and businesses along the nearby streets would generate some leads from the locals who might have seen the unknown beast.

A few minutes later, Tegan dropped the three men off at De Leon's Grocery and Market. Saying her goodbyes, she drove off to make her appointment at the radio station and told the boys she would meet them back at the hotel later that night.

De Leon's Grocery looked like a small-town general store, and that's what it was. A moss-green building with darker green trim, the name spelled out in yellow text outlined in the same green trim. The yellow writing also revealed the store had groceries, fresh produce & deli meats, as well as freshly prepared sandwiches. The outside Vivco Ice upright ice merchandiser would serve as a suitable home for one of the newly printed flyers. Ty suggested they go inside and see if any workers or customers recognized the animal in the brochure. Once inside, they found the story mostly empty.

As they walked through the aisles, they found one man stocking shelves. Frank Jackson turned eagerly to see if the men needed help. Frank was the cashier and night stock clerk at DeLeon's. In his early forties, he was below average height and average weight, with hard features. He had short, strawberry blond hair, and dark hazel eyes.

"Can I help you boys find anything?" asked Frank.

Carson turned and said, "I hope you can."

He handed Frank the flyer.

"Have you seen anything unusual around the area the past few weeks? Anything that looks like this?"

Frank studied the blurry image for a moment.

"No, sir. I haven't seen it… bu-but I heard something was going on. Something with a couple of ranchers losing cattle and some chickens. Folks come in here and talk, so I hear things, but so far, I've seen nothing."

"What did they say?" asked Ty.

"This creature was on the loose. I didn't believe it at first, but it was in the papers. It's mighty scary thinkin' somethin' is out there killing folks' livestock. That's their livelihood!"

While the men listened to Frank, another customer walked in and peered from over the potato chip selection. A Hispanic man of somewhat short stature, he had a plump, round figure, and curly brown hair with a thick beard. He looked over at the men and made his way toward the soda but was listening to the conversation.

"I wish I had seen that thing," said Frank.

"Well, if you hear anything else, can you call me? I'll leave you my number," said Carson.

Kareem looked over at the soda and saw the plump man quickly glance back down at the selection, avoiding eye contact. Kareem walked over.

"Excuse me, sir?" he said as he extended a hand.

The man looked and extended his hand with caution. It was apparent he was awkward and shy around strangers.

"Have you seen anything like this photo?" Kareem inquired as he presented the man with the same flyer he showed Fred.

Jorge Villa studied the picture and his dark features seemed to turn a little paler. He looked up at Kareem with dark gray eyes and bushy eyebrows. He said nothing as he looked back down at the paper.

"Sir?" repeated Kareem.

"Si! I saw it!" said a nervous Jorge with a strong accent.

Ty and Carson overheard Jorge's comments and rushed to join the conversation.

"What did you see?" Carson asked.

Jorge seemed reluctant to continue, but Ty assured him it was okay.

"I like to do the wood carvings and I've got a little shed behind my house." He paused.

"Go on," coaxed Kareem.

"Three nights ago. Monday evening I think it was. I was in my shed working when I heard a noise. It was a sound I hadn't heard before, so it caught my attention," reported Jorge.

"Did you see what was making the noise?" asked Ty.

"Yeah, I got up and walked outside. It was nearly pitch black, but I saw this large animal under the moonlight standing over by a tree at the corner of my property. It looked at me and then turned and ran down a trail and into the woods behind the lot. I was scared! It was night so I couldn't make much of it, but the moon was out, and I could see it had big teeth. But the thing I remember most was the red eyes!" The three men looked at each other.

"Red eyes?" clarified Carson, "That sounds like the same animal we are looking for! Have you seen it since?"

"No, not since that night. And I hope to never see it again. I think it was *El Diablo*!"

Frank joined the group and said, "That must have been some fright!"

"¡Siii! ¡Tengo pesadillas toda la semana!" said Jorge.

Kareem placed his hand on the man's shoulder.

"It's okay, Señor. We're looking for it and hopefully we find it. Can you call us if you see anything else?"

Jorge looked up and shook his head, obviously still nervous from the encounter. He made his way to the cash register with a six-pack of RC Cola and a bag of pork rinds. After he paid, Carson wrote his phone number on the top of the receipt.

"Thank you. You've been helpful! We are having a town meeting tomorrow at 6 p.m. over at City Hall if you guys want to come out. Maybe hear what others are seeing and share your stories," added Carson.

He shook both men's hands and headed back outside. Ty walked back in and purchased a roll of Scotch tape for the flyers. He handed it to Carson who hung the first sign on the outside ice machine.

Heading from the driveway of De Leon's, the group walked down FM 327 toward Tejano's Taco House. Carson looked around as they walked.

"With this area, that thing could be almost anywhere! Each of these places have trees and a thick brush that a sucker like that could hide," said Carson.

The night temperature was warm, but not humid, which was a relief because the walk to Tejano's was a little further than they thought. When they arrived, they were a bit surprised. It was an actual house. Outside, they found a newspaper rack with advertisement papers supporting local businesses. Kareem picked one up and flipped through it. Inside he found a Tejano's coupon for 60% off one entrée.

"Who's hungry?" asked Kareem. Inside, only one customer was dining.

Jackson Lewis sat alone at a table eating a three-enchilada plate with rice and beans. He had a thick afro and a clean-shaven face with smooth features, and he was of medium height with a lean build. The others sensed he had a quiet confidence about him. The server from Tejano's was in the back, leaving Jackson alone in the dining room. Ty approached, apologized for interrupting his meal, but asked if he had a minute. Jackson nodded his head but said nothing.

Ty showed him the flyer and asked if he had seen the animal in the area. Jackson quickly tilted his head and confirmed he had seen the creature in the photo.

"I am skeptical about strange things," he confessed. "I think life has purpose and meaning. I hate that science fiction shit and I don't care much for strange people or things either, but I can't explain the creature I saw Sunday night," he explained.

"Sunday?" replied Carson.

He and Kareem looked at Ty.

"That's just the day before Frank saw it," said Ty.

Jackson told the story of driving home late at night.

"I came around a corner on Old Corpus Christi Road. As I turned the corner, my lights shined on the road ahead, and this thing ran across the street. Damn near hit it!" said Jackson.

"Did you see what it was?" asked Carson.

"I just saw the ass-end of it, but the damn thing was big. Like about three feet tall. It had long legs, slender son of a bitch, and had a long tail," remembered Jackson.

"Like a wolf or coyote, you think?" asked Ty.

"Naw, man. It was taller than that and longer. He

disappeared into the weeds and trees. I stopped the car and tried to shine the headlights on it, but he was gone."

Carson told Jackson about the town hall meeting the next evening and wrote his phone number in case he saw anything unusual again.

"I don't think we're going to get those tacos," said Ty. "We are getting some leads and need to keep going. Whatchu boys think?" Carson and Kareem agreed.

"We could go to the Baptist church or turn back the other way and check out City Hall and Rail Logix," suggested Ty.

Carson said, "Let's go toward City Hall. We can complete details for the meeting tomorrow."

They thanked Jackson for the information, hung a flyer on the bulletin board inside the taco house, and headed back down the street.

Walking down the street toward City Hall, the men rehashed what they learned earlier today.

"I think we are making good progress," said Ty.

"This thing is still here in the neighborhood and was spotted as recently as a couple of days ago! Let's hit up that mechanic shop, then finish up at City Hall," suggested Carson.

The bay door to Rail Logix was open and a pair of legs extended from under a gray minivan. As the men walked up, a voice from under the car greeted them.

"Howdy! It'll be just a minute," the voice said.

"Take your time," said Carson. "We're just here to ask a couple of questions."

The man rolled the creeper from underneath the vehicle and looked up at the three men.

"You fellas cops or somethin'?" inquired the man.

Ty and Carson chuckled. "No, not those kinds of questions!" reassured Carson.

After rolling entirely from under the car, the man stood, wiped his grease-covered hands on his pant legs, and shook their hands.

Philip Cooper was tall and slightly chubby. He had round cheeks and gentle, warm brown eyes. His light brown hair was concealed underneath a John Deere cap that was also slightly stained with grease and oil. He spoke with a slight accent and down-home country charm that undoubtedly made him well-liked in the community.

"We're looking for an animal," said Kareem, showing the photograph. "Can you help us out? Have you seen anything?"

"Well, shit fire!" exclaimed Philip. "Last night, sure did!"

"Here?" asked Ty.

"Nope, but not too fer. Just down the road a piece. I've been working late here the past few weeks. We've been busier than a cat coverin' shit on a rock pile! It's dark when I get home ta work in my garage. I'm restoring a '67 Nova, two-door hardtop coupe. It's real nice!"

He bent over to pick up a plastic Burger King cup on the floor and spit his dip onto the paper towel inside.

"Anyways, I just got out from under the hood and was fixin' to fetch a cold one from the house. That's when I saw it in my yard eating some apples that had fallen from my tree."

Carson was intrigued.

"This was just yesterday," finished Philip.

"How big was it? What happened next?"

"It was every bit three feet tall and maybe four feet long. I thought it was one of them feral pigs, and I thought I could do with some nice bacon. I went to get my shotgun, but that's when he took off."

"A pig?!" Kareem sounded baffled. "Are you sure it's the same animal?"

"Yep, that's him. That spiky fur on the back is the same. It wasn't quite like a pig. It was hairless or short, close hair like a pig. It was shaped kinda like it from the back, but it was skinnier than a rail. It had long legs in the back, but the front looked more like a wolf or one of them hyena," said Philip.

"Well one thing's for sure," said Carson, "there aren't, or shouldn't be, any hyenas around here!"

Ty looked at the guys, "well whatever it is, when we find that thing, it won't be around here either!"

Philip shook his head while he spat in the cup again.

"Yep, that thing had some fierce-looking teeth. I am sure it could do some damage to whatever it gets a-holt of," said Philip.

Carson told him about the cattle over at Fred Dalton's ranch and the neighbor's ranch before that.

"Well you boys better bag him then!" said Philip.

Carson replied, "Hopefully, the people in the area can sleep once we figure out what it is and take it out of here!"

"I'm sure everyone will be happier'n a two-peckered dog when you do," replied Philip.

"Indeed they will!" said Carson.

He invited Philip to the town hall the next day.

"One more stop and let's call it a night?" asked Ty.

"I think we have enough from the talks tonight to set up an investigation," said Carson.

"Yep, and who knows what'll come from Tegan's radio spot," added Ty. "We are going to need some equipment if we stay out here. Some tents, some cameras for sure. Maybe headlamps, walkie-talkies, and a thermal camera. I will make a couple of calls tomorrow, and I think I can get them for a few days while we investigate."

The last stop was City Hall; however, it was already closed by the time they arrived. The doors were locked, and the parking lot was empty. They were surprised it looked like a bricked mobile home that also contained the police department.

"Since the police department works from here, I would've imagined the building to be open," said Carson. "I guess they're out patrolling."

Meanwhile, Kareem stepped aside to order an Uber. They taped a flyer on the front door and waited for their ride to arrive for the return trip to the Red Roof Inn. Ty looked at his cellphone while waiting.

"Tegan texted saying she finished her segment, and everything was ready for tomorrow," he said.

"Great!" replied Kareem. Slapping the palm of his hands against the top of his legs, he asked, "Who's thirsty?"

The trio returned to their rooms and shared a bottle of Jester King's Black Metal Farmhouse Imperial Stout Ty had brought in his duffle bag.

CHAPTER 10

TOWN HALL

FRIDAY, JUNE 19, 2015

The crew arrived at City Hall approximately 4:30 p.m. to set up for the town hall meeting. Carson got a little nervous as they walked toward the building.

"I don't know about this," said Carson to Ty hesitantly. "I was all fired up about it yesterday, but maybe we are in over our heads. I mean, it's been years since you and I did this stuff in college, and maybe I am just not good enough to do it," said Carson dejectedly.

"Snap out of it, man! These people need us. As Fred said, they are out of options, and they think we can help. You and I used to have fun doing this, and that was just for shits and giggles. Now we can help people. You were always so confident of our hunts before, and I admired that about you and looked up to your leadership. I know the past few years have been difficult, but you got this! I am proud of you for getting out of the house, trying new things, meeting new people, and taking the chance on this adventure. Now let's go in there, kick some ass, and take some names," Ty said encouragingly.

The pep talk appeared to work as a determined look crossed Carson's face.

"You're right. Let's do this!" he said with a new sense of purpose.

Entering the building, they met Natalie Simmons to review the room's layout and discuss the evening's events. Natalie had worked with the city for nearly twenty years and thought there would be a good turnout.

"Folks 'round here are plenty scared. This isn't the first time there's been strange animals in the area."

"That's right," said Ty. "About ten years ago there was a creature spotted and they called it the Elmendorf beast. Turned out to be a coyote with severe mange."

Kareem said, "After what we heard last night, who knows what we are dealing with? The descriptions ranged from wolf and hyenas to pigs to kangaroos. That's why this meeting is going to be so important."

Tegan suggested they open the meeting up with only a brief background of why they were there.

"From my experience in therapy sessions, we don't want to give too many details that could inspire their stories. I think we should keep it vague and see what the people have to say."

"That's a good idea," agreed Carson. "We can take notes and ask some people with better leads to stay behind and schedule individual follow-up interviews over the next day or so."

Ty and Tegan finished setting up tables that included soft drinks, water, and snacks donated by De Leon's Grocery.

"There, that should about do it," said Ty, finishing adding some chips to the table.

Soon the door opened, and the first people began trickling into the room. Minutes later, a steady stream entered. After only a few minutes, the one-hundred-fifty person-capacity seating was full, and a few people stood in the back of the room. It was a larger turnout than they expected.

"I hope we can get good leads from the room," said Carson.

The group looked at each other with anticipation. What would the evening bring? It was all new for Tegan and Kareem, and they were looking forward to hearing from the people of Elmendorf. It was mysterious, but exciting for them. Carson gave a quiet, single clap and rubbed his palms together as they began to sweat. He looked at the others and took a deep breath. "Let's do this," he said.

Carson approached the podium and adjusted the microphone to his height. The crowd's murmurs quieted down as he stood at the podium, ready to begin. He surveyed the crowd, cleared his throat, and began to speak. "Wow," he said, then turned to look at his friends and back again to face the audience.

"I'm beside myself seeing the turnout here today. This is great! We didn't expect this many people. Thank you all for coming and taking time out of your evening to join our meeting. We really appreciate your time and assistance."

The crowd clapped.

"My name is Carson Quinn, and I am one of the field researchers for the group. Along with me today are Tyson Carr, Kareem Ortiz, and Tegan Stone. I would like to start things off by saying a special thank you to Natalie Simmons from City Hall for providing the space and helping to set this meeting up on such short notice. We appreciate your hospitality and the generosity in getting this together."

The crowd looked on. Natalie stepped forward and gave a quick nod of her head as the crowd applauded. Carson began again after the applause died down.

"Ty and I started this group several ago when we were in college. We wanted to go out and do scientific research and investigate unique North American creatures that were yet unrecognized by mainstream science. We've heard reports of such an animal in the area, and we brought Tegan and Kareem along to assist in the investigation. We are interested in speaking with anyone here who may want to share their stories with us, and we'd be happy to talk with you one-on-one. You can always count on the fact that any information you give us will be confidential. We will never share your identity, your whereabouts, or anything else. So with that in mind, we'd like to invite you to share your stories. Anything you've witnessed, even if it seems minor. The information you share might help to identify what this creature is and remove it before anything else happens. You know, meetings like this are great because it gets people thinking, oh, I'm not crazy! 'Cause there are people in here who have seen tracks, heard noises, and caught glimpses of this creature. So maybe hearing their stories and experiences can reassure you if you have seen something and perhaps dismissed it as your imagination."

A hand raised in the second row. Ty pointed at the man. "Yes, sir?" acknowledged Carson.

The man used his elbow to nudge the woman beside him before standing.

"This lady here has had a sighting," he said. Ty perked up. "Outstanding! Would you like to tell us about it?" replied Carson.

Lily Shaw shot her husband a quick, aggravated look.

"Jonathan! You tell 'em!" she softly objected.

"No, you!" replied Jonathan.

As she stood, Carson reassured her.

"It's okay, ma'am. Any information you have is fine. Even the smallest detail."

Lily gave Jonathan another irritated look before beginning. She was an average woman of medium height and petite build. She wore a small gold earring in each ear, her blond hair placed in a bun, and light brown eyeshadow around her green eyes. Reluctantly, she began.

"About two weeks ago, we had an incident on our farm where we had a young calf come up missing. We live in a farmhouse on several acres of well-preserved land and have a herd of cattle, some chickens, and a dark brown horse named Nellie. We later discovered something had killed the calf

Jonathan interrupted, "Tell 'em what you seen before that."

"Well, a few days before that," she continued, "I was out picking apples beyond the barn. It was just getting dark. I finished and was walking back to the house and looking at the apples in my basket, planning which ones to use for pie later the next day… as I walked back, I heard a russlin' in the brush behind me. I looked up and turned… I saw this thing standing beside a tree about maybe sixty yards away. It was dark in color and tall. I couldn't tell if it had fur or what from that distance, but what stood out most were the red eyes. I hadn't seen anything with eyes like that before. It just stood there looking at me. I felt hypnotized for a moment, then I just dropped the basket of apples and took off running toward the house. I told myself, don't stop until you get to the door."

"You said it *stood*?" clarified Kareem.

"Yes, on two legs," responded Lily. "It had two front legs too, but the back ones were stronger, and it could stand up, but kind of hunched over," added Lily.

Jonathan stood. He had a medium, solid build, long face, creased brow with hazel-blue, bagged eyes, and a prominent Adam's apple.

"I think that's the same thing that took to our calf a few days later!" he said.

"What did you notice about the calf when you found it?" asked Carson.

"There were puncture marks on its neck, and some deep scratches on its back, but otherwise it was intact. Whatever it was didn't eat it like you would think a wolf or coyote would do. The weird thing was all the blood was gone from it," reported Jonathan.

The guys in the group recognized Jonathan's story fit with the other sightings of the same animal.

Tegan asked, "Have you had any more sightings since then or had any more incidents on the farm?"

"No, ma'am. Just those couple of days. A few days later, I heard my neighbor Fred had some of the same things happen to him on his farm."

The group again turned and looked at each other.

Ty spoke to Carson in a hushed tone, "This family lives close to Fred. We're gonna to want to meet up with them later and get more information."

Carson turned to the Shaws. "Thank you for the information. We would like to speak afterward and see if we can talk to you in more detail, if that's possible."

Jonathan Shaw nodded in agreement.

Another man stood in the middle of the audience. He had a large body with powerful muscles, cold, narrow brown eyes, well-kept black hair, and a thin chinstrap. He appeared to be a fan of Latin jazz, wearing a Tito Puente t-shirt and a pair of jeans. He also sported a fancy watch that gave Carson the impression he was hard worker and career focused.

Taking the microphone, he said, "Hello. My name is Ronaldo Amaya. I saw the animal just last week."

"Last week?" repeated Ty as he jotted some notes on an index card. "Go on. What did you see, Ronaldo?"

"Well, it was in the woods by my house, and it was dark. I had a long, stressful day at work, and I wanted to relax by spending some time in the woods. I get re-centered in the woods," reported Ronaldo.

Carson quoted John Muir, *"The clearest way into the universe is through a forest wilderness."*

"Yes, but this night I couldn't shake an uneasy feeling I had," said Ronaldo. "I felt like something was closing in on me. I pulled out a flashlight from my back pocket. It was dark and creepy, and I started to sweat. I was scared. As I scanned the landscape with the flashlight, that's when I saw it! It was hideous. The most grotesque thing I've seen in my life! It was greenish brown with a scaly, sparsely fur-covered hide. But the scariest thing was the huge red eyes! And an enormous mouth crowded with long fang-like teeth!"

"What was it doing?" asked Kareem.

"It just stood there with its left clawed hand resting on a tree and the right clawed the air toward me. The only thing I could think was to get out of there. I dropped the flashlight and hauled ass toward the house. I turned twice and looked over my shoulder, but it wasn't following. Didn't matter- I continued to run until I made it back to the house, and as you can see, I'm not much of a runner. I remember the low growl and hiss-like noise it made. That's still fresh in my mind!"

"What do you think it was?" asked Tegan.

"I don't know. It looked like a hellhound or something. It was tall but hunched over. On all fours it looked like it would have been big but standing on its hind legs it was frightening!" added Ronaldo.

Carson replied, "Have you been walking in those woods long? Have you ever seen anything like it?"

"I have lived there for over five years and have always enjoyed walking in the woods... but now? Now I haven't been out there since. I haven't seen it again, but haven't gone looking either," stated Ronaldo.

"Hopefully we can find the creature, remove it, and you can get back to enjoying the woods," added Ty. Ronaldo shook his head and returned to his seat.

"Do we have any others who want to share an encounter with us? After we conclude the meeting, we will remain here for some time and can talk to you about any information you have if you do not wish to share in front of the group," said Carson.

After a few moments with no one speaking up, it seemed as if the meeting was about to conclude until another man stood and spoke. Just below average height and lean with soft features, Dexter Allen was in his mid-thirties, had long wavy brown hair, and pale brown eyes.

"If we have time for another story, I'd like to share my experience. I also have some photos that I took," revealed Dexter.

"Photos?! We would be interested in seeing any photographs you have!" said an excited Carson.

"I work for a company just on the edge of town. It is a rural part of town - quiet and with very little traffic. I was making some calls in the evening about a week ago and was leaving the office around 8:45 p.m. As I walked across the parking lot to my car, I was looking at Facebook on my phone and texting to my friends to see if they wanted to meet up for a drink. I looked up and paused because I realized that it was quiet. Like deathly quiet. No birds, no barking dogs, no frogs, or insects making noise. That struck me as odd. There is a pond not too far behind the building and there are always frogs or some insect making noises in the evenings," said Dexter.

"As I scanned the area, I saw nothing at first, but then I noticed a shadow walking around the pond. It walked like a wolf, but longer and taller than any wolf I had ever seen. It was also slender. Like a malnourished extra-large Mr. Bigglesworth. Then the creature heard a noise and stood up on its hind legs. It stayed in that position for a while smelling the air, and looking around," reported Dexter.

"Wow, that's incredible!" said Kareem.

"Yes, and I still had my phone out, so I clicked on the camera app and zoomed in. The photos came out a little green and grainy because of the natural lighting, but the images are clear," said Dexter. "I clicked the video camera and filmed a few seconds as the creature stood on his legs, then dropped, and ran into the woods beyond the pond."

"That had to be scary," added Carson. "What happened next?"

"Well, I just stood in disbelief trying to run through possibilities in my head to explain what I just saw. I had never seen a large animal that was comfortable on two legs as it was four," recalled Dexter. "You never think you are going to run into something unexplained, so when it happens, it's startling."

He described that when it stood on its hind legs, it was not erect but hunched over like an old Hollywood monster movie. He recalled even after it ran off, he walked toward the pond, passing his car by a couple of feet, yet close enough to reach its safety should the strange animal return. But the beast did not return. It disappeared into the rapidly falling darkness that engulfed the woods. He stood in wonderment and a little fear.

"I'd love to look at those photos and video!" said Ty.

Carson called Dexter up to the podium to review his evidence. Kareem assisted by plugging the USB cable to Dexter's phone and Carson's computer. Once connected to the computer and the running projector, Dexter pulled up three photos and a short ten-second video taken of the creature. A couple of photos showed the creature standing on its hind legs and one on all fours. Dexter had zoomed in when taking the photo, so the creature was larger, but the photo quality was grainier. Still, the features and size of the beast could be seen.

The crowd gasped in shock and awe when the images opened, and a low chatter continued as people talked to their neighbors about what they saw on the screen. Looking at the photos, the creature didn't match any animal the group had seen before. It was easy to tell how the reported sightings ranged in comparison from wolf and coyote to boar, alien, devil, and even kangaroo. It resembled a combo of each animal. Like a Texas platypus. The video showed the animal drop from two legs down to all fours, then turn and disappear into the wooded area.

"Wow, I don't know what to say," said a stunned Carson. "Can you email me a copy of those pictures? We'd like to inspect and determine what this might be. We're up against something that looks unknown."

After a minute or two of soaking in everything they just witnessed, Ty stepped up to the podium.

"Well… I think that is a good way to end the session… Wow, I am still shocked. If you have any other information or want to talk to us, we will be here for a while longer. We would also like to have a couple of you stay and get some details from you. We want to speak in further depth with those people and work to set up an investigation to capture this animal. Dexter, if you could stay. Also the Shaws. If anyone else wants to meet further with us, you can stick around, or you can also write your name, number, and a description of your encounter in the notebook on our table up here. Thank you for coming out and sharing your experiences with us. We hope to have some answers as soon as possible," concluded Ty.

The crowd stood and filed out, others waiting around to see who else might offer a story they could eavesdrop on. Dexter, the Shaws, and a couple of other people remained. A small group of people lingered around, unsure of stepping forward or out. Ty unplugged the computer and broke down the presentation equipment as the other investigators packed up and prepared to leave.

Jordan Phillips was a man with deep-set blue eyes, a scratchy unshaven beard, and long brown hair. He had a tall and narrow build, kind of like Shaggy from Scooby Doo, with an equally charming and easy-going personality. He approached Tegan and Ty near the snack table and shared his recent encounter.

"Hello," he said, "My name is Jordan, and I saw that animal."

Ty and Tegan stopped what they were doing and listened.

"You did?" asked Tegan.

"Yes, I am an amateur astronomer and I saw the creature one morning while stargazing… I like to get out of the city limits and look at the stars where it is darker. About six weeks ago, I went out to watch the Eta Aquariids meteor shower. The peak activity was in the predawn hours the morning of May 7. Even though the shower is better viewed in the southern hemisphere because of the later sunrise, I thought with an average near-peak activity of over forty meteors per hour, I stood a good chance of seeing some before heading off to work. So, I drove out to one of my favorite spots, out at Braunig Lake Park."

"The lake? What did you see there, Jordan?" asked Carson as he walked over, joining the others.

Jordan continued, "I walked along the sidewalk and although there were some campers in tents, it was unusually quiet. There are some animals that live there like white-tail deer, some smaller mammals, and many migratory and wading birds like tri-colored herons, common moorhen, red-winged blackbirds, and Harris' Hawk. There are some tree-lined areas and tall reeds along part of the lake."

"Sounds like a pleasant spot to view wildlife," replied Carson.

"It is. And an excellent spot for channel cat fishing. Well, as I came around a bend and into one of these more secluded areas, I heard a rustling noise from the reeds. I had been looking up at the sky the whole time, so I stopped and looked toward the noise. That's when I saw, about twenty feet away, the animal that was in that guy's photos."

"Dexter's photos?" inquired Tegan.

"Yes, ma'am! It was on all fours and appeared to be

feeding on a small deer."

"Did it eat the deer?" asked Tegan?

"No," replied Jordan, "it wasn't eating it, but it looked like it was biting it on the neck. Like a vampire or something."

"I froze with fright when I saw it. It looked up, dropped the deer's neck, and gave a hissing-like noise. It was still early, and the sun was just coming up. I remember the bright red eyes it had as it looked at me. I didn't know what to do. I was far away from the car at that point and not even close to the campers. I thought I might be next, but it turned and disappeared into the reeds. I gave up on the meteor shower after that and didn't even go to work. I called the boss on my way home, told him I wasn't feeling well, and went back home to bed. I hoped to not see that beast again, but when I heard about this meeting, I wanted to come and see if I was crazy. It's nice to know I am not, but I am spooked by all the people here today that have reported seeing it. Makes me nervous going back out at night. I certainly hope you guys find it and kill it, or at least get it out of here!"

Kareem had a map of the town and drew a red X on the map in the location Jordan reported his sighting. He added an X to the site of some of the other stories they heard in town yesterday and in the meeting. He called Lily and Jonathan Shaw over to add their location to the map.

"We want to map out all the sightings so we can see if there is a pattern. Maybe then we can narrow down the search area and get a realistic search radius for our investigation," said Kareem.

Lily pointed to their location on the map, and Kareem

added their neighbor Fred Dalton's ranch. He drew a circle around the region with his finger.

"With two sightings right there, this seems like a strong possibility. Some others are not too far away, so it could be a good sign the animal is staying in that area," analyzed Kareem.

Jonathan wrote the couple's phone number and address in the notebook.

"We'd love to have you come out and look around. See if you find any more clues or locate the animal," said Jonathan.

"We'll call and set something up in the next day or two," assured Kareem.

After an exchange of handshakes, the couple left the town hall hoping the investigators could do something to return the community to the peaceful life it knew only weeks ago.

Two other attendees awaited an opportunity to speak to the team. A short, thin woman with mousy-brown hair, gray eyes, and dark freckles across her nose identified herself as schoolteacher Sharon Chapman. The other woman, a tall, thin lady whose multiple tripping episodes while walking to the podium led Carson to believe she wasn't graceful, introduced herself as Sophie Thompson, lab assistant. Despite the clumsy nature, Carson picked up on her kind-heartedness and dedication to helping others. Plus, her rosy cheeks and her ability to blush added to the appeal of her straight, neck-length red hair and sparkling emerald eyes.

It pleased Carson to see the number of leads that they received in the meeting as he prepared to talk to the two ladies. He glanced over at the notebook on the table, and although he could not see how many people wrote their name, it looked like there were at least a few. He thought ahead to narrowing down the potential interviewees and investigation sites. The anticipation made him both nervous and excited. Maybe with all this information they could find and remove this predator.

Sharon spoke first. "I teach third grade at Freedom Elementary School."

Ty asked, "Where is in relation to these other locations on the map?"

"It's about seven miles away, out South Highway 181. Just under three miles away from Braunig Lake. I arrived early to school one day about six weeks ago. It was still dark outside," said Sharon.

"Three miles, plus the animal would have to cross that highway," said Carson, looking at the map.

"Our school is just off Liedecke Road, and it is quiet out there. Some small businesses, but mostly rural," said Sharon. "I only caught a quick glimpse, but I saw what I thought was a coyote running across the back of the parking lot."

Carson asked, "Have you seen coyotes there before?"

"No, I've seen coyotes, but not by the school. This animal was taller than what I have seen before, and after hearing these people today, I think it may be the same animal. I remember it was fast. It had long, thin legs, but it was agile for its size," recalled Sharon.

"Have you seen it since then?" asked Tegan.

"No, just the one day," said Sharon.

"That's extremely helpful," said Carson. "The other stories didn't talk about how quick it was, so it's good to know what we are up against when we go out to investigate," he concluded.

Turning to Sophie, Carson asked about her sighting.

"I have not seen the creature," she said. "And I hope not to see it alive! I do work as a lab assistant, and I thought if you capture or kill this creature, you will need someone to run tests on it to help identify it. I can help you all with the lab analysis if you need that," she offered.

Ty was excited. "Yes, we need some help with that. I hadn't worked through the problem that far ahead. I think with this information we can set up a pretty good investigation and if he is still here, I think we can catch him. When we do, we will need your help," replied Ty.

Carson added, "Yes, for sure. We appreciate your offer! That will be important in solving this mystery."

She wrote her information in the notebook and left.

Kareem looked at the group and at Natalie Simmons, who remained behind to help with the cleanup.

"I think that went well," said Kareem.

"Yes, better than I expected," said Carson. "We heard good stories and we have some other people to follow-up with tomorrow. Tegan, how many others signed the book?" asked Carson. Tegan pulled the notebook toward her and looked it over.

"Looks like four new people we didn't talk to this evening, plus we have the contact information for the Shaws, Jordan, Sharon, Dexter, and Sophie."

"Well, we've got our work cut out for us," theorized

Carson. "What do you say we call it a night?"

He turned to Natalie. "Do you need us to do anything else?"

"No," she said, "I have put away everything and am ready to lock up for the night."

"Thank you for all of your help in getting this set up," said Ty. "We could not have pulled this off without your help."

Natalie smiled and acknowledged the gratitude. They walked out together into the dark parking lot.

Kareem said, "Hey, what do you say we hit up a bottle shop on the way back to the hotel? I used Untappd and found some Lone Pint Yellow Rose close to here."

Tegan agreed, acknowledging how helpful that will be when reviewing the notes from the evening and planning the next step.

"Let's do it! I'm down for a couple of bottles," said Carson as the group headed back to Tegan's Verano.

CHAPTER 11

INTERVIEW PROCESS

SATURDAY, JUNE 20, 2015

I t was just after 10 a.m. when Carson dressed and headed down to the Red Roof Inn pool where the others were already discussing the plans for the day.

"Mornin', ladies," he said as he wiped the sleep from his eyes.

Ty spoke, "There's Sleeping Beauty! 'Bout time you got your ass up. We've got work to do."

Kareem tossed Carson a packaged blueberry muffin as he sat in a white plastic chair with his face to the sun.

"Have some breakfast. Compliments of the Chef at Valero."

"Yum. Gas station muffins," Carson said sarcastically. "You don't have any more of that Yellow Rose, do you? That was delish!"

"No, 'fraid not," said Kareem. "They don't carry it at the Valero, but I can get you more of that Lone Star you used to love."

Carson looked up and grinned. "I'm good, thanks. So, what's the plan for today? Are we going to meet up with some witnesses from yesterday?" inquired Carson.

"Yes," said Tegan. "I have called Jordan. He's the astronomer guy, Sharon the schoolteacher, because the school isn't too far from where Jordan had his encounter at the lake. We're also going to meet up with Dexter. You remember his awesome photos? And then there are the Shaws - that couple who live next to Fred Dalton. Since he called us in the first place, that should be an excellent area to start," concluded Tegan.

Kareem added, "We can meet the Shaws at their farm. Since we have already been to Fred's, we can get a closer look at that land. Jordan can meet us at the lake, but Sharon isn't working today since it's Saturday, so she isn't in the same area. I set up a meeting at Las Coronas Bar & Grill off Loop 1604. It's a little closer to town, but she lives out that way and we can grab some lunch. We'll wrap up later this afternoon with Dexter over at a place called Papa Woody's Roadhouse on South Presa Street."

Carson pulled his old brown straw hat down over his eyes to block the sun. His opened shirt fell to each side of his stomach as he slouched down in the plastic chair.

"Sounds like y'all got it figured out. When do we get started?"

"It's time to get started now, slack ass," said Ty. "We have many people to interview, and I am sure the Shaws are up and ready for us now. So button up your shit and let's get ta stepping, Skippy."

Carson stood and arched his back as the group made its way to the Verano. "I want to get information that leads to catching this creature, but hopefully it hasn't caused any more damage to anyone in the area. Especially the Shaws and Daltons. They have already been through enough and it will be a hard year for them with the loss of revenue from the ranch," said Ty. "When you're running a tight business with a lot of debt, every little piece of the puzzle is important. We must get this thing before any more incidents happen. Another head or two might just put one of those ranches under. And that would also be bad for Kareem and Tegan's burger appetite."

The sun was quickly approaching high noon when the investigators pulled into the Shaw's *L.J. Ranch*. Jonathan approached, extending his hand to Carson first. Lily smiled and quietly shook Tegan's hand.

"Thanks for letting us come out and look around," said Ty.

"We visited Fred Dalton's farm a few days ago. He is the one who called us down here," said Carson.

"Is that right?" asked Jonathan.

"Yes, he lost a couple calves as well and saw the creature out around the creek. Even put up a couple of trail cams and got a few photos," revealed Carson.

"Well, I hope you get the sumbitch since he's done got three calves right here in the same area," said Jonathan.

Kareem looked at Lily. "Now you say you were down here by below the barn?"

"Yes, I was down picking some apples to bring up and bake a pie for Sunday dinner. First, I heard the russlin' in the bushes, and when I looked up, he was down by that tree over yonder. He was up on the hind legs and sniffing the air," recalled Lily. "I dropped the apples right quick and turned back toward the house. I didn't run, but I moved quickly and kept checking to see if he was followerin' me."

"That must have been scary," said Carson. "What would you have done had it come after you? That's a long way to the house."

"Yes, it is. I wouldn't have made it running. I figured I would have to jump on old Nellie over there," suggested Lily as she pointed toward a tired-looking horse grazing in the pasture.

"Well, I am glad you didn't get hurt and that you haven't seen the animal again," said Ty.

"Me too!" said Jonathan, "But the rest of the area doesn't sound so lucky. Those sightings have been common over the past few weeks. Do you guys have any idea what kind of animal it is?" asked Jonathan.

"Not yet," admitted Carson, "We are still piecing everything together. We have only a handful of blurry photos, a couple of eyewitnesses like yourself, but we haven't checked them all out yet. We're going to get through a few more today and then come up with a plan to do some investigation. Maybe spot this creature with our own eyes," said Carson.

"Are you prepared to kill it?" asked Jonathan.

"We'd rather not, especially if this is something no one has seen before," said Ty. "We will if we have to, but I think I speak for us all when I say we would rather capture this thing alive and see what we have."

"Well, I am fine if you kill it," said Lily. "I don't want to see that thing again!"

Carson and Ty looked around at the distant trees, the barn, and the field where the cows, chickens, and old Nellie lived.

"Do you mind if we walk around and see if there are any clues still here?" asked Carson.

Jonathan approved. "Sure, let's take a walk, but it's been two weeks now. I don't know what we could find. It has rained a few days since then, so I am sure any clues are long gone."

"Maybe, but we could get a feel for the land and maybe see how this thing is traveling the area," suggested Carson.

The group walked along the barn and down a path leading to the apple trees. The cattle remained distant while Nellie raised her head to check out the unknown visitors but seemed to have little interest in checking them out. The walk wasn't too far from the barn to the trees, but far enough that Carson wondered if Lily had mistaken it for another animal. The black bear was eradicated from Texas in the 1950s but had been re-emerging over the past thirty years. Since 1983, the state made it illegal to hunt bears, and sightings have increased. Since the sightings were uncommon, maybe she wasn't expecting to see a bear. It could have stood on its hind legs to reach for some apples. The group continued walking and Carson didn't mention the possibility of a bear.

As they approached the trees, Ty and Kareem searched the ground for clues, but as Jonathan thought, the recent rains left the area smooth with no signs of tracks. Tegan and Carson looked at the trees and noticed some scratches on the trunks.

"Carson, do you have a tape measure?" asked Tegan.

Carson stared at Ty, waiting to make sure he saw him, then reached into one pocket of his shorts.

"Of course, Tegan. I have one right here in my handy pocket," he said, giving Ty an awkward stare.

Ty only shook his head and chuckled, still not buying the usefulness of cargo shorts in 2015.

There were some scratches near the base of the tree, but it surprised Carson to see there were also some as tall as him. Tegan held the tape measure at the base of the tree while Carson extended it toward the scratches.

"These are just over five feet, almost six feet tall!" said a surprised Carson.

Still, in the back of his mind, he thought it could be a bear at that height. He remembered at the town hall Lily said it was a dark animal, which again could be a black bear. But she wasn't sure it had fur, and that sounded unusual. Plus, she mentioned the eyes were unique.

"You said something yesterday about the eyes?" inquired Carson.

Lily grew attentive. "Yes! Those eyes were like nothing else I have ever seen. Bright red like they were glowing," said Lily.

That eliminates a bear, thought Carson.

"And you said it was dark?" asked Ty.

"That's right. It was dark, like a dark gray or maybe brown," recalled Lily.

"Was it furry?" asked Kareem.

"I don't think so. It looked smooth, but there was some spikey fur that was even darker kind of down his spine," said Lily.

Carson kicked at the ground covering while his mind ran through possibilities of what the creature could be. "Some of the other people who saw it said it looked like maybe a boar or a wolf. One guy said a kangaroo, of all things," said Carson.

"I don't know about a boar or a wolf because it was on two legs and those walk on four. Plus, it was slender, not stocky like a boar. And a kangaroo? I ain't never seen a kangaroo except once at the zoo," said Lily.

Carson chuckled, "Yeah, the kangaroo threw me too!" he admitted.

As they continued to walk, Ty noticed some of the brush had been trampled down and made a slight trail through the back of the trees and off the Shaw's property.

"What's that direction?" asked Ty.

"Down that way, about a mile or so, is Fred Dalton's ranch," said Jonathan.

"Looks like whatever was here used that trail to get between ranches. Maybe we should follow it down to Fred's and see where else it goes?" suggested Tegan.

"You are welcome to use the 4x4 if you want to drive it down along the path and see what you can find. Beats walking it," said Jonathan.

Carson agreed. Lily remained with the group while Jonathan went to get the vehicle. A few minutes later, he returned with the 4x4 and a couple of bottles of water.

"You better take some water. It's getting warm out," suggested Jonathan. All four got in with Carson driving and Ty riding shotgun while Tegan and Kareem sat in the back.

"Let's see where this thing goes," said Ty.

With the crew settled into the 4x4, Carson started driving down the path of trampled grass and brush that ran along the property line. The trail down to Fred's ranch was straight, but Carson drove slowly because of the rough undergrowth. It took fifteen minutes to make it down to the boundary of Fred's ranch. Fred was outside working on fence repairs as the unknown vehicle entered his property. Pausing work, he laid down his hammer and raised his rifle toward the unknown trespassers. As they moved a little closer, he recognized Carson and lowered the weapon.

"What are y'all up ta this mornin'?" inquired Fred.

"We met up with the Shaws about their incident with the creature. You see anything else of him since the other day?" asked Ty.

"Nope. Nary a sign," disclosed Fred.

"Well, that's good, but he's still around somewhere," said Tegan.

"Any leads?" asked a hopeful Fred.

"Quite a few witnesses. We're out today meeting with a few of them to see what we can discover as far as clues," said Carson. "But chances are we won't find much because of the rains."

Ty suggested, "Most likely, we will have to camp out and do a field investigation to locate the creature."

"Well, I'm glad this ain't your first rodeo. The feller I spoke to about you said you were good at catching things like this," confided Fred. Ty and Carson turned and looked at each other with a non-confident glare.

Tegan broke the uncomfortable silence by speaking up.

"If the creature is still out there, we'll find it!" assured Tegan.

"I hope so!" wished Fred. "Where you headed to next?"

"We're starting here with a look at the land between the Shaws and your place. Then we'll head out to Braunig Lake, but that's a little far in the 4x4. We'll head back to get the car, then meet our next witness out at the lake. After that we're going to visit the elementary school, even though our witness can't meet us there. She said she saw the creature, so we will look at the area first, then meet up with her later," reported Carson.

"Sounds like y'all've got a long day ahead of you," acknowledged Fred. "Better get to it, I reckon."

The quartet waved as Carson turned the vehicle around.

"We will be in touch," said Kareem as the vehicle started on the trip back to the Shaw's ranch.

Arriving back at the Shaw's ranch, Carson drove the 4x4 up to the barn and talked to Jonathan and Lily.

"Well, we didn't see much, but it is a clear shot between farms. That path was beat down, so it is likely it followed the tree line right down to the Dalton place. We are going to head out to the lake to see our guy out there, but I want you to call us immediately if you have any new sightings or find any clues," said Carson.

Lily assured them they would call if anything happened. The group made their way back to the car and headed out to Braunig Lake to meet Jordan.

As Tegan pulled into the lake's parking lot, Jordan was standing in a ramada close to the water. The team exited to greet him.

"Is this where you were?" asked Kareem.

"Nice to see you again. Yeah, this is about right. I was walking down the sidewalk. Usually on the weekends there're tents set up along this side over yonder," Jordan said as he gestured with his right hand toward the dirt area past the ramada. "As I said yesterday, I was out looking at the sky for the meteor shower and the creature was over in the reeds over there, just barely in the water. When I heard the reeds rustlin', I looked down to see what was causing the commotion," recalled Jordan.

"And you said it was about twenty feet away?" asked Carson.

"Yes, that's right," confirmed Jordan.

"You mentioned it had red eyes, which we have heard from all our other witnesses too, so I think it's the same animal. But you said it hissed at you?"

"It sure did! I was scared and thought after the deer it was feeding on, I might be dessert!" said a nervous Jordan.

"It's still got you shook up pretty good, doesn't it?" asked Ty.

"Yes, sir! Those eyes I see in my nightmares. I don't know how fast it would be if it came after me, but those long back legs looked like they could scoot on down the canyon!"

Ty asked, "Did you get a look at his teeth? You said he had a deer and bit the neck like a vampire?"

"I didn't get a good look at 'em, no. I just saw he wasn't eating the deer, but he was biting the neck. Then he dropped it when he saw me and thankfully skedaddled on into the reeds and off ta who knows where next."

"Well, that was about six weeks ago you saw him, which is around the time when Sharon saw it at Freedom Elementary in the morning. That's about three miles away, so it probably stayed between the lake and the school, I imagine," said Carson.

"All the sightings aren't that far apart," said Tegan. "Within a seven to ten-mile radius, I'd say - and that's not too big of a range for an animal of that size."

Ty glanced around. "Let's walk down to the lake's edge and have a closer look at where that creature was when you saw it," suggested Ty.

The five made their way down the sidewalk and stopped on the water's edge. They got a good view of the area and headed further in the direction Jordan saw the creature. Several of the reeds were broken and the group could see signs that a struggle that took place, but there were no signs of the animal or remaining footprints of the creature.

"A dead animal like that won't stay out here long," said Carson. "Other animals will come and pick apart that carcass and clean it up pretty quick."

Ty looked around the weeds just past the grassy edge of the lake. "They may pick the meat clean, but the bones won't break down that fast. In six weeks' time? Something larger may have dragged it somewhere, but I am sure we might find it around here somewhere," replied Ty.

Laying on the side of the lake, the deer would feed a lot of other animals in the ecosystem: ravens, flies and their maggot offspring, coyotes, and other larger birds of prey such as buzzards would all take part in feeding on the body.

"The circle of life," said Ty.

"It's the wheel of fortune…," replied Carson.

"The coyotes are likely to drag the body off the path and into the underbrush. As they say, Mother Nature is the best clean up for dead animals."

The group dispersed to search for the body, and after a few minutes, Kareem stumbled upon the mostly decayed body of the fallen deer. The skin and meat were gone from the neck down, but some skin was still present.

"Do you have any of those pecker-checker gloves?" asked Carson.

"Do you mean latex gloves?" asked Tegan. Tegan handed Carson a pair of chalky latex gloves from her purse as Carson smiled. Using the antlers to drag the body into the opening a little more, Carson focused on the remaining elements of the body.

Examining what remained of the neck, the puncture wound was still intact. There were two large gashes in the neck, and one slightly smaller in the middle - but the skin around was not torn, showing the killer did nothing more than drain the victim. The other damage occurred later by the other local predators after the deer was slain. Carson was puzzled. An animal would have to eat to survive. How is this creature surviving only on the blood of its prey? All the reports mentioned biting the neck of an animal and draining blood, but not eating the animal.

"Unique," said a puzzled Carson.

Ty pulled out his cell phone. "Let's get a few photos of this. Maybe we can have Sophie look at these and she can get some clues from that."

"Yes, great idea! Take photos," said Tegan. "Because you are not putting that dead animal in the back of my new Verano!"

"So, Jordan," said Kareem, "After the animal saw you and hissed, it dropped the deer, and disappeared this direction?" he asked as he pointed toward the reeds at the back edge of the lake.

"Yes, he turned and moved pretty quickly," replied Jordan. "That's why I was glad he went that way instead of coming at me. That boy can scoot and there was no way I could outrun him."

Ty looked on. "So far, we heard no stories of it attacking people, so maybe it's not interested in humans?" said Ty.

Carson agreed but added, "With those sharp teeth, claws, and quick, long, muscular legs, if he changed his mind, I think a human would be in trouble. Just because he hasn't yet doesn't mean he wouldn't."

Wading through the reeds and flats, the group headed in the direction the creature was last seen. The grasses and cattails were thick along the backside of the lake. The shallow water, dense wetland plants, Crane flies, and humid June afternoon around the lake made for slow progress. Looking around to survey the area, Carson pointed off into the distance.

"What's that enormous building over there?"

"That's Braunig Lake Power Plant," noted Jordan.

"Power plant?" questioned Carson.

"Yes. This park and lake are a reservoir owned by City Public Service Energy. Back in the mid-1960s, San Antonio was booming, but the increased need for power coincided with a six-year drought. Before that they had been using water from Edwards Underground Aquifer, the city's sole source of drinking water, to generate power. But now they were forced to increase power but reduce the usage of the city's drinking water. Producing electrical power takes a lot of water, so they came up with the idea of building a reservoir. Actually, two reservoirs. This one and Calaveras. They cool the power plants with recycled water, which is then released into the lakes. They provide cooling for five power plants, almost five thousand acres for recreational use, as well as creating a fish and wildlife habitat," reported Jordan.

"There's no danger of contamination to the lake? There are many people out here fishing," questioned Tegan.

"Fishing is popular here. It's a major pastime of a lot of folks," said Jordan. "There have been reports of mercury in the past. CPS has taken a lot of precautions to reduce the amount, but they found, about five years ago, low levels of mercury contamination in fish at Calaveras, here at Braunig, and in the upper San Antonio River. After a review, the city said they are safe to eat. This lake is about the best around for catfish. Even in winter, around the hot water discharges next to the jetty and under the bridge at the end of the west end of the reservoir are great fishing spots. Good red drum and bass fishing too," said Jordan.

"Seems like a lot of smoke," said Ty, looking up at the sky.

"That mercury gets blown from coal stacks, gets in the waterways, and is absorbed by fish that can end up on the dinner table," continued Ty.

"Or a bird eats the fish, then something eats the bird, and it can get into the ecosystem," said Carson. "You hear stories about mutated animals all the time. Must be some truth to all the legends. You never know. This animal we are looking for might be a mutated coyote or something because of the water and animals eating fish here," theorized Carson.

"I've been fishing here since I was a tyke," said Jordan. "I think it's fine. I've never come down with anything from eating the fish."

Finally coming to the end of the reeds and back to dry land, the group faced a small, wooded area. "What's out that way?" asked Kareem.

"Nothing for a bit," said Jordan. "But out that way there is Community Baptist Church in that direction, Nando's Icehouse toward this way, and if you keep going, there is the Pilot Travel Center and Freedom Elementary."

"Freedom Elementary?" repeated Tegan. "That's where Sharon works and saw the creature in the morning before school."

"It's about four miles from here," said Jordan.

"Is it mostly backcountry out through there?" asked Carson.

"Mostly. There're a couple of small roads, and the San Antonio River runs out there," said Jordan. "But he would also have to get across I-37 to get there."

"Unless he used the river and went under the highway," said Ty.

"I say we get there using the car," suggested Kareem. "I'm not walking four miles through a river, only to walk four miles back! Plus, I'm getting hungry."

"Sounds like someone needs a Snickers!" quipped Ty.

"You can drive along Frontage Road. There's a Whataburger and Bill Miller's BBQ right next to the Best Western and Pilot Center," said Jordan.

"Let's get the BBQ," suggested Kareem.

"Aren't we going to meet Sharon at a restaurant?" asked Ty.

"Las Coronas Bar & Grill… we can skip the grill and just have the bar!" said Kareem.

"Let's go check out Bill Miller's, then we can walk around the school and head out to see Sharon after that.

With this heat, some cool drinks always hit the spot. And Bill's is a chain, but it's barbeque, so we can't go wrong there," said Carson.

The quintet walked back toward the parking lot where they shook hands and parted ways with Jordan. Getting back into the car, it was a short drive to the restaurant.

"They have a drive-thru," mentioned Tegan.

"Let's go inside and sit for a bit. We can look over what we've seen today, plus plan for the next two interviews later this afternoon," plotted Carson.

Tegan found parking in front of the entrance sign of the brown-brick building. Exiting the vehicle, Carson stood and stretched in the shaded area underneath the covered entrance. Inside, they were ushered to a booth by a young waitress wearing the name tag Alana.

Alana Iglesias was a young, seventeen-year-old Mexican woman working at Bill's during summer vacation from school. She was average height with a heart-shaped face and a small nose. Her thick blue-black hair had faint signs of purple and pink, as if it recently had been dyed. She had dark brown, close-set eyes with pink eyeshadow, dark well-shaped eyebrows, and rosebud mouth with pink shiny lip gloss. A small tattoo on her left forearm and a septum piercing suggested she was a little edgy.

"Can I start you off with something to drink?" asked Alana in a silvery voice.

Looking over the menu, all four selected sweet tea.

"Why don't I bring you a bucket? That's only $3.99 and will save you a little money," suggested Alana.

The guys looked over the menu and discussed what barbeque they wanted. Tegan stood up to go to the restroom, requesting the guys order for her.

"I know you all want barbeque, but I have been craving fried chicken. Can you get me the three-piece?" asked Tegan.

"That has fries and bread. You good with that?" asked Ty.

"Yes, that's fine. Thanks," said Tegan as she exited.

Soon, Alana returned with four cups and a bucket of sweet tea. "What did y'all decide?"

"She wants the three-piece fried chicken. And I will have the Rancher plate with mashed potatoes and coleslaw," said Ty.

Carson ordered the Rancher plate as well and Kareem, with his enormous appetite, ordered the Rodeo plate.

"Since you all want barbeque and are choosing the same sides, you might instead go for the large Bar-b-q Family Order. That's $28.95, but you get a pound and a half of barbeque that you can mix and match, a quart of potato salad, pinto beans, and coleslaw. Plus, you get pickles, onions, and two loaves of French bread. It's cheaper than if you order separate and you'll probably have some left over," suggested Alana.

"Leftovers? You don't know me and Tegan," Kareem jested.

"Perfect!" said Carson. "Can we get brisket, chicken, and ribs?" he asked.

"Oh, and I want a couple of hot links," added Ty.

Tegan returned, sat down, and removed a small notebook from her purse.

"Okay, so what do we know? Should we make a sketch?"

"I don't even know what we would sketch," admitted Carson. "We know it's about three feet tall and four or four and a half feet long, thin but muscular back legs, slender build, kind of darkish-gray, and either hairless or just a little hair on the body except for the dark spiky fur down the back. We know it has big teeth, red eyes, and makes a hissing sound. But we don't know what it looks like. We have heard canine creatures to boars to bears, and don't forget that crazy kangaroo description. We heard he looks like an under-fed Mr. Bigglesworth. It can move on four feet and at least stand upright on two, but possibly even walk as a biped. We know a lot of characteristics, but not the overall general picture," pointed out Carson.

"All the photos we have seen have been too blurry to really know what we are dealing with, but maybe we can use them as a start and add the details we have learned. At least that might be clearer than what we've seen," said Tegan.

"One thing we have seen from Fred's photos, from what Dexter showed us, and even what we learned from Jordan, it seems the creature typically moves on all fours, but when it is checking out the area like catching a smell, looking for the source of a noise, or scouting the area, that's when it goes bipedal. It can probably walk a short distance, but for longer distances I bet it drops back down," suggested Ty.

As the food arrived, Tegan decided maybe two drawings would be better. One walking and one standing. "So maybe the four-legged one can have a body like a boar, but a head like a coyote or dog. The back legs are long, thin, and muscular, with the front legs a little shorter. That is going to make it hunch forward. And the tail we know is long," said Tegan as she sketched a rough draft.

"Where did you learn to draw like that?" asked Carson.

"The Art Instruction Schools… you know, from the television commercials and comic books? I used to draw Tippy the Turtle and that pirate. I just kind of kept practicing," replied Tegan.

"Really? I didn't know anyone actually did that," replied a surprised Carson.

"Yep. Charles Schultz is a graduate, thank you!" added Tegan.

"No shit?" Carson asked as he took a bite from a meaty rib.

Tegan paused long enough to take a few bites of the fried chicken. Her facial expression showed the chicken met the anticipation and cravings she had in the recent days.

"There really is nothing like good, southern fried chicken," said Tegan as she took another bite.

Putting the drumstick down, she wiped her fingers on the napkin, and went back to adding details to the four-legged version of the animal. She added the spiky hair along the creature's arched back, added pointy ears and sharp teeth to the gaping mouth. Alana walked back to the table to check on her guests. She looked down at Tegan's sketch.

"Whatcha drawin'? El chupacabra?" asked Alana.

The table's occupants froze in silence.

"Chupacabra?" asked Ty. "You don't believe in that, do you?"

Alana gave a surprised look back. "Yes, they're around here. Been here for years," said Alana. "They drink the blood of small farm animals like chickens, goats, and so forth. And nothing else but a vampire really drinks the blood of its victims," she said matter-of-factly.

With plenty of food and drink still on the table, she dropped some more napkins and returned to the kitchen.

Kareem looked at the drawings. "Now that she mentions it….," he said.

Carson took the bipedal drawing and stared at it. Tegan had not yet finished the detail on that drawing, but Carson tried to picture it completed.

"Sonofabitch!" exclaimed Carson. "The stories we hear about here in Texas, and the so-called chupacabras that have been reported in the past look like dogs. The Texas chupacabras always look like a canine, a Mexican hairless dog, or a wolf or coyote with severe mange. Even a raccoon with mange recently was thought to be the chupacabra. But that's not what the chupacabra originally looked like when it was first reported in Puerto Rico in the 1990s. Madelyne Tolentino described it like a Hollywood monster with big alien-like eyes on the side of its head, large back legs, short hands with three fingers, about five feet tall, kind of monkey-like with spinal quills. She said the eyes were large oval red eyes that sometimes glowed and the skin bluish gray. It had a snake-like tongue, fangs, and a foul, sulfur-like stench. It was more demonic, like a cross between a vampire and a gargoyle. Come to think of it, the Puerto Rican reports said it hopped like a kangaroo," recalled Carson. "The common feature the creatures share, apart from their name, is their lust for the blood of livestock."

Ty studied the two drawings. "You know… the sightings between the Texas and Puerto Rican versions sound like two completely different animals, and someone might wonder how the story changed over the years. Why was the chupacabra like you described and now people think it looks like a dog? Well, these drawings may explain that. When it is on all fours, it looks like the Texas version, and upright it looks like the Puerto Rican version. That creature caught in Cuero, Texas, was said to be a chupacabra also had three toes. Maybe there really is something to this chupacabra," said Ty.

Kareem said, "Chupacabra means *goat-sucker* and they say it drains the blood of its victims, just like our creature."

"But why blood and not eat the meat?" asked Tegan.

"That is a puzzle," replied Carson. "Maybe the creature has evolved to where it needs that nourishment… maybe it is deficient in a mineral or something that it gets from blood?" suggested Carson.

"Iron," said Ty. "Maybe it's deficient in iron and gets it from the blood. That's the only thing I can think of that would be significantly present in the blood."

Finishing up the meal, Ty called Alana over. She instinctively brought a couple of boxes and the check.

"Thanks for your help with that drawing," said Ty. "That looks like the stories of a chupacabra. Have you ever seen one?"

"No, not personally, but a friend of mine said he saw one a few years ago," replied Alana.

"Well, keep your eyes open," said Carson. "We are just checking out the story from a teacher over here at Freedom Elementary who says she saw one about three weeks ago."

Each person dropped ten dollars on the table and Ty threw in an extra five dollars for an added tip.

"What do you say we give a quick drive by the school to look at the landscape, then head down to Las Coronas? We are supposed to meet up with Sharon in about an hour," suggested Ty.

Tegan took the road in the parking lot, turned right on 1604, then a quick right onto Liedecke Road. The school had two large parking lots up front, and one on the side. Ty speculated those were not where Sharon saw the creature because of the higher levels of traffic.

"She said she glimpsed it running across the back of the parking lot. What's behind the building?" asked Ty.

Tegan drove to the side parking lot and saw the driveway. She continued past a basketball court and behind the school before seeing two large, round parking areas well behind the school.

"That's a little far to park and walk to the school for work," suggested Carson.

"Yes, but she could park here at the far right of the parking lot, and she would have a clear line-of-sight back there. That could explain the distance she said it was observed," said Kareem.

"Those areas look like playgrounds. And look behind them, it's just green woods and what looks like a little dirt road. Perfect spot for the… I guess… chupacabra… to hide," said Carson.

"Oh, so that's what we are really going to call it now?" questioned Ty.

"Why the hell not? We don't know what it is, and that's just as good as anything. We said it fits the legends, so let's go with that until we find out otherwise," suggested Carson.

"No wonder she didn't get a good look at it," said Tegan. "That's quite a distance out to that lot and if it was just dawn, it would be hard to see it clearly."

"Let's head out to the bar and see what Sharon has to say," said Carson.

"Yeah, let's see how she reacts when we spring chupacabra on her!" chuckled Kareem.

Three miles later, the crew turned down an unnamed dirt road with a cow ranch on one side and a goat ranch on the other and headed toward a lengthy building with yellow aluminum siding. There was some shade from a large tree out front and a large outdoor dining area. That would be good in fall evenings, but not a hot June afternoon like today. Opening the door underneath the watchful eye of two faux geckos chasing each other around a Welcome to Las Coronas sign, they found Sharon already inside. The dining area was spacious, and being early afternoon, wasn't too busy.

"Definitely a nice little hideaway bar," said Carson as he walked around, heading toward Sharon's table. Piñatas hung from the ceiling and cowboys sat at the bar. Two dart machines, a pool table, a few bar-top video games, and six televisions scattered around gave more of a Giddy Ups vibe than the craft breweries Carson had been visiting recently with his friends, but it was comfortable. And during happy hour the drinks were $1.50.

"Hello! Nice to see you again," Sharon said in a friendly voice. "Are you hungry? They have good T-Bone steaks."

"That sounds pretty good," said Carson, "but we just had some barbeque down the road. We will just order drinks. How are you today?"

"That sounds pretty good," Tegan said under her breath to Kareem.

Sharon revealed she was doing well and was grateful they were there to help understand the creature.

"We visited the school before coming here," said Ty. "Where was the creature when you saw it? We were thinking you parked on the side, and it was in the back of those playground areas."

"That's right. It was a good distance, but I could see it. I was afraid for the kids because, you know, we have some small children, and an animal that size is a threat. It was early in the morning before the kids got there, so I don't know if it would be afraid of humans or not. You know kids are noisy, so that could scare it away," said Sharon.

As they spoke, Carson was momentarily distracted by the sounds of a fiddle on the television. The bar was showing a music video channel, and the sound of the fiddle stood out over the prior background songs that hadn't captured Carson's attention.

Huh, he thought to himself, *Alabama was right. If you want to play in Texas, you gotta have a fiddle in the band!*

The others at the table continued their introductory conversations while Carson watched a four-member Mexican country band called 8 Segundos play their self-titled song. He was impressed with the speed and artistry of the fiddle player.

"Wow!" he spoke aloud, drawing the attention of those at his table. "This guy is great!" said Carson.

"I didn't know you knew Spanish," responded Kareem.

"No, I don't… my high school Spanish is a bit rusty, but I am diggin' this song, and that guy reminds me of Charlie Daniels."

"How do you like it if you don't understand Spanish?" asked Kareem.

Carson's comparison was even more visible as the next song up was another song by 8 Segundos, *Cuando El Diablo bajo a Georgia*, a Spanish rendition of the Charlie Daniels song *The Devil Went Down to Georgia*. The fiddler flipped the bow behind his back and twirled it in his fingers with an artistry similar to Doc Holliday and the tin cup in the movie *Tombstone*.

Looking back to answer Ty's question, Carson said, "You don't have to understand the words of the song to enjoy it. Karl Jenkins proved that with *Adiemus*."

Puzzled, Kareem asked, "What's *Adiemus*?"

"What? Besides amazing?" replied Carson. "Adiemus was a concept focusing on the music. When we hear a song, we are distracted by many things, including the words. Jenkins sought to remove that and basically created a new language. Singers performed the song in the created language, which instead of distracting us with the words, since we don't know what the words mean, the voice becomes an instrument itself. So, the songs and album were very popular, even though people didn't understand the words," revealed Carson. "I'm gonna have to add these guys to my BandsInTown app," he said.

The discussion was broken up by a young waitress named Letty as she approached the table to ask if the newcomers wanted anything to eat or drink. The group looked over the menu, not seeing many craft options.

"Well… when in Rome," said Kareem. "I'll have a Bud Light."

Tegan looked over the menu and saw few options. "I think it'll be a Bud Light for each of us," she suggested. Ty and Carson agreed, and Letty disappeared toward the back.

Soon she returned with a cold round for the group. A few weeks ago an ice-cold Bud Light would have been refreshing to Carson. Now he disliked it, but hoped he wasn't turning into one of those beer snobs he heard about while trying to learn more about craft beer. He tried to remind himself of the two best types of beers. The first being free, meaning if a friend offers a beer, take it regardless of the style or brand. Second: cold, and this Bud Light, although not free, was cheap, and it was cold.

"So…," started Carson, "This creature, have you seen it since that day?"

"No, I only saw it that once," admitted Sharon.

"You said about six weeks ago. Do you remember the day?" Sharon paused and thought about the incident. "It was a Thursday because I remember it was pizza day at school," she recalled. Looking at her phone she scanned the weeks. "Thursday May 7," she said.

"May 7?" questioned Carson. "Just like we thought, that's the same morning Jordan saw it out at the lake. He said it disappeared into the reeds, and that was early morning. The lake is just a few miles away, so it is possible that it headed here next," replied Ty.

"Do you have any idea what it is?" asked Sharon.

"Well, we're uncertain," said Kareem, "We have a few leads and a lot of clues…"

Ty spoke up, "We think it might be…" he paused as he scanned the faces of those at the table, reluctant to say the word.

"A chupacabra…" interrupted Carson.

The group looked at Sharon awaiting her reaction. She was slightly surprised, but not to the degree they expected.

"I have heard of the chupacabra… but I didn't think I would ever see it," she said.

"You don't seem overly surprised," said Ty.

"Well, there have been rumors of chupacabras around here for years," said Sharon. "I thought it might just be one of those urban legends, but it seems every year or two someone is saying they encountered one, so I guess I thought it might be a possibility. Especially being in that town hall meeting and everyone talking about what they saw, but not knowing what it was," she stated.

"Well we aren't sure yet," admitted Carson. "We have another guy to meet with this evening, but after that we are going to investigate and see if we can find this creature before he does any more damage to the local community and ranches," Carson replied.

"Do you think it's a threat?" asked Sharon.

"So far it hasn't hurt people," said Tegan. "It has only attacked farm animals. A couple of cows, and there may be some chickens. Small animals like goats could be at risk too," continued Tegan. "The chupacabra attacks those type of animals," she concluded.

"We are going to meet our last contact then make some calls to our friends at the university. Tomorrow we set up camp and investigate this creature. We will not leave until we get it. One way or the other," said Carson.

"That's a relief!" said Sharon. "That will at least help the community rest knowing the creature is captured or killed. Maybe life can get back to normal," she said.

After a few more minutes of small talk, Carson spoke up and said they had a lot of information to go on but needed to get to their final meeting of the day and prepare for the upcoming investigation. The beers totaled $6 for the four of them, but he also picked up Sharon's tab. Twenty dollars covered the total check.

The next stop was Papa Woody's Roadhouse, about twelve miles away. Ty said they would be in contact if any additional information were needed. Returning to the car Tegan set the GPS for Papa Woody's and they headed up US-281 North.

Late afternoon and Papa Woody's wasn't to capacity yet, but later in the night it appeared likely to fill up as the Motley Crüe tribute band Looks 2 Kill would be taking the stage. Closer to concert time there would be a five-dollar cover, but now it was still free entry. At a small round, wooden table close to the stage the group located its last contact for the day, Dexter Allen. Carson thought Dexter's long, wavy, brown hair fit with the hair band genre, but the mid-thirties seemed a little passed the peak of Motley Crüe. The band wouldn't play for a few hours, so he wasn't sure Dexter was planning on staying for the band.

Reaching out for a handshake, Carson sat down. "We were really impressed with your photos yesterday," said Carson.

"Thank you," returned Dexter. "I know they were a little blurry, but you can get an idea of the size and characteristics," he said.

"You said you were working late that night when you caught the creature on your phone?" asked Ty.

"Yes, that's right. I was making some calls and came out around 8:30 that night. Trying to set up a get-together with friends I noticed that creature as I walked to my car," recalled Dexter.

"You said it was near a pond?" asked Carson. "What's interesting is you saw it near a pond, Jordan saw it at a lake, and two other contacts Fred and Jonathan have a creek that runs through their ranches. We also think that it moved from the lake to the school where Sharon saw it by traveling along the river. So, it appears to like water," said Carson.

"You described it as a Hollywood monster," recalled Tegan.

"Yes, the way it walked hunched over, it was a slower, deliberate walk on two legs. It appeared able to move faster on four legs," said Dexter.

A young waiter walked up to the table as the group was talking.

"Are you all ready to order?" asked Dexter willing to offer some guidance. "The wings are pretty good here," he added.

"Oh yeah?" asked Kareem.

"Hungry again?" inquired Ty.

"There's always room for wings," retorted Kareem as Tegan nodded her head to support his position.

"And they also have the absolute best homemade chips in town," added Dexter.

"This place is fairly nice," Tegan said to Dexter as she looked around the spacious dining room. She also noticed the large outside patio with multiple televisions and a big fan. "It looks like a popular place," she added.

"Yes, it is. Especially when a good game is on or in the evenings when a band is playing. It gets packed," he said. "It's been here just over four years now and has its share of regulars; me included. And the beer is cheap. Two bucks for beers, including Shiner," said Dexter.

Each member of the group placed an order of wings and a Shiner.

As the group awaited the drinks, Carson filled Dexter in on updates to the case.

"Thank you for those photos yesterday. They helped. We had seen trail camera footage from another witness, but they were grainy and difficult to see. Although yours were a little grainy, they are the best we've seen," commented Carson.

"They came out pretty good for catching me by surprise," said Dexter. "Had I been prepared and looking for a creature, I could have maybe taken some better pictures. When you are preoccupied with your phone and then just happen to see an unknown creature out of the corner of your eye, photo quality isn't the first consideration," said Dexter.

"We've looked at the photos, and we've talked to a few witnesses," said Ty. "This may sound a little crazy, but from what we have seen and heard, we think this might be a chupacabra," explained Ty.

"Chupacabra?" responded Dexter. "I've heard stories of the chupacabra, but I have always heard it described it like a coyote. Not like this two-legged creature," he added.

"That's true," admitted Carson, "That is the typical description here in Texas… but the chupacabra sightings, the first sightings, from Puerto Rico describe a different creature," said Carson. "That creature stood on two legs, looked like a hunched over alien with spiky hair on its spine, red eyes, and fangs. We think that with those big legs the creature can stand either on two legs like a kangaroo or running on all fours like a coyote or boar. That would explain the descriptions of each type of animals in the sightings," concluded Carson.

"Well, damn," said Dexter.

"What's the plan? How are you going to catch a creature that has never truly been caught or identified?" asked Dexter.

"That's a good question," said Carson. "We are going to make some calls to get some equipment and investigate to see this thing for ourselves. If we can catch or kill it, we have a lab assistant that was at the town hall meeting. She will analyze it and see what it is," explained Carson.

"When are you going to investigate?" asked Dexter.

"We start tomorrow," said Kareem.

"Yes," said Ty, "I am going to make some calls here in a bit to friends at the college and get some equipment. We will also stop by and get some tents from buddies in the area who are into camping."

"That's the plan," said Carson. "But tonight we can hang out, have some beer, and listen to local live music."

The group stayed for a few more hours drinking two-dollar Shiners and listening to the tribute sounds of Motley Crüe. Except for Tegan. She switched to sweet tea since she had to drive the boys back to the hotel.

The conversation faded as the band took the stage. The loudspeakers were pumping screaming guitars that made talking impossible. Even the lights seemed to distract from the ability to talk as they pulsated brightly around the group's table. The crowd size increased as the band played on throughout the night. As the evening concluded to the sounds of toasting bottles and Kickstart My Heart, Carson was glad they didn't have to get up early in the morning.

CHAPTER 12

BASE CAMP

SUNDAY, JUNE 21, 2015

Mid-morning, a white Bronco pulled up in front of the group's hotel. It was an old 1993 model that had seen its better days. Two individuals rode inside, but it was not Al Cowlings and OJ Simpson. It was Tomo Watanabe and Fahim Al-Razi, two friends of Ty's whom he met at a teacher's conference in San Antonio a couple of years ago.

Fahim Al Razi was a thirty-two-year-old Iranian male, tall and skinny, with a background in science and technology. He exited the Bronco wearing dark blue jeans, a short-sleeved dark blue button-up shirt, a black cowboy hat, and boots. He hadn't shaved in a couple of days and his dark black facial hair showed a shadow that was closer to 8:30 than 5:00.

Tomo Watanabe worked with Fahim in the science department at St. Philip's College in San Antonio. Tomo was 5' 9", clean shaven, and slender. He too was wearing jeans on his weekend off, with a navy t-shirt of Japanese gaming icon Kirby dreaming of hamburgers, a backward black with a purple bill New Era Tohoku Golden Eagles hat, and black boots. John Michael Montgomery's I Can Love You Like That stopped playing as Tomo turned off the vehicle. The two stepped out looking more like cowboys than scientists. Fahim made a call to Ty as the two stood outside of the truck.

A few minutes later, Ty, Tegan, and Carson greeted Tomo and Fahim in the parking lot. Tegan moved her car next to the Bronco.

"We brought the stuff you asked for," Fahim said to Ty.

"Good! Thank you!" replied Ty.

Carson introduced himself to both men as Tegan opened the trunk on the Verano. "What do we have?" asked Carson.

Tomo removed a large item from the backseat of the Bronco. "Ty said you guys were going camping and needed some supplies and equipment to search the woods," said Tomo. "We brought a Black Pine Freestander Turbo six-person tent that should be big enough for everyone," Tomo said as he handed it to Carson.

"Turbo?" asked Kareem.

"Yes, you can set it up in less than a minute. It's got a system of jointed tent poles, so you just stake out the corners, lock the joints in place, step inside, and push up the top. Attach the rainfly, and you're ready to enjoy the scenery," explained Fahim.

"We also brought four North Face Wasatch sleeping bags," said Fahim. "They have a temperature rating of twenty degrees. You won't need that protection tonight, but these are good bags in the fall and winter, so you'll be warm as you snooze through the chilliest nights."

"And what's the most important part of camping?" asked Tomo.

"The cooler?" asked Ty.

"The cooler!" said Fahim. He pulled out a Coleman forty-eight-quart chest in the standard red with the white top.

"And, of course, we brought it filled," said Tomo as he removed the lid showing a couple of bags of ice engulfing twenty-four various cans and bottles of local Texas craft beer.

"Now we're talking!" said Tegan as she looked on.

"Oh, and you will need this," said Tomo as he handed a long metal object to Tegan.

"What the hell is this?" she inquired.

The metal object was just over twelve inches long with a twisted middle and a harpoon edge. The other end had a downward turn.

"That is a WhaleSlayer, and Ty, don't lose it or it's your ass!" threatened Fahim.

"WhaleSlayer," questioned Ty.

"Yes, it's a handcrafted bottle opener forged out of half-inch steel by this guy out of Mississippi. It's about sixty bucks for a small one, but the larger one like this is one-twenty. The challenge is since it's handmade, the wait list is more than a year long," said Tomo.

"I've had that one for about two years and I love it. I

would recommend getting on the waitlist now. Join the Facebook group and fill out the online form. Then forget about it until he contacts you when you make the short list," suggested Tomo.

"He makes several styles and all of them are incredible. I can't imagine drinking beer without using my WhaleSlayer… so you better make sure I don't have to!" said Fahim, as he gave a steely gaze to Ty.

They loaded the camping equipment and cooler into the Verano, but one large box remained.

Fahim said, "Now for the fun stuff!"

The group looked on with anticipation as Fahim sorted through the large cardboard box.

"We have a couple of audio recorders. They are just standard handheld mini cassette recorders, a few sterile collecting bottles in case you run into some fecal samples, a box of latex gloves so you don't contaminate the DNA, a yellow rigid one-foot wooden ruler for measuring footprints…" Fahim said.

"I recommend you split up to stay in pairs," suggested Tomo. "So we brought two walkie-talkies for communication, four headlamps, a small parabolic mic, two cameras with thermal imagers, two sets of night vision goggles, a time-lapse camera and tripod, finally a remote-controlled drone with an infrared camera, and a few other goodies."

Fahim told Ty they could keep the stuff for a couple of weeks because school was out for summer and the semester's low enrollment meant they wouldn't need anything back until the end of July.

"What are you guys hunting?" asked Tomo.

Ty and Carson looked at each other before Carson answered, "the chupacabra."

"Are you shitting me?" asked Fahim.

"I wouldn't shit you…" said Ty. He left the rest of the one-liner unsaid.

"Do you think that thing exists?" asked Tomo.

"If it does, this stuff should help us find it," replied Carson. "And we've had a lot of eyewitness reports with similar sightings, so something is out there," he added.

"We plan to camp out between these two ranches where recent sightings have occurred, then we are going to walk the woods and see what's out there," revealed Ty.

"If you need any more toys, call us," said Tomo. The two shook hands with the trio and said their goodbyes.

"Be safe out there," said Fahim through the open Bronco window as they backed out. "If that beast is out there, who knows what it's capable of?"

As Tomo turned toward the driveway he reached down between the seats. "Here," said Tomo, "You might need this. Just in case." He handed a revolver to Carson. "Just in case it comes down to it," Tomo said.

Fahim reached into the glove box and passed a box of ammo to Tomo, who handed it to Carson.

"You might need this rifle too," said Fahim as he removed one from the gun rack in the truck. The Bronco drove off as Carson and Ty looked at the weapons and realized shit was about to get real.

Tegan, Ty, and Carson returned to the hotel room after loading the car with the borrowed equipment. They found Kareem looking over the map of the Elmendorf area and measuring distances with a small ruler.

"What's up?" asked Ty.

"I am looking at the map and trying to see where we might set up base camp," said Kareem. "We have Fred Dalton and the Shaws just over Highway 181 off Elmendorf Lavernia Road. They're kind of close to Calaveras Lake. Then you have all the sightings we had around the town of Elmendorf, just a few miles on the other side of Highway 181. A little further past that is Jordan's sighting at Braunig Lake, and Sharon's is just a few miles away at Freedom Elementary. We have a total radius of about fifteen miles. One thing that is common is water. The two lakes, some ponds in town, and the San Antonio River closer to the elementary school. Water not only attracts it but attracts other animals that it might feed on. Just down from Fred and Jonathan, there is an area with a few ponds. The larger ranches stop and the area becomes smaller houses down by the Valero. That gets a little busy because Highway 181 is right there, but there are also three ponds close together between the highway and Fred's place. Those lakes are not only close to Fred & Jonathan's sightings, but they are on the way to the other sightings. I think we should camp out right around that area because there will be plenty of water that will draw potential food for the chupacabra."

"That sounds good to me," said Carson. "We can leave the car at Valero and walk over to the pond. I think I saw a For Sale sign there recently, so it should be vacant land."

"Let's roll!" said Ty. "We can be there this morning, set up the campsite, and maybe take an afternoon nap. It's going to be a long night, I think."

Leaving most of their belongings in the hotel, the crew headed down to the car.

"I paid us up for the rest of the week," said Carson, "so we might as well leave the stuff in the room. Tegan has all the equipment in the car. I think we are good to go. Maybe we can stop by Fred's on the way to let him know, then head down to the Valero."

"I am kind of excited," admitted Tegan as they got into the Verano. "I've never been on a nighttime investigation before. But I always see them on Ghost Adventures and those types of shows. Have you seen Ghost Brothers? I love that one," she said. "Makes me wonder though, do ghosts only come out at night?"

"I don't know about ghosts," said Carson. "I've never seen one. But animals typically hunt at night, so for us it makes sense to be active when they are active."

It was twenty miles from the Red Roof Inn to the Valero. Tegan parked the car near the back of the parking lot. "Do you want anything from inside before we set up camp?" asked Tegan.

"I'm good for now," said Carson. "It's literally like three hundred yards to the front of that first pond. We can go back to the store if we need something."

The group began unloading the car and set up the tent on the east side of the first pond. There was a small strip of land between it and the next small pond that was flat enough to pitch the tent.

"Let's back up here to the pond so we have an excellent water source," suggested Carson. "It's a little shady with the trees, and it's a flat surface which makes it good to set up the tent. We're not too far from where the reports have been. Fred's ranch is just about a mile or mile and a half down that road, and there's a good chance the chupacabra passed by here to head toward the town where the other sightings occurred."

"Right," said Ty. "The first thing we do is set up the tent and secure our base camp. We also need to be mindful of our environment. Being close to the pond, we might encounter snakes, ants, and the bushes are kind of bristly and thorny. We should all wear pants to protect our legs from the briars and thorns," he suggested.

Each member grabbed items from the car and headed toward the pond. It was quiet out and the air was humid, ensuring few onlookers were around to wonder what they were doing. The walk to the pond did not take long. It wasn't a far distance and within two trips from each member, the car was unloaded.

Carson and Ty began working on erecting the tent by dropping the stakes and unfurling the tent from the bag. He followed the directions Fahim provided and in just a few minutes, Carson had the tent in place and was ready for the evening.

Once erected, Kareem moved the box of equipment inside the tent, and Tegan brought the cooler. Just outside the tent, they found four large, flat rocks they could use as chairs while planning the evening's events.

"Let's see that map again," said Ty. "Here on our right we have the other small pond, and just past that are two more small ponds. A few hundred yards east we have a long, narrow pond that's almost like a canal, so when we are out walking around tonight, be careful of all these little ponds. I don't want to fall in one," said Ty.

"I think we head out as a group first," suggested Carson. "That way, we have each other's back and there's protection if we run into the creature."

"I agree," said Kareem, "and an afternoon nap sounds pretty good so we can be alert tonight, but I think first we need to check out this cooler your boys brought," he said as he looked at Ty.

Tegan said, "This humidity is making me thirsty! And it's important to hydrate."

"Knowing those boys - who don't forget came equipped with this awesome WhaleSlayer," said Ty, "there shouldn't be any big market beer in here!"

Opening the cooler, the group gasped as if they just opened One-Eye Willy's treasure chest. A glacial amount of ice surrounded by a mixture of San Antonio bottles and cans stared back at them.

"Look at this haul!" said Kareem.

"I told you my boys wouldn't let us down!" said Ty. Reaching a bare hand into the icy waters, Carson moved in a counterclockwise motion, causing the cans and bottles to dance in the icy bath.

"I have had none of these!" said an excited Carson. Busted

Sandal's Slippery Rock IPA and 210 Ale, Ranger Creek Brewing's Oatmeal Pale Ale, Strawberry Milk Stout, Red Headed Stranger, Love Struck Hefe, and Purple Rhine Berliner Weisse, Freetail Brewing Company Bat Outta Helles, Yo Soy Un Berliner, Texicali Brown Ale, and a couple bottles of #Whalezbro presented the group with a variety of local beers and enough to get through the afternoon and the morning after the investigation.

"Wow! I am excited to dig in!" said Tegan eagerly.

"Let's finish unpacking and getting set up, then we can start the pre-game," suggested Ty.

"Remember that nighttime is when the creature is active, so it's used to the area in the dark. We are entering its terrain during its peak time, so we must be on high alert."

"When you say it that way, it sounds a little scary," admitted Tegan.

"Right. That's why we should stick together. One thing that will help is the night vision equipment will allow us to even the playing field," said Carson.

"We should set the time-lapse camera's tripod right here around these ponds," suggested Ty. "The water might draw him in, and he likely will be curious about the tent that is new in his area."

"We'll divide the other equipment up among each of us," said Carson.

"How about we divide some of these beers up amongst us now?" suggested Tegan.

"I like the way you think!" said Kareem as he shoved a hand into the icy water of the cooler. He pulled out a white can of 210 Ale from Busted Sandal.

"I've heard good things about San Antonio blondes," Kareem said as he opened the beer and took a swig. "A little nutty. Kind of reminds me of a lager. Smooth. A little sweet, but the bitterness from the hops keeps it from being too sweet. I could do this at a beer league softball game all day," said Kareem as he tossed a beer to Tegan.

She reached up and two-hand caught the bottle headed at her. "Aww, aren't you a sweetie?" she asked as she caught a Ranger Creek Brewing Berliner Weisse. "You know I love Berliner Weisse! Cute purple label too. Hand me that Whale-thing?" she asked as she leaned toward Carson and pointed at the WhaleSlayer bottle opener. "How the hell do you use this?" she asked as she looked it over.

She took the hook end and popped the top off as she crooned Prince's Purple Rain. The beer was a nice sour with a hint of lavender, a tart flavor she loved, and an aroma that was amazing.

"I love this!" she said with a smile. "Nice fruity notes, a little carbonation, maybe a bit of pear and honey. When you are thirsty, nothing quite cuts through that like a nice sour beer."

"You ready for one too?" Carson asked Ty.

"Ooooh yeah, hit me, brother!" Ty said in his best Macho Man Randy Savage voice.

Carson tossed Ty a Ranger Creek Oatmeal Pale Ale and pulled out a Ranger Creek Love Struck for himself.

Ty sat down, grabbed the WhaleSlayer, and opened the bottle after seeing how Tegan used it. Taking a sip, Ty decided it was an excellent brew. It was hoppy with a clean flavor with a little bitter finish. He picked up the oatey tones that balanced out the hops before declaring it smooth and tasty.

Carson used the WhaleSlayer on the Love Struck Hefe and was love struck himself after the first sip. Nice and light with the traditional banana and clove tones, a dry finish, decent carbonation that he thought made the beer refreshing and easy to drink. He thought he even picked up some mild pepper and a hint of lemon zest in the mix.

"This stuff is pretty good!" said Carson.

"Better than the Stars?" joked Kareem, making fun of the San Antonio Star's recent loss in overtime Saturday night.

"Hey, I admit I'm hooked. Fred told me he was a big WNBA fan and suggested I watch some games. They are enjoyable, and the Stars are the closest team we have. They are struggling so far, but I think they can turn it around. I have enjoyed watching them play in just the few games I've seen," admitted Carson. "Have any of you ever been to a WNBA game?" asked Carson. Everyone shook their heads no. "I have not yet been to one either, but depending on when we wrap this up, we should go to a game. Next one is Thursday against the Phoenix Mercury," said Carson.

"Sure, why not? Hopefully, we will be finished with this creature by then. And when we get back to Austin, we have to get ready for the Jester King release in a couple of weeks," said Tegan.

"Oh yeah, you mentioned Jester King and their releases

when we were at Black Star last week," said Carson.

"When is the next one?" he asked.

"Friday, July 3," said Ty. "It is their spring beer, the Vernal Dichotomous. That's a farmhouse ale that is a blend of a November 2012 beer barrel-aged in oak barrels. It has barley, hops, lavender, and spearmint. They brewed the other beer just a couple of months ago with kumquats. There is always a crazy line, so we have to go early. They limit it to three bottles per person per day," revealed Ty.

"I'm pretty sure I've never even seen a kumquat," admitted Carson.

Kareem and Tegan finished their beers and were on to round two. Tegan had the Ranger Creek Strawberry Milk Stout and Kareem, a Ranger Creek Red Headed Stranger.

"This is also superb," said Tegan. "Nice stout with dark chocolate, strawberry, some vanilla, and maybe even coconut," she reported. This was one of the best milk stouts she had in a long time.

The Red Headed Stranger was a red IPA, which was something new to Kareem.

"A little sweet," he said.

Malt, grapefruit, lemon, floral notes, and hops gave it balance.

Nice tribute to Willie Nelson, he thought.

Ty grabbed a Yo Soy Un Berliner but put it back in the bath. He knew Tegan loved Berliner Weisse and saved it for her. Instead, he took a Texicali Brown and tossed Carson a Bat Outta Helles. Ty stopped to admire the artwork on the can, a nice Day of the Dead motif. He was impressed with the beer, a nice brown ale with coffee notes. The coffee was a little robust and toasty. Carson's can was also smooth and flavorful. It had the aroma of wheat, grass, and earthy hops. The mouthfeel was thin with a wheat and honey flavor with a sweet finish.

"Okay, so what's the plan?" asked Kareem, "Are we out to catch this thing today or just try to find it for now?"

"We can't cage it right now, and I don't want to kill it. Unless we have no choice. Hopefully, we can spot it tonight and get a feel for what it is. Where it goes, what it does, and what it's capable of so that we are prepared for later. We will have to build a trap or get something to hold it once we know what we are dealing with. We think this is a suitable area based on the prior sightings, but it's not guaranteed. The sightings from Fred and Jonathan happened three weeks ago now. Our more recent sightings have been in town, so if we find nothing, we may have to move. But I think we get a nap then see what's out there tonight," suggested Carson.

"Yes, that's what I was thinking too," revealed Ty. "That's kind of how we did it in college. Get the information, then head out later intending to catch it. We can't catch what we don't know is still out there," he said.

As the group sat in the tent working on the contents of the cooler, Kareem noticed it was getting darker outside.

"Looks like it is getting cloudy. I hope it doesn't rain tonight while we are searching for that beast," he said.

"Not getting much rain during the year makes me a bit of a pluviophile," said Carson. "But rain would suck tonight.

From my experience, a little light rain wouldn't hurt that much and might keep it cooler, but if it rains hard like it usually does during May and June, that will slow us down and make spotting the animals that much more difficult."

Tegan took the last sips of her beer. "Speaking of experience," she said, "how did you and Ty first get into this?"

Ty and Carson tried to recall. "The idea came about over a bottle of gin and a jarful of pennies," quipped Carson.

"Ha! I think it was… Dr. Thompson's social science class, wasn't it?" Ty recollected.

"Dr. Thompson? Yes. Yes, I think that's right. I was in the back of the room, not paying much attention to the lecture. Usually looking out the window in class and drawing sketches in my notebook instead of taking notes," recalled Carson.

"That's right! I remember Bigfoot peeking out from behind a tree!" said Ty. "And wasn't there an alien?"

"Most likely," said Carson. "I was always drawing aliens," he said.

"You were into that shit. Like Project Blue Book or something," said Ty.

"That's because I had a weird sighting once when I was a teenager. Not a first-hand alien or spaceship sighting, but my aunt did and called us out the next day to her farm. It scorched the ground in a circle and there were four indentations in the ground, like legs or something. I remember taking pictures of the grass. Although I didn't see anything else, it still sparked my interest, so I started spending more time outdoors and watching the sky," said Carson.

"I thought you were weird at first," admitted Ty. "I had seen nothing usual and didn't believe in it, but we started talking in the back of the class every day and you kept sketching animals and aliens. I thought you were crazy when you first suggested we go out and look for something after I asked you if you believed in that stuff," said Ty.

"Remember we went out in the woods behind the college and tried to find some mysterious animals?" recalled Carson.

"Ha-ha, yeah, the jackalope! Never found that sonofabitch either, did we?" asked Ty.

"Nope, but they are out there," said Carson as he finished the beer, "They are out there…."

As he crinkled the can, a light rain fell. The sound hitting the top of the tent was a little relaxing.

"Boys and girl… I think I'm going to catch a few hours of shut eye. What say you?" asked Carson.

Tegan unrolled her sleeping bag. "I think that is a good idea. It will be a long night and I am a little sleepy now. A few hours should do the trick," she said as she scooted inside the top of the unzipped sleeping bag.

"Never thought I would sleep and dream behind a Valero," said Kareem.

Within a few minutes, all unfurled their sleeping bags and took a nap. The late afternoon clouds rolling in and the rhythm of the falling rain put each to sleep. They continued to sleep as afternoon turned to evening and darkness began to fall.

CHAPTER 13

NIGHTTIME INVESTIGATION

SUNDAY, JUNE 21, 2015

One by one, the group awoke from the afternoon nap, with Carson being the first to rise. He walked to the front of the tent and looked out as the sun neared the horizon, leaving the sky bright orange. Despite the sun, light rain was still falling, but he concluded it wouldn't be an issue to take the electronics out with them. Since they were not his, he was more cautious. The headlamps would be fine, the microphones and cameras they would have with them, and the drone they would leave in a duffel bag until needed. The only equipment that might be at risk would be the time-lapsed camera that would be out in the open for an extended period. Perhaps he could position it under a tree that would provide some break to the rain?

As the others began stirring, he turned to separate the equipment for their scouting mission.

"Remember tonight, we are looking for information. Our priority is to locate the animal, see how big it is, where it lives, how it interacts with the environment, and then we come back to put together a plan for later. We will need to get some traps in place once we know more," said Carson.

He grabbed the duffel bag and drug it toward the equipment, placing the Phantom 2 remote-controlled drone into the bag.

"Nice sack!" said Ty, "Where's that from? The Gap?"

Carson turned with a sharp look. "As Jacob said in *Crazy, Stupid, Love, be better than the Gap,*" remarked Carson. "For your information, kind sir, it is from my subscription box from Bespoke Post. It's the Standard Issue box, and I can earn $25 if I recruit you to join the club. Maybe then you could get a monthly box of awesome," said Carson with a snarky response.

"How many damn subscription boxes do you get a month? I suppose you do Taste the World and Barkbox too?" Ty shot back.

"No. I don't have a dog," replied Carson. "I just have two for right now. But I am thinking of joining the Dive Bar Shirt Club if you must know."

"Guys, the sun is down and maybe we should get started," suggested Kareem before joining Carson down on the ground to split up the equipment.

"There is a headlamp for each of us," said Carson. "We have a parabolic microphone and a couple voice recorders. Why don't you and Tegan each take one?" Carson said to Kareem. "Let's throw the sterile collecting bottles, latex gloves, and wooden ruler into the duffel bag. I have my cell phone. Anyone else bring a camera?" asked Carson.

"I brought my GoPro camera. We can use that. It has better low-light performance, 4K video capability, and slow-motion, so we shouldn't get those notoriously blurry photos we see of Sasquatch," suggested Kareem.

"That's sweet," said Ty. "We also have these night vision goggles."

"What the hell is this thing?" asked Carson.

Ty said, "This stick? We have one rifle and one pistol. We might need more protection. This is a Streetwise Peacemaker stun baton. It's capable of packing a whopping six million volts. If that beast attacks, this is a good, non-lethal way of stopping it in its tracks," said Ty.

"Put that in your pretty little duffel bag, grab the firearms, and let's get to hittin' the woods," suggested Ty.

Carson grabbed the pistol and Ty the rifle. With the equipment distributed, the group decided it was time to head out and assess the situation. As Carson looked around, he recognized that while the rain was light and would not damage the equipment, it posed some challenges. Having rained for a few hours, the ground would be wet, which would cause footing to be more challenging.

One benefit to the wet ground was an increased chance of footprints. Witnesses reported the tracks of the supposed chupacabra differed from those of other canines such as the coyote. Instead of four distinct toes, the chupacabra had two middle digits that were said to appear joined, almost as if the animal had three toes. The long toenails also were more prevalent than other animals in the area.

Carson knew that on cloudy nights, it was essential to hunt with your ears because you can't always see with your eyes. The deep shadows and the unseen animals lurking in the brush made the thrill of being outside hunting for such a mysterious beast even more dangerous, but also exhilarating. Just the thought of stepping out into the woods and hunting again returned the excitement and adrenaline rush that used to drive him years ago. Just the initial jolt of that rush was a welcomed feeling.

With the sun now submerged, the group exited the tent's and entered the rough terrain south of the two ponds. Medium height, thick grass, roots, and brush on each side surrounded the banks of the pond. The night was filled with the sound of frogs around the water, katydids in the bushes, owls, and other miscellaneous bugs that brought the night to life.

As they made their way through the darkness, walking around the water's edge, Kareem felt nervous. The idea of looking for the creature, the interviews, and everything that transpired up to now was exciting, but didn't quite feel real. At this moment, hiking around the dark Texas landscape with technical equipment, lights, and firearms, the realism hit him like a brick. He indeed had never been part of such an expedition, and even though camping is an often-embellished experience for guys to glorify when telling others. Kareem had only been camping a few times as a kid, and none of the experiences were positive.

He recalled his first experience camping in the middle of summer outside of Austin. Their campsite had no grass, only rocks. And ants. Tons of ants. He remembered a restless night attempting to sleep on the hard ground in the hot Texas air and listening to the unknown sounds on the other side of the tent. He remembered some of those sounds belonging to at least one raccoon who entered their camp and ate all the food because Kareem left it out, even though his father reminded him to put it away before going to bed.

Another camping experience when Kareem was about ten saw an unexpected, horrible thunderstorm pop up on the second day of a camping trip with his family. He remembered the lightning flashed before his eyes and the thunder crashed loudly. He was scared and hiding in his tent, screaming his lungs out.

The sounds of sirens interrupted the terrifying night. An ambulance. Lightning had struck a person camping in the same campsite and they were now unconscious. As the rain slowed to a slight drizzle, those memories of camping in the thunderstorm brought those nervous feelings back. To this day, thunderstorms still scared him.

Hopefully there will be no storm tonight, thought Kareem.

He remained close to Tegan, who was just in front of him in the group's march through the darkness. While Kareem had a couple of other non-eventful camping experiences, the two negative ones stood out more in his memory than the others did.

Kareem snapped back to the present moment as the group continued around the pond in the light rain. He scanned the ground, searching for any footprints, but especially the odd prints described as belonging to the chupacabra. There were still sounds of night animals, which usually showed a predator was not around. The group continued, but the frustration grew. The animal was spotted around the area and the proximity of water seemed to be a good attraction, but as each member continued to look and listen, the creature was nowhere to be found. Carson wanted to ask if anyone had seen anything that might be the creature, but he knew the answer. He half expected that if he asked aloud, he would likely get a response similar to the trooper in Spaceballs.

He elected to leave the question unasked and continue walking.

After another fifteen minutes, the group came full circle around the pond.

"Okay, this isn't working," said a frustrated Carson. "Ty, what do you say we split up? We have enough equipment. Kareem and I can go one way while you and Tegan can go the other way," suggested Carson.

"Sounds good. We can cover more ground that way, and we have radios in case we get in trouble or spot something," replied Ty. Having an experienced tracker paired with a newbie was a good move to remain productive and teach the newer members a little something along the way.

"We have highway 181 to the east and Elmendorf Lavernia Road to the south/southwest. Chances are he won't cross the road unless he has to. It isn't too busy at night, but there may be enough cars to scare him off. That leaves the woods to the west and the woods to the north. I think that is as good of a place to look as any. What do y'all think?" asked Carson.

"Sounds like a plan," said Tegan.

"There's a lot of wooded areas around here where it could be hiding. Let's plan to meet back up in, say, three hours if we find nothing," suggested Carson. "Stay in contact on the radio. They are fully charged and should get us through the night."

"See you soon, bro. Stay aware and be safe out there," said Ty to Carson. After a fist bump, the two groups went separate ways. Carson and Kareem to the west, and Ty and Tegan to the north.

"It is a little creepy out here at night," Tegan said to Ty as they made their way toward the darkened tree line ahead.

Per audacia ad ignotum," replied Ty. "Through boldness into the unknown."

Tegan knew Ty and Carson used to go on frequent camping expeditions hunting for these unknown creatures while in college, but this was new for her. At her job, she was used to handling difficult situations and remaining calm. But here she jumped at every noise, and became nervous when there was no noise. She perceived something was lurking in the shadows, just waiting for something to jump out. While this chupacabra had not yet attacked a person, she wondered what if this was the night it decided to try a human snack? She stayed close behind Ty and continued toward the woods and as ground brush grew thicker.

Just then, she saw something out of the corner of her eye at the same time she heard it. She detected the crash and just caught sight of something running through the persimmon trees parallel to her. It looked like a huge, brown dog. At first, she thought it was a buffalo, but she knew that a wild one wasn't possible in Texas. The beast crashed through the thicket, and she heard it hit the water from where they had just come. It sounded like a herd of hogs plowing the trees, but what she glimpsed was an individual animal.

"Did you see that?" she whispered to Ty.

Ty didn't see the animal but turned after hearing the noise. After the initial loud crash, the animal continued running toward the campsite. He thought he heard the faint splash of animals across the thicket in the pond. The duo turned back toward the direction they came from and ran toward the water back at camp.

As they got closer to the pond, the sound intensified, and even Ty began getting nervous. It was so weird because in his collegiate expeditions, he never felt that way. Maybe it was because it had been several years since going on this type of adventure and his adrenaline was pumping. Or maybe it was because when he and Carson used to go out, they never encountered anything. But this was happening. There was something out there! What he thought could be a group of animals turned out to be one animal. When they got within a hundred yards, he could hear it plain as day.

Whatever it was, it wasn't in a hurry and stayed in the brushes, just out of sight. Earlier in the day, the group had scouted the area and Ty knew the water the creature was in was less than waist deep on him. He could hear the *splash, drip... drip... drip...splash* as the animal put one foot in front of the other, as if it was trying to be quiet.

Probably trying to sneak up on prey, he thought.

Hopefully, he and Tegan were not the intended meal.

He thought it could be another person till he remembered how deep that water was. He would never point a gun at a noise or anything he wasn't planning to shoot, but as the noise grew louder, he raised the rifle and looked down the barrel. Carson was shaking. He just hoped Tegan didn't notice and erode whatever confidence she had in him and his experience in the woods.

The creature reached the edge of the water with about forty yards of thicket before the open ground between where it was and where Ty and Tegan were approaching. It crashed about ten or fifteen yards and then went quiet. Deathly quiet. No frogs, no crickets, no birds, nothing. Ty thought he might have imagined it, but Tegan reported she saw the blur of something from the corner of her eye, and they both heard it crash through the brush and undergrowth. He imagined the beast picked up their scent and could be hiding. That was a dangerous situation where the hunter might become the hunted.

Ty scratched his head and scanned the area, looking for the animal. He thought he could hear something now and then, like it was sneaking up on them. But as they stopped at the pond, there was no sight of the animal. Ty lowered the rifle and searched the ground. He no longer saw or heard anything from the animal but found tracks on the ground. Prints with a combined third digit that fit the description of the mysterious creature. He and Tegan were both shaken but feeling the rush of dopamine released by the pursuit.

"I know it was that beast!" said Tegan, "And we tracked it here to the pond… but where'd it go?" she wondered.

"Beats the shit out of me," responded Ty. "But we should get some photos of these tracks while they are fresh. Look at the distance between them. He was covering some serious ground quickly," he said. "Better call the other guys while we're at it," he suggested.

Tegan grabbed the radio. "Hey guys, over?"

Kareem replied, "Hey Tegan. You guys finding anything over there? It's quiet here, over."

"Keep your eyes peeled. We just had some excitement here. I saw the creature run back toward our camp, but it hid in the covering. We ran after it and heard it, then just when it sounded like we were right on top of it, we came out of the brush and it was gone, over."

"What do you mean there was nothing there? Are you sure you saw it? … Over…"

"We saw it, and something was here because we are standing in a group of footprints. That animal was running fast and had a large gait from the placement of these prints. They dug deep in the mud too, so it's a gigantic beast. Shocking something that big moves that fast. Over," replied Tegan.

"Did you take photos of the tracks? At least we have something to go on. Some type of proof. Over," responded Kareem.

"Yes, we got 'em. But the animal disappeared, so it might be headed your way. Over," Tegan added.

"We'll be on alert. Thanks for the heads up. Over and out," concluded Kareem.

Carson suggested since the animal could be headed their way. Maybe the parabolic mic and thermal camera might help them identify if the creature was nearby. Reaching into the knapsack, Kareem removed the camera and handed it to Carson. He kept the mic for himself and returned the bag over his shoulder. Scanning the open grass and low ground covering brush, nothing showed up on Carson's camera.

Kareem scanned the area with the mic, looking for any unusual sounds. It was surprisingly quiet. He would have expected to hear owls, maybe some frogs, and other night insects around the wet areas. A coyote or even a fox would be expected, but the silence was unsettling. Maybe something the animals considered a threat was in the area. Maybe the chupacabra was nearby?

As Carson scanned the camera back to the left, he saw a red, orange, and yellow figure moving from right to left. Much of its body was red, showing warmth, likely from running. It was distant and covered by the trees and brush.

"I can't tell what it is, but it's in a hurry," said Carson. "This could be the creature the other team saw. Let's go!"

Kareem and Carson put the equipment back in the bag and turned to pursue the creature. They loped through the dense underbrush, attempting to avoid rocks and roots protruding from the ground. Sweat ran down their foreheads as they continued, Carson attempting to keep his breathing in tune with his steps. The damp grass brushing against his legs, the puddles soaking his feet as he led the way into the darker recesses of the woods. He realized months of day-drinking and lounging voided any cardiovascular fitness he enjoyed in his youth as a basketball player in high school.

Now struggling to breathe and talk, he managed, "Shit... I need to put that Shaun T workout DVD on when we get home," gasped Carson.

Kareem was having an easier time and could converse with the slow-jog pace.

"Which one? *Hip Hop Abs? Tilt, Tuck, and Tighten?*" asked Kareem.

"*No. Insanity.* I bought it a while ago but never used it."

"We're in some insanity right here," replied Kareem.

Brush smacked his face as he continued following the trail of the animal. Soon the ground covering became less, and they were in a small area of open field. The animal was not in sight and once again the night air was silent. Taking the camera back out of the bag, Carson scanned the horizon, but nothing showed on the screen.

"Damn it!" he murmured. "I know it went in this direction," he said. He picked up the radio and called over to Tegan.

"Hey guys, let's meet back up. We just saw it run off in the distance. I think we're closing in. Over," said Carson.

He gave their location to Tegan and fifteen minutes later, the groups reunited.

"So what's the plan?" asked Ty.

"It could keep running to God knows where," said Carson. "But I'm hoping it stops and rests somewhere and we can catch up to it. I couldn't get a feel for the size of it because it was so far away on the thermal.

"From what we saw," said Tegan, "it is large and fast!"

"Oh, it was definitely fast," replied Carson. "He shot across the tree line, not worrying about the rocks and branches that slowed us down. He knows the area."

As the two groups continued walking as one, they searched the area for clues, with Ty and Carson taking the lead. "Let's hope this investigation turns out better than that jackalope," Ty said with a chuckle.

They continued through the open ground and back into a wooded area, denser than the first.

"Not much human traffic through this area," said Carson. "Some patches of grass, but mainly dirt," he said, looking down as they slipped through the area.

Carson's headlamp shone down on the ground, and he noticed footprints. They looked like the ones Tegan described near the pond. Each print had four toes, but the middle two digits were combined. The claws were long, and the tracks were deep from the size and speed of the animal as it ran across the dirt floor of the wooded area.

"Let's get some photos of these prints so we can compare it to the ones you took earlier," said Carson. "But I am sure they're the same. Wish we had some plaster that we could have made some casts to get a good size. Where's that yellow ruler?" asked Carson.

Bending down to inspect the tracks, Carson concluded they were like a canine species. He turned toward Kareem and Tegan, who he knew had never tracked an animal before.

"The claws help to identify this as a canine track," he said.

"It is possible to see claw marks in feline tracks, like a mountain lion or bobcat, but this is usually when the animal is running or pouncing. Also, the leading edge of the heel pad on a cat has two parts, or lobes, but you can see in this one a lack of a third lobe on the hind edge of the heel pad. That is another clue it is a canine. A canine track has a third lobe, but here the shape of the leading edge of the heel pad is a single lobe. You can also see at the top of the track the alignment of the front two toes. They are side-by-side, or very close to it, in dogs tracks. There are exceptions, such as when the animal is making a turn or walking on a slope. Here he was likely running in a straight line, so they were side-by-side. But you can see the second and third toe are conjoined, which matches our eyewitness reports of the creature. These outside toes are consistent with canines, almost triangular with the pads. Canines have a little point where the heel pad turns. One thing that is unusual with these front tracks is they usually are larger than hind tracks. These larger ones appear to be the hind tracks, which would support the reports that the creature has strong back legs that allow it to stand on its hind legs. They have to be muscular to support its weight," said Carson.

Kareem took several photos of the track with the ruler laid out beside the print. "From the heel to the toe, that's about four inches long and five inches wide," said Kareem.

"The average adult cougar tracks average three-and-a-half inches tall by four inches wide, so we are looking at something bigger than that," said Ty. "Male coyotes are about three inches by two inches and a standard walking stride is about forty or forty-two inches apart. This guy was running, so the stride would be longer. We also know this creature is five feet long, so running stride is likely around eighty inches," calculated Ty.

"Let's get moving while he still may be in the area," suggested Carson.

Looking at the surrounding trees, there were occasional branches that were bent, showing something large passed through. The tracks continued in the same direction. Continuing walking in the same direction as the evidence, the group came to an area that looked like an enormous field. There were trees in the distance and ankle-high grass, more maintained.

"This might be someone's property," said Kareem. "It looks like a field, but it's too dark to see if there is a house."

Ty stopped and looked around. There was no sign of a building, but it could be the backside of a large plot of land. He wanted to continue following the tracks to see if the animal was still in the area.

"Let's dig in the bag and get that drone out," suggested Ty. "We can fly it over the area to see if the creature is still there and maybe we can see if there are any buildings."

Kareem removed the Phantom drone equipped with FLIR thermal and electro-optic cameras. The thermal imaging was helpful for spotting livestock on large ranches, or, in this case, feral animals such as the chupacabra. Some of the high-tech ranchers also used drones for crop inspection and monitoring field irrigation. With the controller, the user could toggle between thermal and regular camera images, making it useful in ranch management.

"We can also live stream thermal images or capture photos and video," said Ty. "I got to use one of these bad boys after a conference last fall and I would love to have one, but they are pricey. About $3500, so don't break it or Tomo and Fahim will have my ass!" replied Ty.

Soon a light humming sound signaled Kareem brought the propellers on the four arms to life. The drone rose and glided out over the open field.

"We can get about seven-hundred meters' distance with this before it gets out of range with the radio transmitter," said Ty.

Carson pulled up the app on the smartphone to watch the video and guided Kareem toward the search area.

The drone disappeared into the darkness as Kareem guided it toward the distant trees. A couple of large images appeared, but Carson identified them as horses. He also saw a barn near them.

"It looks like this is a small ranch or farm," said Carson. "Just a couple of horses, but there is likely a house closer towards the road. We can check that out later."

Dark trees appeared in the live stream and under their cover, the team saw a bright red and orange figure. It was panting and standing next to a tree on two legs. One of the front legs rested on a tree trunk, as if to prop the animal up.

"That's got to be him!" said Carson. "It's not a bear and I haven't seen another animal stand against a tree like that!" he said. "Let's go!"

He turned to dart off in the animal's direction, but Ty reached an arm out to stop him. "If this is someone's property, we can't just run across it. This is Texas. For trespassers, folks 'round here, they let their shotguns do the talkin'!" Ty said.

"We're close to the creature and well behind the house. Besides, the owner is probably asleep. I am sure we won't get in trouble. We'll be in and out before they know it," responded Carson.

"Right, and if we catch it, then what? How are we going to extract the animal from their land?" argued Ty. "Remember, you said we were just collecting information. We are in no position to bag this dude tonight."

"It might not be trespassing," said Carson. "If we didn't have that drone, we wouldn't know it was someone's property. It might just be an open field," he offered.

"I don't know, but I know someone who would know," replied Kareem.

"At this hour?" asked Tegan.

"Yeah, he's always around and available. Let me give him a quick call," responded Kareem. He took out his phone and dialed a number. Seconds later, thunder crashed, and a bolt of lightning struck a nearby tree. An eagle shrieked. A man with a tattered gray suit with ash marks covering his face walked toward them from behind a tree.

"SOMEONE JUST CALLED ME!" he bellowed as he continued walking toward the group.

The other group members looked at Kareem, then at the man.

"Are you the Texas law eagle?" asked Tegan.

"RYAN PILSON! THE TEXAS LAW EAGLE!" screamed the man. The eagle cried out again.

"Um… Mr. Law Eagle… can we go chase that creature hiding over there in the trees?" asked Carson.

Calmly, the man replied. "You could be charged with criminal trespass and more serious property crimes throughout San Antonio, Bexar County, and the surrounding areas in Texas under Texas Penal Code Section 30.05. Under the penal code criminal trespass includes the following elements: the person *'enters or remains on or in property of another; without effective consent; and when the person had notice that the entry was forbidden or received notice to depart but failed to do so'.*"

"We saw a barn on the drone, so it likely is the property of another, and we will only remain there long enough to get the animal… but no one told us we could not enter or were forbidden. So we're good, right?" asked Carson.

"For the criminal trespass statute, they define the term *entry as the intrusion of the entire body. And notice must proceed the criminal trespass allegation*," replied the man.

"Yeah, like I said, no one gave us notice," retorted Carson.

"It's not that simple," said the man.

"*Notice* is defined as *'include an oral or written communication by the owner* or someone with apparent authority to act for the owner'. That can be the property is surrounded by *'fencing or other enclosure obviously designed to exclude intruders or to contain livestock'*," replied the man.

"No fence here, or at least if it is, then it's broken and none right here where we might realize it is someone's land," said Carson.

"A second form is a sign or signs posted on the property or at the entrance to the building, that would likely come to the attention of intruders, indicating entry is forbidden," said the man.

Scanning the trees and surrounding area with the flashlight from his phone, Carson replied, "No signs here…"

Looking at Carson, the man continued.

"The visible presence on the property of a crop grown for human consumption that is under cultivation, in the process of being harvested, or marketable if harvested at the time of entry is also considered notice."

"Just grass over there. No crops that we can see. Looks like we are good to go," replied Carson.

"A final method of notice can include the placement of identifying purple paint marks on trees or posts on the property," added the man.

"Purple paint?" asked Carson.

The man stated, "HB 793 took effect in September 1997, under the Texas Penal Code 30.05 Criminal Trespass, Section 1, subsection D. The law requires that the purple paint markings must be vertical, at least eight inches long and one-inch wide. The bottom of the mark should be between three and five feet above the ground. The markings can be no more than one hundred feet apart in timberland and one thousand feet apart on open land and must be in a place visible to those approaching the property. Ranchers across the state had contacted their state representatives and stated that they were having problems with getting trespass cases filed because signs were torn down and fences were cut; thus rendering the property not properly posted. The presence of purple paint is identifiable and unique. Purple paint should be taken seriously. Trespassing is a Class B misdemeanor in Texas unless the intruder is carrying a firearm, which you have, then it stands as Class A misdemeanor. Both are punishable by fines and imprisonment," added the man.

Ty shone his phone around the area where the field began. He noticed on two nearby trees a vertical stripe about ten inches long.

"Well, there's your sign," said Ty.

"Best to go knock on the door," suggested the man.

He walked behind a tree. Another lightning bolt struck down. A hawk screamed a third time, and the man was gone.

Looking down at the phone app, Carson noticed the animal was gone. Dejected, he said, "Better fly that drone back in here before we lose the signal. I guess we should return to camp and visit the house tomorrow. It's too late to knock on the door tonight. Besides, the animal is gone, so…."

"We had some excitement tonight, didn't we?" said Tegan as the group turned and sauntered back toward their campsite.

"How do you two feel?" asked Ty.

"Not bad for our first time out," smiled Kareem as he gave Tegan a high five.

"I am tired," said Ty. He continued, "Plus, all that excitement got me thirsty. Who's up for a beer?"

"I could use one before bed. Maybe two. Let's finish those beers and hit the sack," said Carson as they continued walking.

CHAPTER 14

FLUTTERS IN THE BASEMENT
MONDAY, JUNE 22, 2015

Tegan awoke to the smell of bacon. She looked around to assess the situation and saw the guys were already awake. Ty and Carson were cooking over a campfire, and Kareem was looking at the footage from the time-lapsed camera left at the camp last night while the groups hunted for the creature. She looked at her watch and saw it was 8:45 a.m.

"Good morning, guys. You're up early," she asked sleepily.

"Just getting a little grub going," said Carson. "We walked over to the Valero and bought some bacon, eggs, bread, and orange juice. Had to get paper plates, forks, and a pan too."

"Wow, what a pleasant surprise," said Tegan.

"So, anything on the camera?" asked Ty.

"Mostly nothing," said Kareem. "A lot of darkness, but there are a couple that have some promise, and one that is the best photo we've seen of the creature yet."

"Let's have a look," said Ty.

Kareem scrolled through dozens of photos before coming to one that showed a blurry animal close to the camp in the water. The next one was amazing. Something must have made a noise. Maybe it was Ty and Tegan, as they were running back toward camp, but the animal was standing still, upright, and looking toward the camera. It was a clear photo that showed the animal in detail. The red eyes that were described by prior witnesses were radiant, almost as if they were glowing.

The animal had one foot in the water and one on the muddy ground outside of the pond. Its mouth was gaping. Enough to show the front fangs that extended long, almost like a saber-toothed tiger. The night vision of the camera made the animal look green, but they could tell the figure was dark and mostly hairless. There were patches of fur along the spine, and while bipedal, it hunched over.

"Holy shit. That's our guy! It's just like all the reports said. I can see why they described it as all those different animals! It has characteristics of all of those and if you just see it for a second, I think you could imagine it was any of them," said Ty.

"That proves this urban legend is a real animal, and it's here in these woods. Imagine the scientific aspect of this find and what it would do to bring cryptozoology to the forefront of discussion," said Carson enthusiastically.

"Or we could get eaten," said Kareem pensively.

"I'm sure he won't eat all of us," Ty said snarkily. "Someone has to live to tell the tale in the movie."

That didn't make Kareem feel any better. The group continued to eat breakfast and review the photos. Carson picked up a piece of crisp bacon with his fingers. He savored the moment as he took a bite.

"Damn, I love bacon," he said with an ecstatic smile on his face.

"So, plan for the day… we need to visit that house down the street and see if we can talk the owner into letting us check out that area past the barn. Then we can look for clues, figure out how to catch it, and where to go from there. Agreed?" Carson asked.

"I had a hard time getting to sleep last night," revealed Ty. "I didn't used to feel that way when we were in college, but then we really were that close to finding something. Yesterday, both groups saw the creature and then we saw it again at the end of the night. My heart was racing, my mind was spinning, and my blood was pumping all night," confessed Ty. "When we used to do it before, I think what we felt was us psyching ourselves up, but last night was real. We now have the photo to prove there is something out there," concluded Ty.

"We know he is big. We know he is fast, and he is familiar with the terrain. He's going to be a hard beast to catch," pondered Carson.

"Do you think the homeowner will even be home now?" asked Tegan. "It is Monday morning. They're probably working."

"Good point," said Ty, "What can we do?"

Carson looked at his phone. "I don't know about now, but tonight Whitesnake is performing at the Majestic Theatre," said Carson.

And with that he went into an air guitar motion and sang

Here I go again on my own…

"I used to love that song," he said.

"I say we just go over, knock on the door, and see what's up," suggested Ty.

"Maybe wait until noon or so. But I don't want the trail to get too cold," confided Carson.

After finishing breakfast, they checked out the house. "We should at least see if someone is there," suggested Kareem.

They cleaned up the breakfast remnants and other trash in the campsite, running it over to the trash bin behind the Valero, then walked along Highway 181 to the driveway of the house. Walking down the long driveway between rows of trees, they saw a single-family house that looked to be built in the late 1980s. A brick house with an asphalt roof that looked to be over 2500 square feet. Carson knocked on the door and waited. He turned, talked to the group, and after a few minutes, knocked again. Still no answer.

Another pause, then Carson said, "Third time's a charm," and knocked again. "Looks like no one is home," he said. "Let's go back to camp, then maybe head into town and think about traps and where we can put them since we can't get on this property."

As the group turned to walk away and took a couple of steps in the driveway, the front door opened. A fit, average height man with striking features, medium, curly, light brown hair, and blue-green eyes stood in the doorway.

"Can I help you?" he asked.

Carson and the others stopped and returned to the front door. "Hello, we didn't think anyone was home. We're investigators in town checking out reports of a mysterious creature in the neighborhood," said Carson.

"Oh, the guys from the town hall meeting?" the man asked.

"Yes, we met with some people after that meeting and checked out the areas where they reported seeing the creature. We set up camp yesterday in the woods out by those ponds behind the Valero," said Carson.

"Yeah, I meant to go to that meeting, but I got busy with work and couldn't make it out," the man said. "Sorry, I didn't hear when you first knocked. I was downstairs in the beer cellar with a couple of friends."

Carson looked back with a raised eyebrow. "Beer cellar?" he inquired.

"Yeah, I'm a graphic designer and work mostly from my home office. Well, home office/man cave/beer cellar/garage," he said. "A few of my friends who also have flexible schedules came over for an early-week, near-mid-day bottle share," he added.

"Right on!" said Carson.

"Last night that creature was in the woods around here and we chased it, but it crossed over into your property. We didn't want to trespass, so we came to ask permission to check it out," said Ty.

"Sure, no problem. I have almost nine acres out back. A barn, a couple of horses. And I don't want it attacking my horses. I heard a few ranchers lost cattle because of that thing," the man said. "Hey, listen, you guys want to come in and meet my friends? I don't know if you are into beer, but we're about to dig into these bottles. We have several, and they are all pretty good ones," the man added. He stuck out his hand and introduced himself. "I'm Freddie Marshall."

Carson shook his hand, as did the others, with Carson introducing each one.

Freddie led the visitors into the three-bedroom house, the kitchen, and through a door that led into a converted garage. A life-sized Fathead poster of Tim Duncan and another of Manu Ginobili graced the wall of his man cave. A sixty-inch television, a PS4 console, and a framed poster of the USFL San Antonio Gunslingers logo completed the wall on that side of the room. A desk with a computer monitor rested in the back of the room behind a yellow bean bag chair. The other long wall continued with wooden shelves and two double-door wine refrigerators. A leather sofa, love seat, and chair completed the room. Another man and two ladies were sitting down, each with a glass in hand.

Freddie introduced the group of investigators to his friends, mentioning they were searching for an unusual creature in the area. Ellie Barnes was the first to introduce herself to the group. A lady in her late thirties with a small, delicate build, dark brown eyes, and thin dark eyebrows. A light, natural tan, and shoulder length straight brown hair with straight bangs. She mentioned she worked as a realtor and just a few weeks ago, she saw the creature while out showing homes in the area.

"It was off in the distance, so I didn't get a good look at it," she admitted. "It looked dark gray, and I thought it was a coyote, but it was a little skinny. Like it was malnourished."

"I am amazed at how many sightings have happened in the area," said Kareem.

"It is surprising people have seen it frequently, yet it hasn't been captured or identified," said Freddie.

"We are hoping to end that this week," said Carson.

"I hope you guys put an end to it," said the other lady.

Caitlin Turner had dark black hair with platinum streaks and hazel eyes. She was of medium height, thin, and had a small birthmark on her wrist. Carson could tell she was creative.

Maybe an artist or a musician, he thought.

As they continued to talk, he perceived her to be eccentric, maybe a little weird, but lovable. She said she was in her mid-thirties and unemployed.

"I too am between jobs, although it has been some time since I was in one," said Carson. "What did you do before?" he asked.

"I've tried a few jobs, but few fit. I'm jobless 'cause I feel lost in this world. I don't want to work in an office. I don't want to do any paperwork, and I don't want to work on a computer. I want to work with animals or plants or do something helpful for our Earth. Something like that. I also write poetry and play the guitar and sing at local bars. I like the freedom, but it doesn't come with much of a paycheck," said Caitlin.

"I know that feeling," replied Carson.

"I have thought of opening my own business. Perhaps a teahouse with a hippie-style shop sounds appealing. That thought brings peace and satisfaction to my mind. But I have no money to start. Continuing to perform songs around town in the evenings would make me happy. But an artistic career is always difficult and uncertain," Caitlin concluded.

"Moving from a science teacher job to a mysterious animal hunter is hard and uncertain also," replied Carson. "Many people are reluctant to talk about what they've seen because they are afraid of what others will think," he continued.

"I haven't seen the creature, but I enjoy hanging out with these folks and having the occasional bottle share," replied Caitlin.

"This is my first bottle share, so I look forward to it," said Carson.

"We should take a group selfie to mark the occasion," suggested Kareem.

Caitlin described the rules: everyone brings at least two bottles of a barrel-aged beer or something with limited availability.

"Or at least not available here," spoke up the yet-to-be-introduced man. "It can be a shelf beer from another state that isn't distributed to Texas," he said. "Hi, I'm Emiliano Rivera," he said with a firm handshake.

"Look at you, talking to strangers!" quipped Freddie. "Emiliano takes a while to warm up to others. He is serious, quiet, and has definite loner tendencies. He enjoys solitude and sits back and observes. He's private, rarely talks about his feelings, and can be insensitive to the hardships of others, but when he gets comfortable and opens up, he is knowledgeable and funny. I always invite him to bottle shares because he dutifully shows up, is consistently punctual, and always follows the rules," said Freddie.

Emiliano was in his forties, gestured quickly while talking with his hands, had a long stride, but was diminutive in stature, and had a soft tending to rounded build with tanned dark brown skin.

"It's essential to follow the rules," said Emiliano. "The purpose of the bottle share is to introduce the group to new beers, so that's what I try to do. I try to find beers that none of the others have had so that we can enjoy the experience."

Freddie added, "We like to hold these bottle shares regularly. Sometimes they happen because we enjoy getting together with friends, some of whom we don't get to see often otherwise, or as in today, it's a good way to meet new people."

"I wish we brought some beers along, but we didn't know anyone was home," said Ty.

"Please. You are our guests and welcomed to share. We also have a few random extra beers that are not as limited. You know just in case we run out and are still thirsty! We also have some food. Any good bottle share host knows you need a foundation. We have some platters of cured meats and veggies, cheese, and, of course, Texas barbeque," said Freddie.

"Let's get our cups! I will go first," said Caitlin.

"There is a half bath just outside the door so we can rinse the glasses," said Freddie.

"First up, I have a 2013 bottle from Freetail Brewing here in San Antonio," said Caitlin. "I love ales, and I love sours… I also love wine. This is an excellent combination of all of them."

She passed around a bottle of Ananke, an American wild ale aged in wine barrels. With the unexpected increase in attendance, it meant each pour was just under three ounces. Not enough for a solid drink, but enough to enjoy a taste of something new.

The beer poured a hazy, golden straw hue with a small ring of pure white head, even in the small vessel. With her love of sour beers, it excited Tegan to try it.

"This is fantastic!" said Freddie.

"Oh my God, this beer is amazing," said Tegan. "This has a little funk, lemon, white wine, hay, and sweet tarts smell to it. I can even taste the oak flavor coming through," noted Tegan.

Kareem smelled it and agreed with Tegan's notes. "Sour, with some tangy citrus notes. A touch of oak with a nice Brett presence. Light to medium in body with a puckering finish. Pretty tasty!" decided Kareem.

"I'd say you folks know your beers!" observed Freddie.

"We've had a bottle or two in our day," replied Ty.

"It's interesting because a lot of the barrel-aged programs use whiskey or bourbon barrels," said Emiliano. "This use of wine barrels stands out."

"I get a little vanilla in the aroma too," said Ty. "Sour light fruits and a bit of citrus, oaky vanilla… and a bit of coconut."

"It has a dry finish like a white wine," said Carson. "It is refreshing and I could see myself enjoying it on a hot Texas day."

"Two years and this is drinking well," Ellie said. "I wonder what another year would do with that oak and wine."

"Let's go light to dark," suggested Freddie.

"Then I think I am next," said Ellie. "Since we started with a wine barrel-aged beer…" She produced a brown growler and introduced the beer as being from a new hot spot. "It's from Red Horn Coffee House & Brewing Company in Cedar Park," she said.

"Hmm. I haven't heard of them yet," said Freddie.

Ellie responded. "These guys just opened March 11, but I enjoy it. This is a Belgian-style red ale that's aged in red wine barrels from Hilmy Cellars in Fredericksburg. It's called You Be Forty. It's aged for only three and a half months in the barrels, but I think it brings out the wine in aroma and the flavor."

Each participant received their share, swirled the small glass, and placed their nose above the rim. Ty took a sip and offered, "Nice twist on a Red Ale. The dryness of the Cab barrel balanced by the malty Red Ale."

"Tastes like a slightly sour dark beer," said Carson.

Caitlin enjoyed the beer as well, adding "I'm getting a lot of dark berries, cinnamon, and toffee,'" she said.

"The amber color is nice, but for me the red wine is strong and makes it a slow drinker," said Tegan.

The group took a quick break to wash out the glasses and prepare for the next tasting. Emiliano picked up a brown bottle with a white label and poured for his new friends. "This is a bourbon barrel-aged imperial bottled brown ale from Ranger Creek Brewing that was brewed in November 2014," he said.

Kareem looked at the glass of jet-black beer with light cocoa colored foaming head and smelled it. He noted a warming bourbon aroma, with hints of oak and vanilla, before taking a small sip.

"I get some heat on the palate, with a pleasing warm caramel and vanilla flavor," he said.

"That one aged in two barrels," noted Emiliano. "First a Four Roses barrel, then Ranger Creek 44 and Rimfire Barrels."

Ty took a sip and reported, "the bourbon dominates but doesn't overwhelm the base beer, which I don't think seems like much of a brown ale; there's no nuttiness or English brown malts. Instead, I find dark malts, faint tobacco, toffee, cream, and a hint of dark malts."

"Man, I love the bourbon on this. I bet this gets better as it warms up," said Carson.

"It has everything you look for in a barrel-aged brown, so smooth! Not too much bourbon, although using two different ones gives the distinct notes that add to the flavor," said Caitlin.

As they finished up the imperial brown, Freddie looked over at Carson and Ty.

"What are you going to do when you find this animal again?" he asked.

"We would like to capture it alive," said Ty. "We want to look at your land and see where it has been traveling, what's in the area, and where a good place to put a trap might be."

"We've seen it in a photo and from a distance, but not up close to understand its size," said Carson. "That could determine our trap plan. But once caught, we hope to have it analyzed to see what it is and where it came from," finished Carson.

"I hope you catch it," said Ellie. "A lot of the ranchers live on tight budgets and losing part of their herd is difficult. And for me, if word got out a monstrous creature was in the area, it would reduce the number of real estate showings I had. Few people would want to move into an area with an unknown, lethal creature."

Freddie offered a tray for each participant's glass. He took them into the kitchen for a quick wash and returned to continue the party.

"Hopefully, my first bottle won't be as scary as that monster," said Freddie with a grin. He held up a dark bottle with an artistic label.

"Being a graphic designer, this label stood out to me," he said. "The label has a nice graphic, eight colors -which is unusual for graphic print, and an interesting name. This is Branchline 5 a.m. To Midnight dark ale," said Freddie.

Carson looked at the bottle and agreed with the review of the label design: a graphic of a number like those on an old alarm clock or gas station pump rolling over from four to five.

He was curious about the name 5 a.m. to midnight.

What does 5 a.m. to midnight mean?

A note on the label stated it contained cocoa, espresso, and mint. Espresso and 5 a.m. could show a cup of morning coffee, and perhaps the mint and midnight related to a relaxing cup of mint tea to end the day around midnight? But then why not chamomile? That sounded more nighttime tea-like than mint. He pondered for a moment, then turned the bottle.

The commercial description provided the answer: *"In order to brew beer, you need to be both an early bird and a night owl. Get up early, drink coffee, eat tacos, drink beer, brew beer, clean up, drink beer, fill kegs, drink beer, stay out late, drink beer, drink beer, and tomorrow do it all over again. So here at Branchline we brewed a seasonal beer to make it a little easier to wake up so early and stay up so late. You are holding a sweet, dark ale brewed with mint, cacao, and locally roasted espresso beans. A wonderful espresso aroma and milky mint on your tongue awaits. So stay up late, or wake up early, or both from 5 a.m. to midnight."*

"Clever!" Carson said as he returned the bottle to Freddie for the pouring. Freddie poured a serving to each guest and awaited the results of their review.

"I like the dark brown hue with small fizzy diminishing head," said Ty. Taking a sip he continued, "Initial flavor is moderate sweet with a light bitter finish. It has a lot of tastes in this one - chocolate, light mint, molasses, brown sugar, espresso, and dark bread, a medium bodied with light carbonation."

Caitlin smelled the glass and noted a minty, fresh-brewed coffee, and Mexican chocolate with a faint smell like Kahlua.

"I like this," she said. "I think it's well done, nothing dominant. It's a balanced beer. Not overly sweet. The mint tastes like fresh mint rather than cheap candy or flavoring. There are even black pepper and chili overtones that blend in nicely, as well as a creamy texture and a long, smoky finish."

Kareem agreed with Caitlin. "Like an Andy's mint but refreshingly smooth," he said.

Emiliano offered, "This is a super interesting, unique beer. I think it's perfect to share with others as the flavors are a little strong. Not sure I could drink a whole one myself, but it has a solid coffee kick and light mint. Outstanding balance to those two flavors."

"I enjoy the darker beers the most," said Ellie.

"Me too!" spoke Carson. "I just recently started into the world of craft beer, thanks to these guys, but I have enjoyed the dark beers more than anything else," he concluded.

"That beer is a good transition into the next round of beers we have," Ellie said. "These are smaller bottles, 12.7 ounces, so I brought two of them," she said as she removed two brown bottles from a paper bag. "This one is also from Ranger Creek and part of their barrel-aged small batch program. This one is marked as bottled November 26, 2012, and is Small Batch Series No. 4."

She passed one bottle to Kareem, Tegan, Emiliano, and Freddie while she did the honors of pouring for Caitlin, Carson, Ty, and herself.

"Ranger Creek has some advantages over others in the barrel-aged program," Ellie said. "It has a whiskey distillery side and always has barrels available to use for aging beer. These bottles are ten percent, so it packs a little kick."

The beer gushed when opened, indicating a bit of over-carbonation.

"Cleanup on aisle two!" said Emiliano.

Freddie grabbed a towel from the dryer in the other room and used it to wipe up the spill.

"Looks like we have a little less now," said Ellie.

A hard pour into each of the snifters generated a decent-sized head, even for such a small pour. Ty took the glass and let it rest a moment. "Good head retention on this, likely because of the carbonation. A nice thick head of khaki," he said.

"What type of beer is it?" Ty asked.

Ellie responded, "The label doesn't say, but at the brewery they said it was an imperial mesquite smoked porter aged in Ranger Creek bourbon barrels."

Tegan agreed, "It has a nice medium body, but the high carbonation leads to a pure foam mouthfeel all the way to the finish, a bit over-carbonated."

"But it has a wonderful taste," said Kareem. "The mesquite gives some woodsy and herbal flavors. I've had the base porter before, and it is simple with some light chocolatey notes. The mesquite smoking compliments the base beer well, without being overbearing."

Caitlin agreed it wasn't overbearing, but added, "The barrel notes are lacking, leaving this feeling like a smoked imperial porter - not a barrel-aged one. I would have liked to see a little more oak and bourbon in this."

"I was definitely looking forward to it," said Carson. "This was a nice concept, but I don't think that they got enough influence from the barrel to match up with the smoke of the base beer."

"Let's have another rinse break and I will pour my second one," said Caitlin.

Carson took the time to review the pitching match-up for the Houston Astros vs. Los Angeles Angels game. Emiliano took notice.

"Are you an Astros fan?" Carson looked up and smiled.

"Yes. Since I was a kid, and they were in the National League. Nolan Ryan. Cesar Cedeno. Ken Caminiti. And later Craig Biggio, Jeff Bagwell, Billy Wagner… but my all-time favorite was Jose Cruz. I used to do that high leg kick when I played Little League."

Emiliano agreed with the historic choices. "After a couple of rough years transitioning to the American League, I am glad to see they are doing well now. What about that Carlos Correa kid? He's off to a great start in his rookie year. I think he's the shortstop of the future. He's shown he can hit at the major league level, and with power."

"We've got good, young arms too. Collin McHugh is pitching tonight and already has seven wins," Carson stated.

"I want to rinse the cups before this one because it should have a unique taste and I want to see how it stands up," said Caitlin. "This is Lakewood Brewing Company's Mole Temptress Imperial Milk Stout. Bottled earlier this year, so not a lot of age, but it should be good. I've left it out on the table to get closer to room-temperature, so it should open up nice."

Tegan's eyes lit up, and she smiled as the dark liquid poured into her snifter. "We might need some tacos to go with this," Tegan said. The pour was a dark brown/black, but not pitch black, as Tegan was expecting.

"I am a big fan of mole," noted Emiliano. "In cooking, there are many variations of recipes, but common ground includes chilies and nuts along with a touch of chocolate to tame the heat of the chilies."

Taking a sip, he paused with a surprised stern smile. "Vanilla and cinnamon at first, changing to smooth chipotle spice with chocolate. The chocolate also has some cinnamon with it, but then the chili peppers hit you at the end along with what seems to be nutmeg."

He took another sip. "I've tried every pepper beer, and this is possibly the most well balanced I've ever had. This is my favorite of the night so far!" said Emiliano with a satisfied smile.

"That Temptress smooth chocolate milk stout base is solid, but then a nice earthy flavor profile hits you in the middle, which I expect from mole. At the end, it finishes with a slight burn from the dried chilies. The only chili I can pick up is adobo, but maybe there's some poblano too. The spicy finish is nice and not too powerful, which is a good thing for me," said Freddie.

Tegan continued the positive reviews, following Emiliano's comments. "It balanced the earthy spices, peppers, and chocolate well, without overpowering any of the three. This may be the best pepper-ish stout I have tried," she said.

"Cinnamon is one of my favorite spices," said Carson. "The pepper is light while it goes heavy on the cinnamon and sweetness. There is some chocolate and the slightest bit of roast. This would be a great nightcap. What's the alcohol on this one?" he asked.

"That's just over nine," said Caitlin.

"The alcohol masks beautifully in this, and I agree with the guys. I think this is the closest I have come yet to finding the *perfect* pepper stout," said Ellie.

Still smiling, Emiliano looked around at the group enjoying themselves.

"It will be hard to top that last one," he said. "We are getting down to the end, but there's still plenty of excellent beer to come. That last beer was nine-point one percent and as Emeril said, *'Let's kick it up a notch!'*"

He reached into a brown paper bag of his own and grabbed two twelve-ounce bottles with his left hand and dropped the now-empty bag with his right.

"How about a little Russian Imperial Stout?" he asked.

Carson sat up tall in his seat. That last beer was fantastic, but from his brewery tours earlier in the week, he already knew he liked Russian Imperials.

"Even though these pours are small, I'm starting to feel it," Carson said, but still extended his glass for the offering.

As Emiliano poured the beer, he said, "This is St. Arnold's Bishop Barrel 8. They take the Divine Reserve No. 5 Imperial Stout recipe as the base beer in this one."

Carson looked like a child at Christmas unwrapping a new PlayStation console. Immediately he smelled it, taking in the Chocolate bourbon aroma. Tegan commented it smelled like raisins, toasted coconut, and vanilla.

Emiliano added, "This was aged in Woodford Reserve barrels." Everyone commented positively on the smell, Carson lingering a little longer than others, just taking it all in.

Ty tasted it and revealed, "There is plenty of bourbon up front to give it strong flavors of barrel juice, charred oak, caramel, and toasted coconut. The dark chocolate mixes with fig and date, along with a hint of toffee & coffee, the finish gives flavors of toasted nuts with hints of caramel and straight bourbon on the linger. I'm not sure what barrel juice is, but I hope it's tasty."

With that, Carson took a sip.

"Oh my. Electricity on the tongue! The barrel aging plays well with this one!" he said with happiness.

Freddie suggested the taste included molasses with a little peat and charred malt. While Caitlin felt that what set it apart from the other stouts was the rich thick body and excellent mouthfeel.

"I think there's some baker's chocolate," said Ellie.

"For the high alcohol content and the bourbon smell, the taste is silky smooth, with no hint of alcohol," marveled Freddie.

Ty looked at his watch and noticed it was well into the mid-afternoon hours. This drinking party turned into a longer-than-expected event. Freddie saw Ty looking at his watch and felt the group might be ready to get going. After all, they came to just ask permission to check the backyard for the animal. He commented that there was one bottle left.

"Why don't we crack this last bottle, then I can walk you to the back of the property to look around. There is plenty of beer to go around if you want to stay longer after we come back," said Freddie. "We can get some pizzas from down the street, watch the Astros game, and make a day of it," he offered.

"Last, but not least, I offer Freetail Brewing's Old Bat Rastard. This one is a 2012 bottle," said Freddie. "I admit I have had this before. I have it every year and buy a few bottles. It comes out on New Year's Day and is labeled as a winter warmer. I know kind of unusual to have a winter warmer in the middle of a humid Texas summer, but it is one of my favorites," said Freddie.

Freddie poured the drink and Carson took a deep breath as he prepared for the final round. His head was already tingling, which he speculated should make searching the woods interesting.

Hopefully the chupacabra doesn't pick that moment to attack, he thought.

"So, what's with the label?" asked Carson. "It looks like a bat in a leisure suit."

Freddie read him and the group the tale printed on the back of the bottle:

"So, kind of like Groundhog's Day?" said Tegan?

"Yes, but grumpier. An old curmudgeon is how the brewery describes him," said Freddie. "They release the regular version on New Year's Day, then they come out with a barrel-aged version in early February. That one is limited to two hundred bottles, so it is hard to get."

"Have a whiff of this," Freddie said to Caitlin as he poured her a taster. She sniffed and had a pleased look on her face. "Smells bready and nutty, like almond butter spread on toast," she said.

Freddie passed one to Emiliano, who enjoyed the malt aromas and caramelized sweetness.

Tegan took the smell in and found a lot of bread and caramel malt along with fruits and an almost port-like smell. Kareem caught the caramel sweetness, but thought notes of grapes, figs, and apples followed it. Ellie thought the smell was tough for her to pick out, but detected fruits and dark roasted malts.

Ty smelled and asked, "You said it's a winter warmer?" He thought it could almost pass as a barleywine with rich molasses, licorice, and caramel, giving it a big aroma. Not quite barleywine material, but in the vicinity.

Carson found the smell to be enjoyable and complex. He detected smells of dark fruits, raisins, figs, caramel malts, bready malts, and toasted malts. He eagerly took a sip. His mind raced, trying to place some of the lingering tastes coming forward. Almost like burnt sugar, a tangy dark malt, some type of metallic roastiness, but a big chocolate taste mixed with a mild spice, caramel, fig, and plum.

Others noted it had a nice hop hit in the middle, but also a great mouthfeel with a slight boozy taste making it feel big. Ellie called out a smooth herbal earthy bitterness and nuttiness. While others enjoyed it, Carson was extremely pleased.

"This has flavors of caramel, cocoa, cherry, brown sugar, raisins, roasted malt, and herbs with a somewhat dry finish. It's really complex with the subtle undertones," he said. "It is full and slightly bitter, not too strong, but I can get the alcohol and I think if a winter warmer means giving you a nice warm feel on a chilly winter day, this would do the trick. I did like the other two beers, but this might be my overall favorite. Nectar of the Gods! I think those tones of apricot, cherry, and currants make me look forward to spring and to hope… to new beginnings!" he said as he raised his snifter.

Freddie was glad his friends enjoyed the beer event, and Carson especially liked the Old Bat Rastard. "Freetail makes a lot of excellent beers," Freddie said, "But that one might be my absolute favorite in the lineup. I look forward to it every year."

"I don't blame you," said Carson. "I am new to the craft beer scene, but that was one of the best I have tried so far."

"You're new? How new?" asked Freddie. Ty spoke up.

"About three weeks now. He was a regular beer drinker at a dive bar when we found him. We introduced him to a local brewery in Austin and blew his mind. Now we are stuck with him, and I think we have to take him to hit up some bottle releases around Austin. Maybe a beer festival or two to give him the full experience," Ty said.

"Do you have a beer cellar yet?" asked Freddie.

Carson chuckled. "Definitely not. I need to learn about cellaring and beer trading. It sounds so foreign to me, but also interesting," he said.

"Tell you what, since you are here to help the community and find out what the animal is that has been wreaking havoc here, and you are a nice guy who is just starting out, let me give you something," said Freddie. "A little thank you for your work and a welcome to our craft beer world. Something to start your beer cellar," he said. He walked to the temperature-controlled refrigerator.

"We can keep it here until you are ready to go back to Austin, but since you enjoyed that Old Bat Rastard so much, I will give you one from my collection." He pulled out a bottle and handed it to Carson.

"It's a 2010 Barrel-Aged Old Bat Rastard," he said. "As I mentioned, they only make about two hundred per year, and this one is now five years old, so that reduces the number available in the secondary market. I still have one left, but you're welcome to have this one," he said.

"Wow! I don't know what to say. Thank you! I appreciate your generosity. Inviting us into your home, to the bottle share, introducing us to your friends, and now this. I am grateful," Carson said humbly.

Freddie smiled, slapped Carson on the shoulder and said, "No problem. Now… let's look for that chupacabra!"

Carson, Ty, Kareem, Tegan, and Freddie walked out of the back door and into the ankle-deep grass behind the house. The walk was more challenging than it would have been earlier in the day when they first went to the house. Even though the pours were small, eight of them added up because of the variety of beer and the alcohol volume.

The horses were grazing behind the barn and didn't come around to see who the strangers were. Walking past the barn, the group made it to the back line of the property. Ty looked toward the west side of the property.

"This is where we were yesterday," he said. "We came from over there, saw the animal on camera, and chased it over the property line. We flew a drone over the area and saw that it was propped up against a tree back here somewhere."

As they continued the walk, the whole group, including Freddie, searched the ground for any clues to the animal. Kareem kicked a pile of fallen leaves looking for tracks the animal may have left.

"Look here!" he said, pointing with his shoe to a pile of scat that laid on the ground. "We know the animal was here. I bet that is his droppings. Did anyone bring those bags?" asked Kareem.

"I have a couple of bags and a pair of the gloves," said Tegan. "I like to be prepared for anything." She put on the gloves, bent down, and collected the sample.

"We can save that for Sophie and the lab," said Tegan.

Ty shined a flashlight around the trees. "Look over there! Claw marks on the tree. Those are higher than most animals," he said.

Freddie looked at the evidence in disbelief. He didn't frequently spend time on the back of his property. Just enough to tend to his two horses, but to think an animal such as the mythical chupacabra was that close to him made him nervous.

"What is that?" Freddie asked, as he continued to help the group. "My God, that looks like a nest," said Carson.

The limbs from saplings, leaves, dirt, and other collected materials formed into a large matted down pile. Something that looked like where the chupacabra slept.

"Some of the recent chupacabra findings have come back after analysis saying they were raccoons with mange or scabies, but this nest… whatever slept here is bigger than a raccoon. And that animal we saw last night wasn't a raccoon," said Carson.

"Bigfoot sleeps in nests, but does the chupacabra?" asked Ty.

"Coyotes are one animal they have speculated to be the chupacabra to be, but they rarely live in nests. They use dens to give birth to their offspring and to sleep," said Carson. "Some have described this animal as resembling a boar. Boars and other wild pigs sleep covered by thick brush," continued Carson.

Kareem knelt and started searching through the nest. He discovered it contained chicken feathers, leaves, twigs, more scat, and footprints matching the animal Tegan and Ty encountered around the pond. There was also the body of a small chicken. It was still intact, but puncture wounds around the neck drained all the blood from its body, matching the evidence found on larger animals.

"Looks like it was here, and this is the nest of the chupacabra," said Kareem.

"What will you do?" asked Freddie.

"We have seen it and know it is big. We have seen it run and know it's fast. It is also strong and knows its way around these woods. We have to trap it, but the trap also has to be strong," said Carson.

"We could dig a hole and cover it with leaves," suggested Tegan. "Then it would run across and fall in," she said.

"We would have to dig a deep hole, then it may still jump out. It is about six feet tall and with those long legs, who knows how high it could jump. Plus I don't want to dig up that much of Freddie's land here," said Carson.

"How about a snare trap?" suggested Kareem. "We could have a loop on the ground, he steps in it, and it snatches him up in the air," he said.

"That could hold him because he wouldn't be able to run if he is hanging in the air. It could take away his power, but the challenge is getting him to step in that snare loop and pull it closed in time," said Carson.

Ty thought for a moment. "I think a big spring-loaded box trap would work best. Those doors come down quickly, they are steel so they are strong, and we could put some food inside to trap him. Once he walks in take the food, the door will close behind him," suggested Ty. "They make traps here in Texas for catching feral hogs. I think one of those would work well for this guy," suggested Ty.

"I think that might work, but where can we get one?" asked Carson.

"I know some friends at the Texas A&M AgriLife Extension Service in Bexar County who use them. I could make a call. Or we could buy one from a local store. I think that Producer's Co-Op in Seguin and New Braunfels carries traps made by Texas Hog Traps," suggested Ty.

"True…," said Carson, "but if we don't have to buy, that would be better. We are only going to use it once, plus we don't have a lot of money. Can you call your friends at Texas A&M and see if we can get one or two here tomorrow?" asked Carson.

"Definitely! I'm on it!" Ty said as he walked away and removed the phone from his pocket to make the call.

"This creature is about the size of a large feral hog, so a hog trap should hold him. We only need to get him inside," said Carson.

Ty returned to the group and confirmed the delivery of two traps for tomorrow.

"We should be ready to bring this creature in," he said.

The news pleased Carson, who returned to the enjoyment of the beer and new friends. An uneasy feeling settled in now that the moving parts were coming together, and it was almost go time. Reviewing the team, all except Ty had an uncertain look on their faces, worried about what was to come next.

Yesterday's hunt was challenging. What would tomorrow's hunt bring?

"Speaking of bringing it in…" said Carson. "How about we rejoin the others inside and finish that beer?" asked Carson.

"I can make a call and have some pizza delivered," suggested Freddie.

They walked back to the house as Carson checked the Astros pregame on his phone. "The game is about to begin," Carson said.

"In more ways than one," suggested Ty.

As they returned to the house, Freddie turned on the Astros game, Caitlin handed each person a Horchata Porter from Alamo Beer Company, and they sat on the leather furniture enjoying the game and conversation until the pizza arrived.

Carson thought about the Old Bat Rastard and the new beginnings of a cheerful spring day he imagined while drinking it. Once again craft beer and meeting new people had brightened his day and the pensive thoughts that three weeks ago were a regular part of his day were fading like a morning hangover after a big greasy breakfast.

CHAPTER 15

TRACKING THE BEAST

TUESDAY, JUNE 23, 2015

Morning arrived and a white 2011 Ford F-350 Flatbed pulled into the driveway of Freddie Marshall's house. Freddie walked out to greet the truck, and the group of Carson, Ty, Tegan, and Kareem walked down the road to join them. Freddie had offered to let the group stay in his house after the bottle shared the previous night, but they returned to the campsite to monitor the equipment.

The driver was a large white man in his early thirties named Charlie Bennett, but everyone called him Tater. Many considered him a good boy. He worked on the farm, hunted, and fished when he could. He loved country music and momma's home cooking. He had a big heart and was always willing to help his friends and neighbors. Ty met him at an education conference in Abilene in 2013. Tater was a service staff with the Texas A&M AgriLife Extension in Bexar

County where he worked to educate Texans in the areas of agriculture, environmental stewardship, youth and adult life skills, human capital and leadership, and community economic development.

Tater exited the truck wearing a camo print long sleeve crew shirt, baseball cap, and Vital pants. A couple of rifles were mounted on his inside gun rack. 40-Hour Week by Alabama played louder until he closed the door behind him.

"Mornin' boys," Tater said. "… and ma'am," he acknowledged with a tip of his cap to Tegan.

"I almost didn't see you with all of that camo," joked Ty.

"I figured on dropping these cages off to you, then headin' out and doin' a little elk hunting since I have the day off," Tater replied. He turned toward the bed of the truck, loosened the straps, and climbed up on the platform.

"We use 4' x 8' heavy duty cage box traps with spring-loaded lifting gate entries," he said as he removed the straps holding them in place. "What you wanna do is deploy these in an open area with scattered brush cover. You have to pre-bait the trap. Trapping is a process, not an event, and pre-baiting serves to both attract the animals. For these feral hogs, it gets them accustomed to entering the trap. Before you set the trap, place the bait near the gate and inside the trap," he guided.

"Are you trapping more than one hog?" Tater asked.

"Um… We're not looking for hogs," said Carson. "And we think there is only one."

"If there are more than one, that could be difficult. One drawback to drop gate box traps is that they do not allow additional animals to enter once the trap is sprung… so you're not huntin' hogs? Whatcha huntin'?" inquired Tater.

"We're going to trap the chupacabra," Tegan said.

Tater looked at her for a few seconds before giving a jolly laugh, his massive belly shaking.

"Woo. That's a good one, Missy…. chupacabra. Now I done heard it all!" he said dismissively. "I mean, I used to hear stories, but I thought it was old men sitting around tellin' their tales," he said.

"I thought it was a tale too, but after the past couple of nights, I can tell you for certain… it's not a tale." said Kareem.

"That's right. We saw it night before last, right out here in these woods," said Carson. "This was not an animal that I've ever encountered in the woods, and I'm pretty sure I've 'bout come across everything you can come across in Texas," said Carson.

Tater slid the first cage toward the edge of the truck while Carson and Kareem reached up and carried it down to the driveway. Ty and Freddie took the second cage. With the truck unloaded, Tater jumped down

"I don't think you are going to find any chupacabras, but good luck with whatever is out there. I don't care what you catch. Just don't beat my traps up too bad."

Tater said he would come pick up the cages later in the weekend.

Freddie informed the group they could leave the traps beside the house when finished, and Tater could get them anytime. Climbing back into the truck, Tater waved as he drove off.

The sun continued to climb during the mid-morning hours as the men carried the cages to the back of the property. Unfortunately, the temperature and humidity also continued to climb, and carrying the large cages proved to be a strenuous task. Each cage took a person on each side. They made their way through the backyard, occasionally sitting it down to catch a rest. Tegan guided the way and provided encouragement as they again picked up the cages and inched closer to their goal. After three brief breaks, the group made it to the desired locations.

"Remember, we have to cover them with brush," said Ty.

Kareem, Tegan, and Freddie began walking around and collecting leaves and small brush to help camouflage the opening of the traps. Carson looked toward the wooded area they encountered the creature two nights before. He looked in the direction the animal ran and where they saw it on the drone. The spot the creature rested after the chase was right where they found the clawed tree yesterday, and close to the nest.

He speculated the trail was a regular route the animal knew well. Setting one trap near the trail would be an excellent location. The second trap they would place further along the running trail, just past the barn. The trap would not bother the horses, and even if they came up to inspect the cages, they were too large to worry about getting caught. That was another advantage of using a box trap instead of a snare trap. The latter might catch the horses, and that could injure Freddie's animals, as they would struggle to break free.

"After the other night, seeing those eyes, seeing the animal run, we know this thing's out here. There have been sightings around town, but it's right here. We have it on thermal video, we have it on photograph, and we found the nest and tracks. We are this close to proving the chupacabra exists. We need to finish setting up these traps ASAP. I'm a man on a mission to prove these things are real. Nothing's stopping me. We've dug too deep and invested too much time to not catch this thing. About the only thing you can trust in the world is your gut, and I know we are close to getting this animal," said Carson.

Ty helped place mud and leaves around the front of one trap.

"I agree. You and I have hunted creatures for years and we've never been this close. We know something is out in these woods."

"And we're going to prove it to each other, this community, and to the rest of the world," Carson interrupted.

"You have got to stop caring what other people think and fight the urge to always prove them wrong. It's going to get you, or us, in trouble one day," warned Ty.

Kareem and Tegan looked on with a nervous agreement. They found the experience the other night to be scary, but they knew they had to settle their nerves. There was something out there, it was harming the animals in the community, and causing people to fear leaving their own homes. They knew they had to do whatever it took to capture this creature. But what then?

All the sightings before were people spotting the animal but being non-confrontational. The other day, they gave chase to it but didn't threaten it. What happens when they try to pursue the beast tonight and capture it? And when the animal realizes it is being hunted and can sense a trap? What happens then when it becomes a fight-or-flight situation? Will it flee, or will it turn and fight? They continued to work as the thoughts flooded their mind.

Carson looked around at the trap by the barn and decided the brush had adequately hidden it. They walked back to the first trap and examined it with equal scrutiny.

"The traps are ready. We're going to get him! We are going to show people this shit is real. And when we do, everyone who is sitting around saying Oh, he's crazy will change their tune. That's what they said about Nostradamus until his predictions started coming true. Then it's like, *"Fuck! We shoulda listened to him!"*" scoffed Carson.

For Carson, this was more than just a job or some adventure to him. It was about credibility and being taken seriously in the scientific community.

"I hope we see it again tonight," said Kareem. "But I have just one question. If it's active at night and sleeps during the day… and if we are saying this is its nest…. where is it now?" he wondered aloud.

"Just because it is daytime doesn't mean it's sleeping. Many coyotes are killed during daylight hours, and with feral hogs they don't have regular habits like deer," said Ty. "He could be maybe two miles away right now and have no intention of hitting this place until it wanders over here again. It might have another nest somewhere and only sleeps here when it's in this area. If there is food around, then it will return," said Ty.

"We need to bait the traps," said Carson.

"What are we going to use for bait?" asked Kareem.

"I've heard people catch boars with a bucket of mash or strawberries and sugar. Coyotes will go for canned dog food or scraps from the butcher shop… but this, we know he hasn't eaten meat so far. It seems to only feed on the blood of livestock… I heard a couple years ago that a group in Brazil called the Association of Haunt Mariana offered money to people to serve as bait to catch a monster they called Caboclo D'Água. Papers reported it as their version of the chupacabra, but it lived underwater and came up on land only to attack humans. But our monster has not yet attacked humans," said Ty.

"How about a baby goat?" asked Tegan. "I mean, its name is supposed to mean goat sucker, right? So why not give it a goat?"

"Well damn," said Ty. "Maybe I can get Tater back on the phone. The Texas A&M AgriLife Extension Service has a goat project," he said. He pulled out his phone and left a message for Tater.

"Hopefully he will get that and come back before sundown. I'm sure he won't think too kindly of using the goats for bait, but we just have to be ready to protect it," said Ty.

"We've done all we can do right now," said Carson. "Until we get the goats later today and until this sun goes down, I think we're in a holding pattern," he said.

Carson advised Freddie they would be out later that night and suggested he stay inside the house tonight in case they angered the animal. He agreed and wished the team well on their hunt. Freddie returned to the house and the group to the campsite.

Settling back into camp, Ty suggested they get some rest to prepare for the hunt tonight. Two nights ago they were rested and found once the hunt started, adrenaline kept them alert, and all-in-all it was a successful night. They hoped for similar luck finding the animal tonight, but this time with a better result. One that would lead to a caged animal that could validate credibility not only for them, but to all those who search for animals that until now had remained off the radar of modern science.

As the group prepared for a nap, Carson stirred around the site and looked over the equipment. Each member needed a headlamp and the other equipment such as the thermal camera, night vision goggles, the firearms, the stun baton, and the GoPro would be split amongst them. Feeling satisfied with the planning, he climbed into the sleeping blanket and closed his eyes.

When he awoke, it was after sundown and the hot temperature from the afternoon sun had already loosened its grip on the land. The group stirred in the camp. Ty woke up and looked at his phone, noting a text message from Tater saying he dropped two goats off at Freddie's house.

"Looks like we're set," said Ty.

Carson grabbed the rifle and a headlamp. "Let's go!" he said. "I think we're ready to get this investigation started."

Ty grabbed the pistol and a headlamp, then helped Carson attach the GoPro to the chest strap. Kareem took a headlamp and the camera, leaving Tegan with a headlamp and the baton. Carson put the night vision goggles in his cargo shorts pocket and the group headed over to Freddie's to get the goats. They found two small kids tied to a roped stake on the side lawn. Kareem and Tegan each took a rope leash from a goat and led them into the woods.

"You're going to be okay tonight, little guy," said Tegan to her goat.

With only the light from their headlamps to shine the way, they navigated through the darkness to the cage nearest the barn. It was undisturbed and the door was down as they had left it.

Opening the door, Carson crawled inside, took the leash from Tegan, and used a nearby rock to hammer the post into the ground. With the goat tied to the post, Carson crawled out and loaded the spring door. It was ready to catch its prey.

"Sucks for the goat," said Kareem.

"Yeah, but he's just to attract the creature. The plan is to get here before anything happens to him," said Carson.

They walked toward the nest where the other trap lay in waiting. Again Carson crawled into the cage, hammered the peg, and secured the second goat. Exiting the cage, he loaded the door as he did on the first cage.

"Goats are ready, traps are ready… are we ready?" he asked as he searched the faces of his partners.

The group members nodded in agreement, and they set off to begin the hunt. As they took a few steps Carson looked down and noticed a small hatchet that must have belonged to Freddie laying in the grass. He remembered how fast the animal was the other day.

"What if the animal avoids our trap?" asked Carson. "We know he is fast and big. If he goes on the run, we are going to have a hard time keeping up with him. We have to slow him down," said Carson.

"How do you plan on doing that?" asked Tegan.

Carson looked around at the trees, then at the hatchet. "Punji sticks," he said.

"What the hell is a Punji stick?" asked Kareem.

"It is something used by the Viet Cong during the Vietnam War," said Ty. "They would sharpen sticks and place upright in the ground, in large numbers. We could use these around a camouflaged pit, or they could hide them in an area where the target might take cover. Back in the war, soldiers diving for cover might impale themselves."

"We don't have time to dig a pit, but we can make several sticks and hide them along the trail before the cage," said Carson. "Maybe he steps on the sticks and runs into the cage. But if he misses the cage, it might still slow him down, and we can capture him."

Carson used the hatchet and chopped off several small sticks about eight to ten inches. He chipped the edges to a fine point and tossed them into a pile, making about thirty spikes overall before concluding that would be sufficient. They gathered the newly created spikes and found a location in the bend of a trail where they would be unseen once camouflaged with leaves.

"Just remember if we come chasing the animal through here…," said Ty, his voice trailing off.

Everyone understood the message and the danger it may be for them if they forgot. Satisfied with their work, they set off in a group back toward the ponds near their campsite.

"The water is a good place to start. If this animal is thirsty... There aren't too many places around here to get water. Not like the pond at Fred's house, the lake, or the river on its way to the school. Chances are if he's here, and he's thirsty, he will be around here tonight," said Carson.

Moving around the pond, the team saw no sign of the creature. Frogs were chirping, katydids and crickets were singing, and owls were hooting. A good sign that no danger was around. They circled the three ponds, looking in the thermal camera and the night vision goggles, but saw nothing. Carson led the group into the woods, following the route he and Kareem took the other night. The woods were quieter than around the pond, but they still heard an occasional owl. For more than an hour, they journeyed through the dark woods without sight nor sound of the creature they sought. Deeper into the woods they walked, further than their first hunt.

"We have to remember where Freddie's house and our traps are. We can't get too far out here, forget where we are, and chase the animal in the wrong direction," warned Carson.

Now more than a mile away from their campsite, the group continued, turning to look at every noise they heard. A sign that showed they were all nervous and jumpy. The group drifted toward the east and the far depths of Freddie Marshall's property as the hunt continued.

"It's like looking for a needle in a haystack. Hunting a dark animal in the dark woods with lots of cover," said Kareem.

They walked east for a while, then back south toward Freddie's house. The woods grew quieter as they moved through the night. They came upon the trail they found in the woods earlier.

"This looks like the trail that heads back toward the traps," said Kareem.

As they walked around the corner searching for tracks or broken branches, Tegan's headlight shone on a tree right beside the trail. Just two feet from her, the quiet creature stood on its hind legs. Detecting the human invaders before they noticed the creature, it disrupted the quietness of the woods by letting out a loud growl, causing Tegan to jump in horror as she stared into its glowing red eyes and saw its sharp fangs and extended claws.

Startled by the intruders and Tegan's scream, the beast lunged toward Tegan. Instinctively, she reacted by jumping back and swinging the stun baton into the beast's midsection. It screamed in pain as the weapon instantly flooded the beast's body with six million volts of electricity. The creature dropped, then attempted to get up and escape in a gingerly trot down the trail into the darkness. The animal was much slower than before it received the surprise intense jolt. "Holy shit!" she exclaimed.

"Oh my God! Are you alright?" reacted Carson.

Kareem grabbed her as she shook from the initial shock.

"Yeah-Yes, I'm fine... I'll be fine! We've got to go after it! I think I got it and it's slowed down now!" she said.

The woods filled with another loud yelp. Ty speculated the creature found the spikes along the path.

"I bet the stun baton weakened its vision, and it didn't see camouflaged spikes. This might be our shot!" shouted Carson.

He turned and ran into the darkness. Ty paused for a second, looked back at Kareem and Tegan, and then ran following Carson. Moments later, a loud metallic sound rang through the night.

Carson stopped, turned toward Ty and said, "That's the trap! Let's go! Get the gun!" The two ran off to investigate.

"Are you planning on shooting it?" huffed Ty as he tried to keep pace.

"That thing almost had Tegan!" Carson said. "The time for preppin' is over. It's do or die tonight! That thing has seen its last day! Get up here!" yelled Carson.

"We can't just leave Kareem and Tegan alone in the woods!" replied Ty. Where are you going?" yelled Ty.

"We've got to check the trap!" Carson shot back.

As the two men reached the cage near the nest, they found the door closed, but the cage was empty. No goat. No chupacabra.

"Fuck! He got away!" yelled Carson. "How?!" He turned frantically, looking in each direction at the trail and the leaves.

"He's been here, and he's injured. Tegan hit it with that baton but look – there's blood all around here. It must have run into those spikes!" he said. "He got away, but he hasn't gotten far. Follow that blood trail!" he said before running off alone in pursuit.

Ty yelled to Carson, "We've got to stay together! You can't go running your ass off alone! He's injured, so he's pissed, and he's in fight mode! If we split up, it's easy pickings for him!" Then the severity of the situation sank in for Ty. "Jesus. We hit him with six million volts, speared it with the spikes, and put a cage right in its running trail, yet he still got away. How do we catch this monster?" Ty questioned.

Shaking off their fear, Kareem and Tegan caught up to the two men and looked around at the cage and the bloodied leaves. "Isn't that a sign we should just get the hell out of here while we still can?" asked Kareem.

"We're in its territory now!" said Ty.

Carson kicked a rock that was on the trail. "Damn it!" exclaimed Carson. "It cannot get away! It will not end like this!" he yelled. Suddenly, he ran off once again into the night down the trail.

"Carson! Damn it! Get back here!" yelled Ty. "This fucker's gone crazy!" he said to Kareem and Tegan just before he left to chase after Carson.

Kareem and Tegan soon followed to stay close to the others, but they were still nervous, and were in no position to be helpful. But they knew being alone in the woods wasn't a good decision. "There's safety in numbers," said Kareem.

Carson juggled, but managed to put on the night vision goggles as he ran down the trail, closing in on the second cage.

"Look!" he yelled out to the others. "Glowing eyes ahead!"

"I'm scared to death, and I really want to get inside the house!" wavered Kareem.

"Ty! Get up here!" yelled Carson. "Can I get a little fucking backup?!"

Ty ran up with Carson.

"I'm right here, man!" he said.

"I'm a little scared too right now!" admitted Carson. "All these years of hunting animals like this and we never found shit. I doubted myself, but here we are knee-deep in shit's creek and I'm not sure how we get out!" admitted Carson.

"First, you gotta calm your ass down, buddy. No more runnin' off into the night like goddamn Braveheart! That shit will get you killed… or me killed… or someone killed," said Ty.

"Damit!" shouted Carson as he raised his rifle and fired two shots into the night out of frustration.

"What the hell are you doing?! Stop shooting!" shouted Ty.

"I locked eyes with something up there in the bushes," Carson said.

"You're either going to scare it off or injure someone!" said Ty.

"Shhh! There's something over there… in the bushes," quieted Carson.

"What? Are you serious?" asked Tegan.

"Yes!" said Carson.

"I see it too," said Ty.

"You're just kidding me right now, right? We scared that thing off and it's run away. Hasn't it?" asked Kareem.

Carson and Ty stood at the front of the pack and continued to stare off toward the dark bushes ahead. Carson cocked his gun.

"What's the deal, Hoss?" asked Ty. "What is it?!"

"Something just ran right through here," Carson said in a hushed voice. "The trees are still moving."

Ty looked into the darkness and saw the moving branches, but no sign of the creature. Carson turned toward his partner.

"You go that way, and I will circle around this way," suggested Carson. "You guys stay back," Carson said to Kareem and Tegan.

As they began making their separate paths toward the bushes, Carson yelled out to Ty, "You see anything?"

"I think…" he said as he spun. "I just saw that sonofabitch go this way. Just to the right of me!" said Ty.

Carson turned in Ty's direction to see if he could provide his friend with some guidance.

"Ty! Look out!" Carson yelled as the creature leapt from the shadows directly at Ty.

"Oh Shit!" exclaimed Ty, as he back peddled in reaction to the beast's sudden appearance.

Gunshots rang through the night as Carson aimed his rifle in the commotion's direction. The creature lunged on top of Ty, snarling and growling as he knocked the startled man down. Ty struggled to fight off the animal, overpowering it only enough to free the hand holding the pistol. The beast continued to snap, gnash, and bear teeth in Ty's face as he held the vicious animal back with one hand and drew the pistol close to the beast's face. The creature continued to display hostility and the readiness to fight until…

BANG! BANG!

Carson fired two shots.

BANG! BANG!

Another two shots, but not from Carson's gun.
A loud groan.
A thump.
Then silence.
Carson ran in the shot's direction.
"Ty?!… Ty?!"

He continued to run as Kareem and Tegan ran in shock toward the bushes. They reached the scene as the bloodied gray creature laid on top of Ty.

Ty whimpered as the heavy animal knocked the wind out of him. He tried to sit up, but his ribs were sore - possibly bruised or cracked. The beast had sunk his teeth in just below the shoulder, leaving his arm bloodied and with an open wound. The animal was dead and the trio standing above Ty struggled, but managed to push it off their friend.

Ty attempted to collect his breath and his thoughts as he remained on his back, looking up at the dark starry sky. Covered in sweat, drool, and dirt, he lay on the ground with his eyes closed and breathing heavily.

"You okay, brother?" asked Carson. "I thought you were fixin' to be dinner!"

He reached his hand down to his friend. Ty's eyes drifted down to lock onto his friend's. He reached his hand up to take

Carson's. Tegan and Kareem rushed over to help pull Ty to his feet. He stood gingerly as best he could, with an arm draped over Carson's shoulder and another across Kareem's. He took inventory of his injuries: sore ribs, sore chest, and sore arm with trails of blood. He exhaled deeply, fighting off the pain from ribs that were likely broken, but managed to free one hand to wipe his brow.

"Yeah, man…. I'm good," he said as he turned and looked at the body on the ground. "That's not how we drew it up, is it?" asked Ty.

Carson looked down at the animal and then up at his friend. "Not exactly," he said, putting a comforting arm on Ty's good shoulder, who could now stand on his own accord.

The group stood around, a little worse for wear, looking down at the creature that had terrorized the local community. Even dead, it was frightful. They got a good look at it under the light of their four headlamps and they saw the reports were accurate. It was about three and a half feet tall and over five feet long, its gray skin now covered with open wounds and blood. It had gunshots on the upper back, its rump, and two in the head that Ty got off. Those were the killing shots, they speculated.

"Now what?" asked Tegan.

"I don't think we should leave it here," said Carson. "Something might come along and eat it… let's drag it back and put it in the cage."

Carson looked at Ty. "Not you, big man," he said. "We've got this."

Tegan reached into her pockets and removed three sets of latex gloves.

"Put these on first," she said.

They reached down and grabbed the legs of the dead animal and dragged its body toward the cage.

"This monster's heavy!" said Carson.

They reached the cage and pulled the body inside. Carson used a long stick to hit the release and dropped the trap door. "That will hold him until morning," said Carson. "We can see if Fred can come out here with that 4x4 and load him up. We might need Tater's flatbed truck to haul it over to Sophie at the lab," he suggested.

"We need to get Ty to a doctor tonight too," said Carson.

"Naw, I'm good," Ty replied, assessing the damage.

"That's a nasty bite on your arm," said Tegan. "That fucker might have rabies."

"Fine. I'll get it checked out tomorrow," he said.

Carson checked his phone. "Looks like urgent care closes at 10 p.m. The nearest doctor's office is closed too. We could go into town and take you to Baptist Health System at Southcross Boulevard," said Carson as he searched the options online.

"I am sure I will be fine until tomorrow morning," said Ty.

A cry echoed through the night, causing the group to stop. Carson looked at his friends, then over toward the second trap by the barn.

"Someone get that goat!" he said.

CHAPTER 16

EXPLORING THE EVIDENCE
WEDNESDAY, JUNE 24, 2015

Wednesday morning at 8 a.m. Sophie Thompson poured a cup of coffee from the coffee machine at the University of Texas Health Science Center at San Antonio Nucleic Acids Core Facility breakroom. She was sleepy from staying up late the night before attempting to finish the final chapters of The Stranger Beside Me by Ann Rule.

With her profession as a lab assistant, she loved true crime and envisioned herself being the one to solve the mystery and save the day. She closed her eyes and sipped from the cup, analyzing her senses to see if she had attained the perfect combination of coffee, milk, and sugar in her mixture. It was good, and a smile graced her face.

The vibration of her cell phone in her lab coat pocket brought her back to her senses. She sat the coffee on the counter and looked at the phone. It was Carson Quinn calling.

"Hello?" she answered.

"Sophie, it's Carson. We met at the town hall meeting Saturday?" he said.

"Yes. Yes. I remember. How are you? Did you search for that animal yet?" she asked.

"Searched for it…. and found it!" he said. "It didn't go quite like we had planned. We had to shoot it… but we have the body. I wondered if you were still willing to help?" he asked.

"You got it?! What is it?" she wondered.

"Well, that's what we were hoping you could tell us. It is like nothing I've ever seen, that's for sure. We'll need your expertise to run some tests on it and see if you can identify what it is. We could bring it over to the lab today. We have to swing Ty by the hospital on account of the thing bite him pretty good in the shoulder. He's got some sore ribs and lungs too, but I imagine he will be fine in a few days," said Carson.

"My gosh! Sounds like it was exciting!" she said.

"Yep. But now it's over. We just have to figure out what it is and where it came from. That's where you come in to solve the mystery," he said.

"Solve the mystery?" she repeated. "Oh, I do like the sound of that. You can bring it by today. We are kind of slow right now so I can get started," she said.

"He's a big guy. Over three feet tall, five feet long, and nearly a hundred pounds, I expect," reported Carson.

"Bring him over. I can look at Ty too. Save you an extra trip," she offered.

Carson's next call was to Fred Dalton. When Fred picked up the phone, Carson filled him in on the night's events and asked if he could bring the 4x4 over to the Valero to pick up the carcass.

"How are you going to get it to the lab?" asked Fred.

Tegan, sitting beside Carson, overheard Fred through the phone.

"It's not going in the Verano!" she yelled for Carson and Fred both to hear.

"Me and my buddy Eric were going to get some breakfast. We can load the 4x4 in the back of his old truck and then haul the animal in the bed," he suggested.

"Sounds like a winner winner chicken dinner!" said Carson.

Within an hour, Eric's old '79 Scottsdale truck pulled up in the parking lot of the Valero where Carson, Tegan, Kareem, and Ty were standing. Eric and Fred walked toward the group, noticing Ty wearing jeans and a sleeveless white undershirt t-shirt. They saw his visible wounds.

"What the hell happened?" inquired Fred.

"The damn thing tried to give me a kiss last night," Ty joked.

"You better get the shoulder looked at. Looks nasty," Fred replied.

"We are going to do that when we drop the big guy off at the lab," said Ty.

Tegan, Eric, and Ty stayed by the truck in the parking lot while Fred, Carson, and Kareem got on the 4x4 and made their way off to retrieve the body. Fred had hitched a trailer to the back of the vehicle so they could put the animal on it. They drove down the road to Freddie's house, then through the side yard, and into the back, where the creature remained in the cage.

"We thought best to drag him out here and leave it in the cage so coyotes or vultures wouldn't get to him before we got him to the lab," said Carson.

"That's smart thinking," said Fred. "Nature has a way of taking care of its own, and it moves quickly," he said.

They opened the door of the cage and grabbed the animal by its feet, then pulled. They drug it out of the pen, and between the three of them, could carry it to the trailer behind the 4x4.

"Well, I'll be damned!" said Fred. "That's the thing I saw that night around the pond. Ugly sombitch, isn't he?"

Fred placed a hand on the animal's mouth and moved its lip up to reveal its large teeth.

"Those will do some damage," he said.

"No shit." responded Ty.

The trip back to the truck was much slower because of the extra weight of the animal on the back trailer. Once back in the parking lot, the three of them, along with Eric and Kareem, could lift the body into the bed of the truck. Everyone circled the vehicle to get their first actual glimpse of the beast in the sunlight.

Carson suggested they take two cars since Fred and Eric were headed to breakfast. Then they could go from the lab and the others could drive back.

"If that shoulder is still bleeding, you're ridin' in the back with the chupacabra," Tegan said to Ty.

Tegan led the way, and Eric followed with the animal in the back. Thirty-five minutes later, they pulled into Floyd Curl Drive and phoned Sophie. She directed them to the back of the building, where she opened a door and pushed a hospital gurney into the parking lot.

"We can put him on here," she said.

Lowering the tailgate of the truck, the creature was once again drug by its feet and the group of men lifted it onto the gurney. Sophie looked at the animal with a surprised look and slowly pushed her glasses back up the bridge of her nose with her index finger.

"Oh…," she paused, not knowing exactly what to say. She gulped as she tried to find the words. "Let's get him inside before anyone out here sees him," she suggested.

With the help of Carson, she wheeled the creature into an exam room. "We'll just leave him here for now," she said. "Let's have a look at you," she said to Ty.

He removed his shirt and hopped up on the exam room table. She pushed on his chest and stomach, asking where it hurt, then focused on his shoulder.

"Doesn't look infected, but I would put some peroxide on it and keep it clean. I suggest going back to the hotel tonight and no more camping outside while this is still open." She wiped up the blood and cleaned the wound. "Looks like it's just those puncture marks from the fangs, but you tore it a little in the struggle," she said.

She grabbed a clean bandage from the drawer and wrapped it up.

"You'll be fine if you keep it cleaned and change the bandages. Here, take a couple more for later," she said as she handed him a handful.

Ty scooted off the table and put his shirt back on over the freshly covered bandaged shoulder.

"So, what's next for this guy?" asked Ty, smacking the rear of the chupacabra.

"Well…," she said as she studied the creature, "I'll look at its body and see if we can identify it from that. We'll have to take some tissue samples and run them through some tests. We have a Beckman-Coulter DNA sequencer here that I can run DNA sequencing and fragment analysis on the samples. Once I finish with the tests, I can put that information into the database and search online to see what animal or animals it matches to," she said.

"How long will it take?" asked Carson.

"If we had to send it out, it would take a few weeks. But we have equipment here, so I can start on it this morning, so we can make some at least preliminary findings tomorrow," she said.

"Thanks! Keep us posted if anything turns up," said Carson. "Thanks for your help on this. I appreciate it."

The investigators returned to their car.

"Now what?" asked Tegan.

Carson looked at the Google map on his phone

"I think Ty needs a beer!" he said as he looked up into the mirror above his seat and saw Ty's reflection from the backseat. "We're up on this side of town… Freetail Brewing isn't too far away," he said. "Which reminds me, we can't forget to pick up that bottle Freddie gave me before we head out of town."

Tegan looked down at her phone. "Hey, I know what. Let's make a pit stop on the way to the brewery," she said. "We've got plenty of time."

"Where do you want to go?" asked Ty wearily.

"There's this place I saw on Fact or Faked a few years ago, and it's just nine miles from here," she said.

"I loved that show," said Carson. "What place?"

"It's called Gravity Hill," she said.

"I remember that one!" replied Ty. "That's the one where you park below the train tracks and the ghost children supposedly push the car uphill," he responded.

"That's the one, and it's nearby. We have to try it out," she said excitedly.

"GPS says it's at the southeastern edge of the city, at the junction of Shane and Villamain Roads, 410 exit 42. Turn south onto Southton Road, then take the second right onto Shane Road. Drive about three-quarters of a mile. We just have to take Highway 181 down to 410 and we'll take the first exit," said Ty.

As they arrived at the scene of the former train tracks, Carson suggested Tegan turn on the hazard lights.

"I was just checking it out online as we drove over here and the websites say the road is still in use and curves once attempting the roll, which could put you into oncoming traffic," alerted Ty.

"For full effect, does anyone have any powder?" asked Tegan.

"There should be some Johnson's baby powder in my duffle bag if it's still in the trunk," replied Kareem.

"Why do you have baby powder?" asked Carson. "Dare I ask?"

"You know… for chafing when I run. It's good for the nether regions," replied Kareem.

With a stern smile Carson replied, "Good to know…"

The bag was still in the trunk and Kareem removed the white bottle. He shook it toward Carson.

"With Aloe & Vitamin E," he teased.

He sprinkled it across the back bumper of the car, giving it a generous coating. The guys stood around the back of the car while Tegan got inside, slowly drove to the top of the hill, and put the car in neutral.

As the legend stated, the car slowly rolled up the hill and over the would-be train tracks. Tegan turned the car into the curve and parked on the side of the road. As the guys ran up to the car, they inspected the back bumper, and noticed as also stated in the legend, fingerprints appeared in the powder.

"That's so cool," said Carson.

"It is an amazing and thrilling effect," said Ty.

"What the Fact or Faked team discovered was the trees were causing an optical illusion regarding the angle or direction the driver is looking as they are sitting behind the wheel. At first glance, it appears you are going up the hill, but it's downhill. The car rolls down the hill because gravity catches enough momentum to push it over the tracks. After the show's tests came back, it was agreed upon that they could debunk the paranormal aspect of the story. The handprints in the powder are real, but they are not ghost children. They are your own oily prints from all the times you opened your trunk or touched the back end of your car," said Tegan.

"But a pretty cool story none-the-less," said Kareem.

Back in the lab, Sophie prepared the creature's body for examination. It was lying on its back with its legs up drawn in like a burglar about to jump from the bushes. She put on a surgical mask and latex gloves, then adjusted a surgical headlight to her head. Prior to starting, she paused and thought this could be her true-crime-novel moment. Except it was an unknown animal rather than a person, and for the cause of death, they already knew whodunit.

She knew people were calling it a chupacabra, but what does that mean? Science had never identified an animal as a chupacabra before. There were many sightings and speculations, but animals thought to be the mythical monster have always turned out to be a common animal. She knew this animal differed from those because of the reported ability to walk on its hind legs.

She began with a careful inspection of the body. In a true crime setting, this could be important in the victim's identification, locating hidden evidence, and finding the cause of death. Here it would be for classification. She walked to the desk and removed an audio recorder so she could record her findings as she worked, then later write up the paperwork.

She would first weigh and measure the body and record physical characteristics such as eye color, hair color, and length. Measuring from the top of the head to the feet, the creature measured sixty-two inches long, about the size of her. This would be the size of the creature standing on its hind legs. Measuring the size of the legs to the shoulder and adding the head, she approximated the animal stood about forty inches tall, walking on all fours like a coyote. Lengthwise, it measured fifty-two inches. The scale showed the animal's weight to be ninety-four pounds.

Studying the body, she searched for identifying marks such as scars and signs of injury. There were the two bullet wounds to the head, one in the forehead and one just above the orbital socket of the left eye. There were also wounds on the legs and stomach, most likely from running through the spikes planted by Carson along the trail. She rolled it over to the X-Ray machine where she planned to do a few scans to see if it would reveal bone abnormalities and the locations of bullets or other objects. She would get one of the skull as well to get images of the teeth.

One of the legendary attributes of the chupacabra had been the large, fanged teeth, characteristics which caused it to appear different from a coyote. A coyote has forty-two teeth, which are adapted for eating meat. It has large, round, pointed canines for grabbing and stabbing prey, and blade-like premolars and molars for both shearing and crushing bones. This animal had an enormous head that was thirty inches long and made up of a large jaw with two wide zygomatic bones. Its massive cheeks housed powerful biting muscles.

The animal's mouth contained a mixture of different tooth types, which seemed to match more closely to an omnivore capable of foraging for plants, certain plants like roots and tubers, but also scavenging carrion, just like African warthogs. Yet the long canine teeth on the top of the jaw gave it characteristics of a saber tooth cat. A third smaller fang was on the top jaw between the two much longer fangs. She found evidence for an omnivorous lifestyle coming from the animal's pointed incisors, recurved pointed serrated canines, serrated premolars, and a mobile jaw joint.

She examined the mouth and jaws of the animal. The legend said the animal fed by draining the blood of its victims. The design of the front teeth allowed the animal to pierce the skin of livestock. Following analysis, animals examined in reported chupacabra cases were ruled to be common animals. Studies showed those animals were physically incapable of sucking blood because the mouth and jaw structure prevented the animal's mouth from forming a seal that would allow it to suck the blood. The structure of this animal was different, but with the two wide cheekbones, Sophie could not determine if it had the ability the other suspected animals did not have. The unknown structure of the jaws did make it more likely than a coyote.

The skull also had unusually pronounced eye sockets that housed brown eyes that glowed red at night. At the top of the head and running down the length of the animal's back was a pronounced spinal ridge with scruffy, black, coarse hair. Other than the spine, the beast was mostly hairless, with a leathery greenish-gray skin. Prior investigations revealed that the animal was some known animal with various stages of sarcoptic mange, but looking with a magnifying glass there were no signs this animal ever had hair.

She analyzed the claws of the animal. The claws on both the hands and feet were like a wolf or coyote, except the second and third toes being nearly conjoined. The animal possessed long, sharp claws on each foot. Its front legs were significantly smaller than the rear, causing the animal to lean forward when on all fours like a hunkered down dog ready to pounce. The hind legs were thin, but muscular and strong. Its hips allowed full rotation for the animal to not just raise up on its hind legs for short periods of time like a bear, but was capable of full locomotion on two legs. Sophie recalled many reports of the chupacabra being like a dog or coyote, but the tail of this animal was much larger. The tail was thirty-eight inches long and was thick enough to provide some sense of balance to the animal while on its hind legs.

Sophie removed her gloves and looked for a few syringes to collect blood. She paused and thought about the creature's habitat. An animal that was thought to be a chupacabra just last year turned out to be a raccoon, and the characteristics of that animal, other than its appearance, matched those of a raccoon. It lived in a tree and ate food with its hands.

A true chupacabra, at least based on the urban legends, would not live in a tree, or eat in that manner. The animal on the table was too large to live in a tree, and Sophie knew from her conversation with Carson that this lived in a nest, like a coyote or a boar. She was aware that over the last couple of weeks, eyewitness reports and newspaper articles verified the animal had attacked livestock. That was another discrepancy from the Ratcliff raccoon chupacabra that ate corn like a regular raccoon. While no one reported seeing the animal in the process of attacking livestock, it attacked Ty by grabbing at him with its front arms, then moving in with the large teeth.

Some say the legend of the chupacabra began after a woman in Puerto Rico saw the movie Species a few weeks prior. The description of the creature she said she saw attack her livestock, a bipedal creature with a spiked back and glowing red eyes, became the basis of the urban legend. The internet was new and untamed then, and the legend of the chupacabra rapidly spread in popularity. It is one of the earliest examples of something going viral online.

This popularity of the creature and limited fact checking caused sightings to spread to other countries, including the United States, especially in southern Texas. But this creature was real, and it was dead on her table. The physical makeup of this animal also appeared to answer the question of how the chupacabra transitioned from a Hollywood monster to a dog-like creature. What on the surface seemed like two distant descriptions made sense with this animal's ability to move efficiently on two or four legs. But she still didn't know what the creature was.

Sophie put on a fresh pair of gloves and prepared to take blood samples. She drew six vials, which would be sufficient for analysis. She used tweezers and sterile plastic bottles to gather hair samples from the spine to be used in the DNA testing. Using the forceps, she removed two of the animal's front claws and dropped them into a sterile bottle. Looking over the animal, she paused to ensure she hadn't missed anything. Satisfied with her examination of the animal's external characteristics, and the blood, nail, and hair collection, it was time to look inside the beast.

Before cutting, she placed the animal on a rubber block to extend the body's arch and to provide greater access to the chest and abdomen. Sophie began the chest and abdomen autopsy by making a Y-shaped incision, the two arms of the Y running from each shoulder joint, to meet at mid-chest and the stem of the Y running down to the pubic region. Next, she examined the organs in place by removing the rib cage using a rib cutting saw. This allowed her to begin an abdominal examination and free the intestines by cutting along the attachment tissue with a scalpel. The animal's organs were examined within the body, removed by the Virchow technique, then weighed and examined in further detail. She took tissue samples from the organs, including the brain, and tested the stomach contents.

Sophie kept the organs outside of the animal for testing. After the completion of the examination, she planned to send the body to a taxidermist for preservation, or cremate the remains, including organs not used in the analysis. That was a decision she would leave for Carson. She was there only to analyze the body and determine the identity of the animal.

She had everything she needed for the DNA testing, but the examination would take the entire workday. Testing would have to wait for tomorrow. She removed her gloves and turned off the light in the exam room.

Following a quiet night at home watching *Law & Order: New Orleans on Netflix*, Sophie returned Thursday morning and prepared for the testing. Some tests set up the night before were ready for analysis today. She jumped into her work, eager to see if she could solve the puzzle. A complete blood count analyzed the red cell and white cell count of the animal. The tests returned numbers that made it appear to be normal for a wolf, but the lymphocytes were high, showing a potential infection, stress, cancer, hormonal imbalance, or other conditions within the animal. Analysis of the blood samples revealed high levels of mercury.

Brain tissue analysis revealed no signs of rabies, which would make Ty feel more comfortable. The stomach contents analysis revealed the animal's stomach only contained large levels of blood, but also plant matter, including apples.

"Interesting," she said. "The animal is an omnivore that eats many roots and tubers, but also supplements itself on blood. It must have a mutation that causes it to be deficient in some vitamin or mineral," she thought.

The analysis of the animal's claws revealed dirt between the nail and skin, showing it pawed the ground to dig up food, but also it contained fibers that matched other animals. Hair and skin samples matching cows, goats, and a human, that was most likely Ty, were detected. To Sophie, this showed that the animal used its front legs to hold its victim prior to giving a killing blow with the teeth.

To begin the DNA sequencing, Sophie placed the collected DNA on the end of a slab of a gelatin-like substance. She placed electrodes at one end of the gel and applied an electrical current. This caused the DNA molecules to move through the gel, and smaller molecules move through more rapidly, allowing her to separate the DNA molecules into different bands according to their size. Electrophoresis can only separate about five hundred bases into clear bands— causing the need for chopping DNA up into small pieces to sequence it.

Following sequencing, she entered the results into the online database and waited for a match. She let the system run and continue searching throughout the day as she carried on with other projects she needed to complete. She expected results by the end of the day and planned to check before going home.

Late that afternoon, she returned to check the results of the test. The online database showed a high similarity to a known match. She stared at the findings with a surprised look and a crinkled brow, then sat down. She thought for a minute, then turned to the computer and searched online for further information.

"This makes little sense," she said under her breath.

Thinking about possibilities for potential answers, she picked up the phone and called a friend to help with the information. After providing some initial details, her friend stated she would call her back after she reviewed an account that may answer some of Sophie's questions.

An hour later, Sophie's phone rang with the information she requested. Satisfied with the findings from her friend, she ended the call, and called Carson.

"Hello?" answered Carson.

"Hello? Hello?" Sophie replied, having difficulty hearing Carson. "What's all that noise?" she asked.

"Oh, sorry. Let me step outside," he said.

"What?" asked Sophie.

Carson walked to the nearest door and stepped outside Freeman Coliseum.

"Can you hear me now?" asked Carson.

"Yes, that's better. Where are you?"

"Fred Dalton gave us some tickets to a WNBA game, and since we've never been to a game, we decided to go before we wrap up and head back to Austin this weekend," Carson replied. "Tonight the San Antonio Stars are playing the Phoenix Mercury, so it should be a good game," he said. "Any news on the animal we dropped off?"

"Yeah. That's what I was calling about. I examined the body and dictated the physical characteristics of it, took blood work and tissue samples, and ran the DNA tests like we talked about," said Sophie.

"Sounds thorough," replied Carson. "What'd'ya find out?" he asked.

"The findings were unusual. The bloodwork showed high levels of mercury. There is a chance there was contamination from the lake water near the power plant. There were a lot of sightings in the area, so it spent a lot of time passing through there and drinking the water. That could have caused some slight mutation, but I am uncertain how much. I found that besides blood, it also eats plants. The blood likely helps it fulfill some missing nutrients it didn't get enough of in its diet. But those aren't the strange things," she said. "We got a match with the DNA in the database… but it made little sense at first," she reported.

"What didn't make sense? What does it match to?" asked Carson.

"It matched the DNA of a hyena," she said.

"Hyena? But there are no hyenas that live in Texas," said Carson.

"There's something else unusual with that too," she said. "Hyaena is the genus that includes two living species. There's the striped hyena and brown hyena," she said. "They are mostly from Africa, but the striped hyena also inhabits western Asia. There is another genus called Crocuta that represents the laughing hyena, also of Africa. And there is genus Proteles which has the aardwolf hyena. It sometimes called a jackal and lives in Africa," she added.

"Okay, but none of those are in Texas," injected Carson.

"Science recognizes those animals as four species of modern-day hyena, and they have similar shaggy coats. But… There is evidence of a fifth hyena. It is one that has largely been unstudied and forgotten," she said.

"What is that hyena? And did it live in Texas?" asked Carson.

"No, still Africa. This was a creature depicted in three different illustrations from a 19th-century book, Volume II of The Natural History of Dogs... Including Also the Genera Hyaena and Proteles. It was published in 1840 with illustrations by Charles Hamilton Smith and engraved by William Home Lizars. It showed an animal that was mostly hairless, except for a coarse dorsal mane and some tufts of fur on its tail. It was called the naked hyaena of the deserts of Nubia," she reported.

"And the DNA of this chupacabra matches the naked hyena from Nubia?" clarified Carson.

"Yes, but our guy is much thinner, likely from some level of malnourishment. And our guy is not a guy. It's a girl…. and she is pregnant," revealed Sophia.

"Holy crap! So that means there are more of them out there?" asked Carson.

"Wolves and hyenas are separate species, so they cannot breed, so likely, yeah… it means there are probably more in existence," she said. "Or someone artificially inseminated it."

"But one thing is still not clear," began Carson. "How did this animal from Africa get to Texas?"

"That was odd to me too, so I called my friend Valerie at the San Antonio Historical Society. I asked if she had ever heard of hyenas being in Texas."

"Did she have any information?" asked Carson.

"Just in the past month the Historical Society received some items from an estate sale and recently finished cataloging them in the system. One thing was an old journal from Ephraim Fontaine," she said.

"Who is Ephraim Fontaine?"

"In the late 1860s a Swiss landscape designer John J. Duerler wanted to open the first zoological exhibit in San Antonio. He thought it would be a huge attraction for people to see animals from around the world they would otherwise never see. It was going to be a private exhibit, but he petitioned San Antonio to allow it to be housed in San Pedro Park, near where the zoo is today. Humphrey Whitman and Ephraim Fontaine were businessmen who moved to the area from Adams County, Ohio and they saw the opportunity to make money if they could open an exhibit of their own in Bexar County before Duerler received approval for his. They didn't seek the city's permission and tried to do it themselves. They were in a hurry and hired cheap labor to build the exhibit quickly. Whitman and Fontaine tried to find the rarest of animals to bring in so that after Duerler opened his, they would still be the better exhibit. Two of the animals they acquired were naked hyenas from Nubia. Fontaine acquired them from an expedition to Africa just months before and had them shipped to the United States," she added.

"That explains how those animals came to Texas." "What happened once they were here?" Carson inquired.

"According to the journal, because of the shortcuts in construction and the use of cheap labor, there were some issues. They managed to get their exhibit up first, but a fire destroyed it before they had the chance to open to the public. Many animals died, but some escaped, including two Nubian naked hyenas. Fontaine's journal said he and Whitman formed expedition parties to search for the missing animals. They caught and killed some of the wild animals, but they did not find the hyenas and a couple of other animals," she concluded.

"So likely the creature we found and called the chupacabra are descendants of those missing unknown species of hyenas that were never recaptured? Somehow, they survived in the wild, breed, and lived undetected for the past one hundred years," said Carson.

"Yes, that's what it looks like," said Sophie. "The DNA matches up to the little-known records we have, and the journal explains how the animals got to San Antonio… and we have one here so it must mean they survived," she said.

"That is a wild story," he said. "I will have to Google some images of this animal, but just a few questions come to mind. There have been hundreds of sightings, but everything previously captured was later identified as common animals. If these things are out there, and if ours is pregnant… why hasn't anyone else caught one before?" wondered Carson.

"It could be there are more out there, but this one became more active in the community where people could see it, and you just happened to shoot one," Sophie responded. "Or maybe it was created and introduced into the ecosystem."

"That seems farfetched, but we will share the details of the case, present the evidence, and I guess the rest of the scientific community can come up with theories and further research," said Carson. "Thanks for all your hard work on this. We couldn't have done it without you."

"What about the body?" asked Sophie. "What do you want to do with it?"

"I think we should send it to a local taxidermist and let the town keep it. I'm sure people would like to come and see this animal once word gets out. Might help the local businesses with increased tourism," he suggested.

"There's Black Feather Taxidermy on US-181. We can send her there."

Still scratching his head from Sophie's findings, Carson went back inside the arena to join his friends. He sat down just as the horn blew to signal the game was about to start. Throughout the first half, the team talked about what Sophie's findings meant and their experiences over the past week. They also enjoyed their first WNBA game, as San Antonio took a 19-7 first quarter lead and were still up 32-27 at the half.

Carson was a little sad Dianna Taurasi, a player he was familiar with from online videos, was not playing this season.

Leilani Mitchell was filling in for her and put up fifteen points during the game. DeWanna Bonner had seventeen, Cayla Francis thirteen, and Candice Dupree twelve, but the home crowd got to go home happy as Sophia Young-Malcolm scored twenty-one, Danielle Robinson with fifteen, and Kayla McBride with eleven. Danielle Adams only had five points, but she made a three-pointer and recorded six rebounds.

The Phoenix Mercury had a strong third quarter with twenty-seven points, which marked their combined scoring in the first half, and took a 54-48 lead heading into the last period. But the Stars rallied and finished with an exciting 76-71 victory. The investigators were elated with the game and came away with respect for the play of both teams.

"Wow! I didn't know the WNBA was this exciting. I will come to more games," said Ty. "These women play hard and are exciting to watch!"

"Agreed!" said Carson as he tapped the edge of his plastic beer cup against his friend's cup.

"This will probably be our last night in town," said Kareem. "We should get a group selfie of our first WNBA game."

"Who's up for hitting a couple of downtown sites? The night is still young!" said Carson.

"We probably should at least visit the Alamo," suggested Tegan.

"You're right, and it's about five miles away," Ty said as he consulted the mobile map on his phone. "Let's just take Houston Street over… and guess what is close to the Alamo?"

he asked with an inviting, upbeat tone. The other three looked at each other, uncertain of the correct response.

"Alamo Beer Company!" Ty said enthusiastically.

"Since we're this close…" said Carson.

On east Houston, Tegan stopped at the light to turn right onto Chestnut Street. On the corner was a Red Roof Inn.

"Why didn't we stay at this one?" she questioned Carson.

"This would have been a better fit for tonight," he said, "but overall, the other location worked better."

She continued down Chestnut and four streets later made a right onto Lamar. The brewery was on the right-hand side and well-lit giant letters on the side of the building spelling out ALAMO provided an inviting entrance. The bar was crowded because of the game, nearby concerts, and the events from Beer, Bacon, and Bingo were continuing, but the team were lucky enough to find a table.

Kareem's eyes widened, and he turned toward Tegan as he noticed the offering of candy-coated, chocolate dipped bacon. The Box Street Social food truck was there, and Myles Smith was playing guitar and singing Ants on the Melon. They each ordered a different beer: Tegan the Golden Ale, Kareem the Amber Lager, Carson the Pilsner, and Ty the German Ale. As they drank and enjoyed the beers, Ty was pleased with the German pale ale, noting the traditional style that isn't often found with the balance of hops balanced with the malty finish.

"We should just stick around for one since we want to hit up the Alamo," said Tegan. "I mean, it will be closed, but we can walk around the outside of the plaza."

"Plus, there is a haunted saloon right there near the plaza," mentioned Carson.

"How can you beat ghosts and beer?" asked Ty.

Kareem dropped twenty dollars on the table, placing a salt shaker on top, and the group headed back to the car.

Driving back down Chestnut Street, Carson noticed something out the car window.

"What is that?" he asked. "Let's check it out!"

Tegan steered the car toward the strange object.

"It's a giant buffalo nickel!" she said.

Indeed it was. Outside Old Time Wooden Nickel Company on 345 Austin Road stood what was described as the world's largest wooden nickel. Carson imagined that was an accurate description as it measured three feet, four inches in diameter and five and a half inches thick. One thing was for certain, it was a photo op he was not about to pass up. He tossed Kareem his cell phone and bolted out of the car to stand beside the roadside attraction. Tegan parked the car, and the group joined him for a selfie with the nickel.

"Check!" he yelled as he returned to the car and continued the journey to Alamo Plaza.

"Wait, we need to get a selfie with the Alamo in the background," replied Kareem.

"We can park here, walk over to the Alamo, then walk over to the Menger Hotel Bar across the street," suggested Tegan.

As they walked the plaza, it surprised them how small it seemed. The image of the Alamo and the status it achieved in

American history caused them to picture a large facility. And once it was. What remained today were just two buildings: the Alamo Shrine, or church, and the Long Barracks. The plaza itself was once part of the original courtyard of the Alamo. The grounds were lovely, and the ancient live oak was an awesome sight.

Carson could feel the history and passion of those who fought in the Texas Revolution of 1835. They observed the plaque and bronze line in the patio that marked the spot where in 1836 Col. William Travis used his sword to draw a line in the sand and asked his men to join him in the battle that would become the fall of the Alamo.

"It would be cool to do some EVPs and thermal imaging around here," said Carson. "Another time…"

Content with their time at the plaza, they continued walking, crossing over East Crockett Street, and coming to the Menger Hotel Bar. It was reported to be the most haunted hotel in San Antonio, and the bar still contained bullet holes from the Old West days. The hotel contained an elaborate stained-glass ceiling and lighted columns in the lobby, but the group was more interested in the bar. It was the bar that was modeled after the bar in the British House of Lords and is also a spot where Teddy Roosevelt recruited the Rough Riders. Legend proclaimed it to be the spot where more cattle deals went down in Texas than anywhere else in the state, even today. It was San Antonio's oldest continually operated saloon and the first bar in Texas to have ice, which was great with the saloon's margarita on the rocks.

The history was present in the air. Looking at the bar's decorations, the bullet holes in the wood, and knowing the pieces of American history that took place inside the walls added to the paranormal attraction of the building.

"I don't know if we will see any spirits tonight, other than some tequila or whiskey, but this is a cool place," said Ty.

"Spirts sound good," said Carson, "but I will stick to beer," he said as he ordered a Saint Arnold Elissa IPA. Kareem also stuck with beer and ordered the Pedernales Brewing Company LOBO Negro.

Tegan continued the trend with a Real Ale Fireman #4, and Ty made it unanimous and found a Jester King Biere de Syrah.

"Now this stuff right here, this is the shit! A little tart, subliminal funk, and lots of fruit. Plus it's a bomber, so good score!" exulted Ty.

"Here's to a good and successful adventure," said Carson.

"And we all survived, at least mostly in one piece," said Ty.

"Let's wrap it up this Saturday with a town hall meeting to let the community know what we found, then we can head back to Austin and maybe get some rest after this," he suggested.

CHAPTER 17

LAST DROP

SATURDAY, JUNE 27, 2015

News spread through the small town of Elmendorf, and for the second weekend in a row, locals packed City Hall to hear about the creature that had been terrorizing the community. This time the creature was dead and there were several reporters eager to learn more about the animal. Many wanted to see the animal and asked where it was. Carson reassured everyone they could see the animal one day.

"It is with a local taxidermist, and he should complete the work in between eight to twelve months," he said. "When it's ready, we will come back down here for the unveiling. Since our investigation wrapped up and we were able to preserve the body, we have had talks with Mayor Michael Galvan. Plans are under way to build a room onto the side of City Hall. This room will house an exhibit for the animal once they receive the mount," Carson revealed.

The team showed a presentation that included photos of the animal, information about what they learned, and an artist rendering of what a naked hyena looked like. The findings were unexpected, and some final test results were still outstanding. Carson confirmed additional tissue and hair samples were sent to three independent labs for further analysis. This would allow analysis from multiple sources to verify the team's analysis. Sophie sat with the team during the press conference to address questions related to her part in the DNA testing and analysis.

After the presentation, most of the crowd remained, hoping to get a chance to talk with the men and women who had captured the creature and eliminated future threats to the livestock in the community. News reporters interviewed each member of the team, the flash of lights from cameras filling the room. This would be a big story for the local print media and the TV news. The immediate media frenzy threw the team into a spotlight they expected, but it turned out to be far greater than they imagined.

Once the word spread online, it would bring people from far and wide to town, even more once the exhibit opened. Lily & Jonathan Shaw were in attendance, as were Jordan Phillips, Philip Cooper, Ronaldo Amaya, and Sharon Chapman. Each thanked the team for meeting with them and working to solve the mystery. Dexter Allen was there to compare the photos of the animal captured to the one he photographed weeks ago. The match satisfied him.

As the crowd finally dwindled, Fred & Jess Dalton stepped forward to greet the crew.

"We can't thank you enough," said Fred. "I hope this takes care of your expenses," he said, handing Carson a check for ten thousand dollars. "But it's more than just us. The entire community appreciates what you've done here. Yesterday we put together a car wash and we held a collection with some of the local businesses. People chipped in to say thank you," said Fred. He handed Carson a second check for another thirty-five-hundred dollars.

"'Preciate it! I'm glad we could help, and the community can get back to normal not worrying about livestock or what's out there in the night," said Carson.

As Fred and Jess left, Freddie Marshall, Caitlin, and Ellie came to say their goodbyes.

"Hey, Freddie. We'll stop by tonight and move those cages and the goat up to the side yard. Tater will come by in the morning to pick them up," said Carson.

"We really appreciate your hospitality," said Tegan.

Natalie Simmons stood ready to lock up the building. Carson, Kareem, Tegan, Ty, and Sophie walked out with her and stood at the front door thinking about their week-long adventure.

"We can clean up the campsite tomorrow, then head back to Austin," suggested Carson. "But what about tonight?"

"Whatcha say we stop for one last San Antonio beer?" suggested Kareem.

"I am in," said Ty.

"Join us?" Tegan asked Sophie.

"I don't know," she said with a shy chuckle as she pushed her glasses up. "I don't drink beer very often," she said. Carson put an arm around her shoulder. "You were a big part of this team and our investigation. It's time you learned!" he said.

"Where shall we go?" asked Kareem.

"Let's hit up the northwest side of town," said Ty. "I heard a new place just opened up last week. We might as well break them in while we are introducing Sophie to craft beer," suggested Ty.

"I'm game," said Carson.

"Mad Pecker Brewing it is!" said Ty. "They just opened July 18, so it is a new hot spot."

Arriving at the pub, they walked in and found an open table on the outside patio. Being a new location, it was busy, as locals wanted to check out the newest entrant in the craft beer scene on that side of town. A young, short-haired brunette server named Paige approached the table to take their order.

"Good evening, y'all. Can I get ya started on something to drink?"

Looking over the menu, Ty asked, "Do you have any house beers?"

"We have a twenty-four-tap system that's filled with local, state, and national craft beers. Right now we don't have any of our own beers on tap yet, but they're coming soon," said Paige. "We have a one barrel, thirty-one-gallon system and will be using it to brew rye IPAs, English-style beers, and a cucumber wheat beer with orange and lime notes that have been winning local home brewing awards for a couple of years," she said.

Kareem noticed a flyer for Freetail Brewing Company night on August 19 and pointed it out to Carson. They would hand free glassware out to customers ordering one of three Freetail beers on tap.

"Might have to drive back down for the glass," said Carson. "Something to drink that Old Bat Rastard in perhaps?" he said.

Ty replied, "It is important to have the proper glassware."

"Yesterday was our Ranger Creek glass night featuring Purple Rhine, one of the newer beers from Ranger Creek," said Paige.

"I'll have one of those," said Tegan.

Kareem ordered a Real Ale Brewing Company Full Moon Rye IPA and Ty an Oasis Texas Brewing Company Meta Modern IPA. That left Sophie and Carson to still order.

"Do you like sour things?" asked Carson.

"I guess so," said Sophie. "I don't really know anything about different beers. Just what comes in the can from the gas station."

"That Rogness Sophina might be a good choice then," suggested Ty. "It's a sour beer that's not too assertive, so it's a nice refreshing taste without being like a Warhead or Sour Patch," he said.

"And it's like my name, almost," Sophia said with a giggle.

"I guess that leaves just me," said Carson. "How about a Guadalupe IPA?" he selected.

"Sounds good," said Paige. "I will be right back to take your food order," she said.

"This adventure was more than I could have imagined," said Tegan. "But in the end, I learned about cryptids, and I learned a lot about myself. I learned that even though I was scared during the investigation, I was able to mostly handle it enough to contribute to the team," she said.

"Me too. I know at first I thought it was going to be just a fun beer trip, but it was great to look behind the curtain and see what's out there in the world," added Kareem.

"We had just one mishap," replied Ty, touching his shoulder. "And that's not terrible. I am already feeling better. It was great getting back out into the woods and this time finding something," he said.

"I think once the news breaks, we will get a lot of calls," said Carson. "Who knows what is out there? You hear stories of unknown creatures from every culture in the world. I think this will prove that these things are out there, and people will take sightings more seriously. I like the way we functioned as a team. It would be better if we didn't almost sacrifice Ty, but I think we can improve over time," said Carson.

"What happens when the press asks about our background and who we are?" asked Tegan.

"We should come up with a team name," suggested Ty.

"Yes, maybe we could come up with an acronym. You know, how the Ghost Hunters are T.A.P.S., and the Mountain Monster guys are A.I.M.S."

"What would we be?" asked Kareem.

"Something with cryptids… What works have a C? Or Austin and A? Austin Cryptid… but what else?" brainstormed Carson.

"Maybe the acronym itself could be a cryptid, like YETI," suggested Ty.

"YETI… I like it," said Tegan. "But what would it stand for? Texas for the T…" she followed.

"Yeah, and maybe Investigation or Investigators," added Kareem.

"Excellent suggestions. But the Y and the E are challenging. Enigma? Entity? Hell, I don't know," Carson said as he sipped his beer.

As the group pondered the possibility of a name, they heard loud music from a car radio from someone driving past the brewery on South Presa Street with their windows down and the Jungle Love by Morris Day and the Time blasted from the sound system.

"That's it!" said Ty.

"What's it?" replied Carson.

"TIME… Texans Investigating Mysterious Entities," suggested Ty.

"Hey, that's not half bad," said Carson.

"I dig it," replied Tegan. Kareem was also in agreement.

"T.I.M.E. it is," replied Carson.

"So if we go with T.I.M.E., who is Morris Day and who is Jerome?" asked Ty.

"Don't ever say an unkind word about the Time!" said Carson quoting the beginning line from Jay and Silent Bob Strike Back.

"I'm not sure who will be Morris Day or Jerome, but let's get a group selfie here at the brewery to celebrate our first adventure as the T.I.M.E. Agency. Sophie, you get in here too. You're part of this adventure," said Kareem.

Five minutes later, Paige returned to the table.

"Are we ready to order?" she asked.

"Can we get two orders of the Texas poutine steak fries, three orders of the citrus marinated chicken street tacos, one croque monsieur, and a pepperoni pizza?" asked Carson.

"You got it!" Paige said as she returned behind the bar to place the order.

Looking at the people around the table, Carson reflected on the past three weeks.

"Here's to new friends, new adventures, and to the T.I.M.E. Agency," he said, hoisting a glass. Everyone at the table raised their glass to meet his.

"About three weeks ago, I was alone, depressed, and uncertain of the future. Then one night I ran into Ty after several years. Even though we all have only known each other for a few weeks, we've already been through a lot together. A lot more than most people who have been friends for years," he said.

"Cheers!" everyone said as they clinked glasses and took a drink.

As they waited for their food to arrive, Carson's phone buzzed with a notification. He continued the conversation with the group, but picked up the phone to check the message. It was an Expedia sale alert, which he usually would dismiss, but after this crazy week, he looked. He scrolled through the destinations listed as on sale in the email.

"Maybe a trip would be nice," he said aloud.

"A trip?" questioned Ty. "To where?"

"I don't know," pondered Carson as he continued to look at the list. "I can book the trip throughout the end of the year.... a fall trip sounds nice. Maybe to peep a leaf?" replied Carson.

"Peep a leaf? Where would you do that?" asked Kareem.

Carson took a sip and contemplated new adventures

"New England sounds nice.... what do you all say?" asked Carson.

BEER LIST

Alamo Beer Co. Amber Lager

Alamo Beer Co. German Pale Ale

Alamo Beer Co. Golden Ale

Alamo Beer Co. Horchata Porter

Alamo Beer Co. Pilsner

Anheuser-Bush Bud Light American Adjunct

Anheuser-Bush Budweiser North American Lager - Light

Austin Beerworks Peacemaker Pale Ale

Austin Beerworks Pearl Snap Pilsner

Black Star Co-Op Brimstone B.A. Cantankerous Dockhand Porter

Black Star Co-Op Brimstone B.A. Crotchety Dockhand Porter

Black Star Co-Op Brimstone B.A. Insubordinate Dockhand Coffee Porter

Black Star Co-Op Brimstone B.A. Rebellious Dockhand Porter

Black Star Co-Op Brimstone B.A. Recalcitrant Dockhand Porter

Black Star Co-Op Conceit Pale Ale

Black Star Co-Op El Vulcano Rye IPA Cask

Black Star Co-Op Epsilon Scotch Ale

Black Star Co-Op Moebius Russian Imperial Stout

Black Star Co-Op Waterloo Berliner Weisse

Branchline 5am To Midnight Dark Ale

Busted Sandal Brewing 210 Ale Blonde Ale

Busted Sandal Brewing Slippery Rock IPA

Freetail Brewing Co. #Whalezbro American Wild Ale

Freetail Brewing Co. Ananke (2013) Aged American Wild Ale

Freetail Brewing Co. Bat Outta Helles Lager

Freetail Brewing Co. Texicali Brown Ale

Freetail Brewing Co. Yo Soy Un Berliner Berliner Weisse

Guadalupe Brewing Co. Guadalupe IPA

Guns & Oil Maverick Lager

Independence Brewing Co. Austin Amber Red Ale

Jester King Black Metal Farmhouse Imperial Stout

Jester King Biere de Syrah Saison

Jester King Vernal Dichotomous Saison

Lakewood Brewing Company Mole Temptress Imperial Milk Stout

Lone Pint Yellow Rose

Naughty Brewing Bourbon Barrel-Aged Kentucky Streetwalker
    Imperial Vanilla Porter

Naughty Brewing I Think She Hung the Moon Saison

Oasis Texas Brewing Company Meta Modern IPA

Pabst Brewing Company Lone Star Beer North American Adjunct

Pedernales Brewing Company LOBO Negro Dunkel Munich Lager

Ranger Creek Brewing & Distilling Bourbon Barrel-Aged Imperial
Brown Ale

Ranger Creek Brewing & Distilling Love Struck Hefeweizen

Ranger Creek Brewing & Distilling OPA (Oatmeal Pale Ale) Pale Ale

Ranger Creek Brewing & Distilling Purple Rhine Berliner Weisse

Ranger Creek Brewing & Distilling Red Headed Stranger IPA

Ranger Creek's Small Batch Series No. 4 Small Batch Series No. 4

Ranger Creek Brewing & Distilling Strawberry Milk Stout

Real Ale Brewing Company Fireman #4 Blonde Ale

Real Ale Brewing Company Full Moon Rye IPA

Red Horn Coffee House & Brewing Co. You Be Forty Red Ale

Rogness Sophina Sour/Wild Ale

Saint Arnold Brewing Company Elissa IPA

Saint Arnold Brewing Company Bishop's Barrel 8 Imperial Stout

Southerleigh Brewing Co. Darwinian IPA

Southerleigh Brewing Co. Dog Ate My Alarm Milk Stout

Southerleigh Brewing Co. Putin's Revenge Russian Imperial Stout

Southerleigh Brewing Co. Seawall Belgian White Blonde Ale

Southerleigh Brewing Co. Smoke on the Water Rauchbier

Southerleigh Brewing Co. Straight Outta Hopton Double IPA

Spoetzl Brewery Shiner Bock

ABOUT THE AUTHOR

Mark Trollinger is a fan of cryptozoology and craft beer. He grew up in Yellow Springs, Ohio and attended the University of Rio Grande in Rio Grande, Ohio - not far from Point Pleasant, WV, thus igniting Mark's interest in cryptozoology, beginning with Mothman.

He is the author of *The Chupacabra and the Bat Rastard, Champ and a Bit of Sunshine, The Red Ghost and a Chocolate Bunny, The Loveland Frog and the Narrow Path,* and *Tegan Stone and the Gibson County Beast* - all books in the Texans Investigating Mysterious Entities (T.I.M.E.) cryptozoology and craft beer adventure series.

The Chupacabra and the Bat Rastard is the first title in the T.I.M.E. series

Mark Trollinger's

Website

Mark Trollinger's

Amazon.com Author Page

WORDS FROM THE AUTHOR

This book is a re-release and revision of the original *The Chupacabra and the Bat Rastard* book, released on my birthday September 25, 2016. Since that time, there have been slight revisions in different editions of the book. With the release of book four, I adjusted the overall size of the book to a smaller size. I liked the look of it and re-released the first three books in the series in the new format. While making that revision, I made some content revisions as well. The Field Notes section that follows in one such addition to this format.

This craft beer-inspired edition cover reflects a chalk-like design used by many breweries on their signs and menus. Nyssa Iniguez created the cover design.

FIELD
NOTES

The purpose of this section is to give a behind the scenes look at the chapters from the author's perspective. There are a few things that are probably viewed as odd that I include in this story. To give you a glimpse of how I approach a story, I keep a couple of short lists such as breweries and locations for the characters to visit. Then I have a list of odd and/or forgotten words that I attempt to work in somewhere. A third list is one of random objects that I also tried to work in. The words were things like pluviophile, ultracrepidarianism, and uhtceare. The random object list included were five hard candies, a 60% off coupon, and a Fingerhut catalog. Both lists include more examples than just these. My attempt for each book is to include random words, objects, and places in the storyline.

The goal of this series is to introduce readers to cryptids around the country. Maybe you are familiar with them, maybe you are not. I attempt to put them in a real-world setting with real life places, events, and craft beer breweries and beers. Throw in some roadside attractions, oddities, and pop culture, then you have a travelogue, if you will, of a specific city or region. Names included are not an endorsement but used to give a realistic sense of the area and what I might do on a trip if I were to visit. I would drink local beer, see local sights, and look for unique things along the road. I hope you will too.

This edition of the book features a different cover. The goal was to create a chalk-like cover that was inspired by the signage and menus used by many breweries. Nyssa Iniguez created the cover. I appreciate all her hard work and communication on this project.

One thing I plan to do is give back to the community through donating a portion of sales from every book to a non-profit cause. This book largely takes place in San Antonio, and there is mention of the San Antonio Zoo. The zoo's mission is to inspire its community to love, engage with, act for and protect animals and the places they live. That's a mission I support. For every copy of this book sold, either print or digital, I will donate 15% of the sales to the San Antonio Zoological Society. With the purchase of this book, hopefully you get a story that you enjoy, but you also support a great organization.

Dedication

I dedicate the book to my family: my wife, Susana, her kids, and her mom. Additionally named, my mom and a few friends I have met along the way in my introduction to craft beer.

Prologue

In the very first version of this book, it didn't have a prologue. One reader provided a review in which he said he wanted some action at the beginning of the story, and he had trouble understanding the time span of the story. With that, I revised it to include a prologue where we see an unknown animal kill a calf that we later learn more about in the story. I also added the second line under each chapter's name, which gives a date that the chapter occurs. That helped address the reviewer's concerns.

Chapter 1

We get a detailed look at Fred Dalton and his wife Jess in this chapter. It may be unusual to start the story without our main characters, but it was an attempt to build the drama around what was happening in the community. Some other reviewers commented that this is a book about craft beer, and we get Budweiser. The craft beer inclusion takes some time to get started. Not everyone in the book drinks craft beer, and Fred and Eric are down-home guys who enjoy the regular beer.

Chapter 2

We first meet Carson Quinn, who is as the main character in this tale, or at least one of the main characters. Right now, he isn't much of a leader. The details in the chapter regarding the layoffs and budget cuts at Round Rock schools are accurate information. I wanted to set the story in as much of the real world as possible. That's why the things mentioned in the chapters are based on real things. Carson has been lonely and depressed for some time, even though in his younger days he was optimistic and full of life. Here we get a chance encounter with his college roommate. This is the opportunity to interject craft beer into the story for the first time and show how far down Carson has fallen from the days he used to hang out with Ty.

Chapter 3

One thing I should point out is I have revised this story a few times. Initially, it went from Chapter 2, jumped right into what is now Chapter 6, and then Chapter 9. Carson's depression we pick up in Chapter 2 appeared heal immediately and he was meeting new people in Chapter 3. Looking back, it that felt inaccurate. In a story that is supposed to be based on realism, with a turn to fantasy at the end, that seemed like a fantasy world. The transition from deep depression to fully inclusive leadership of a group of people unknown to him and without experience with hunting unknown creatures could not happen that quickly. Therefore, this was an adjusted in a revision. We saw Carson have some moments of fun meeting Ty, but I wanted to show that when he got home and was alone again, he struggled with his depression.

Chapter 4

The chapter title is an homage to the episode styles from the old Bullwinkle cartoons. The episodes were named one thing, but then added or and an alternate title. I wanted to show Carson slowly coming to realize he has a problem. Looking in the mirror was a sign. So I entitled it I Saw the Sign, but then included the Bullwinkle aspect and made that or. Of course, Ace of Base sung the song I Saw the Sign, so that's why I added it. This chapter continues a back-and-forth internal struggle Carson has with himself, trying to overcome his depression. Maybe he sees this chance encounter with an old friend as a safety net that has cast to save him. Despite the occasional optimistic tones, there is the dark side that continues to pull at him.

Chapter 5

The feelings in this chapter turn upbeat. Carson remembers both he and Ty enjoyed football while they were in college, and maybe they can hang out again and have fun. Similar to the earlier chapters, a dark feeling still nags him, and the internal conflict continues. Each year, millions of Americans face the reality of living with a mental illness. Although this story takes place in June, May is Mental Health Awareness Month. During May, the National Alliance of Mental Health joins the national movement to raise awareness about mental health. Each year, they fight stigma, provide support, educate the public and advocate for policies that support people with mental illness and their families. September is Suicide Prevention Awareness Month.

If you or someone you know is in an emergency, call The National Suicide Prevention Lifeline at 800-273-TALK (8255) or call 911 immediately.

Chapter 6

The chapter title reflects that when putting something together, there is always some assembly required. The goal is to create a cryptozoological investigative team, but we have only Carson and Ty at this point in the story. There needed to be more assembly to create a team. When Ty invited Carson to hang out, he mentioned in Chapter 2 that he meets up with a few friends who like craft beer. Here we meet Kareem and Tegan, who not only help with the craft beer integration, but round out the team's formation. Tegan is a therapist, and I wanted to use that professional experience to play against Carson's depression. She helps people at work with those issues and she can help Carson. We also learn that she is a big eater, even though she's petite. In stories, they frequently show women as people who only eat salad and are afraid to eat in front of others. Why? Tegan can throw down while eating as well, if not better, than any of the guys. She can certainly hold her own and that doesn't make her any less of a woman. Always ordering a salad and water is more of a fantasy than any cryptid. At the end of the chapter, we have the call from Fred that launches the adventure.

Chapter 7

Although Carson said yes to Fred in Chapter 6, and the newly formed investigative team was down to start this adventure, Carson has second thoughts. This is his depression and internal monologue trying to convince him that this is too much, and he should just remain alone and in his house. The worries about what others will think of him creep in again and he considers calling Fred back to tell him they can't do it.

Chapter 8

This chapter is another attempt to right the ship and overcome the self-doubt feelings. He wakes up feeling good, does some chores, and gets outside. Doing so, Carson views the day with positive thoughts. After a brief internal conflict, again with thinking of cancelling the trip, Carson receives a call from Tegan, and it prevents him from doing so. Perhaps another sign of universe intervention.

Chapter 9

Waelzbro was a cool name because it kicked in a good discussion on craft beer and the pursuit of whales. Also, the book is entitled The Bat Rastard, which is a beer called the Old Bat Rastard made by Freetail Brewing in San Antonio. Another beer Freetail made was called Waelzbro. This is a lengthy chapter in which the team arrives in San Antonio, has an investigation at Fred's and later begins searching the town for witnesses. It also provides insight on Untappd if you would like to track your own craft beer journey. I created Untappd accounts as listed in the story, but it wasn't possible to keep up with those accounts. Instead, you can follow me under VanillaHeat on Untappd.

Chapter 10

The town meeting is common in many cryptid investigations, and we have one here where the team can hopefully find some leads on what people are seeing in the community. Here we pick up a couple of new characters that later appear in the story as new leads revealed.

Chapter 11

Following the Town Hall meeting, we follow up with interviews of some witnesses and gather more details about this creature. Sometimes I am not sure what direction my writing takes. I have the plan outlined when I start, but then it goes off on its own in a new direction. Where we meet the waitress in Miller's BBQ, the drawing and identification of the creature by her was unplanned, but just happened as I started writing it.

Chapter 12

Base camp starts us on the field investigations for the creature. In most shows, there are multiple investigations, and the first one is a fact-finding mission for the team to find what they are up against. That happens here as the team sets up a camp behind the Valero. Originally, I placed this location using Google maps, but later I visited the area and discovered its private property. So don't trespass • When Carson mentioned a scorched circle with indentations inside, that's based on an experience that I had. My great-uncle called my dad following a night where his wife was home alone at their farmhouse in Ohio and heard noises and saw lights that she couldn't explain but was too scared to look out the window while it was happened. When we went to their house the next day, that is what I saw.

Chapter 13

Speaking of trespassing, this chapter includes the night investigation for the chupacabra, where the group splits into two teams and each has an encounter. As the creature escapes, Carson wants to continue the hunt, but I added official Texas law to show they could not continue.

Chapter 14

The title to this chapter, initially, just popped into my head as I was writing it. But I think it popped into my head because it made sense. The scene takes place in a basement, and we learned the Old Bat Rastard has some mighty leathery wings, and wings flutter. I brought Carson's emotion back as a reflection comparable to the beer's origin of the Bat Rastard story. Jose Cruz was a favorite baseball player of mine as well.

Chapter 15

This chapter includes the last investigation and battle with the chupacabra. We could break out the traps, some investigative equipment, some personal protection, and a bit of plans gone awry.

Chapter 16

This chapter describes true life scientific data and processes about DNA analysis. The description of the chupacabra changed in a later version. When I wrote it originally, I pictured the chupacabra as an Entelodont or Daeodon, which are prehistoric creatures dubbed terror pigs. I was looking for a predator that had strong back legs and could stand up. When people think about the chupacabra, there are two versions: the original Puerto Rican version, which looks like an alien or Hollywood monster, and the more recent Texas accounts that are more like hairless dogs. When I received the artwork for the original cover from the original cover artist, Abir Hasan, the animal was thinner than the animal I described in the story, so I revised the description of the chupacabra. It could no longer be a daeodon, so I had to find something else. The naked hyena appeared as Plate XXVII in Volume II of The Natural History of Dogs Including Also the Genera Hyaena and Proteles, published in 1840, authored by Hamilton Smith, and part of a major series of animal tomes edited by Sir William Jardine and entitled The Naturalist's Library. This is a creature that existed but has faded from the body of literature except for rare internet mentions. The text is available on Amazon.

Chapter 17

To conclude the adventure, the team hits up another brewery and reflects on the adventure. Carson especially experiences gratitude for the changes to his life over the weeks of meeting Ty, Kareem, and Tegan. The reintroduction to cryptozoology and the introduction to craft beer have given him something to look forward to with his new friends who shared similar interests. In the original story the idea of the name of the investigative agency occurs in book 2, but now that I am re-releasing these books, and started using the round icon on the covers (originally starting in book 3), I thought it might be difficult for readers to identify book one and two in the series. I took the portion from the original book 2 and worked into this book so that I could add the series icon to the new cover and clearly show this is the first book in the series. The ending where Carson gets a notification and contemplates peeping a leaf is a lead into book 2.

 **Beer List**

This is a list of beers named in the story, even beers that are not craft beer. The intention of the beer list was to serve as a checklist for readers. Perhaps you are visiting San Antonio and want to try some of the beer you read about in this story. Here's your chance – an alphabetical list of every beer mentioned. I recommend check marking or highlighting the beers you try.

Let me know on Instagram or Twitter what your thoughts were on those beers.

 **Photo Challenge**

Another way I wanted to make this series interactive was to

use one of those daily photo challenges consisting of a word or phrase related to the book. Readers could post a daily photo to their Instagram page with the hashtag

#chupacabradailyphotochallenge and we could see what other readers are posting. I will start this up in January 2023. Check out my Instagram page for details: **mark_trollinger**.

SELFIE LOCATIONS

This is an Easter egg in each story. It may be something that is often passed over in reading, but in each book, there will be multiple mentions of taking a selfie. Usually by Kareem, and typically at least five. This may seem odd to include in a story about cryptids and beer. The intention with the selfies is to make the book somewhat interactive. My goal was to include spots within the location where the characters would take a selfie (they are traveling and seeing new places, after all). I thought perhaps readers would take their own selfies at those same locations and upload to social media sites using #chupacabraselfiechallenge to build a community and make it more realistic. Even though only one book was about the chupacabra, it has become basically a mascot of the entire series.

1. If you missed the locations in the story, here is a list including in this book:

2. Barney smith's toilet seat art museum (San Antonio, Tx)

3.   A group of friends at a bottle share (your choice)

4.   At a WNBA game (your choice)

5.   World's largest wooden nickel at old time wooden nickel company (San Antonio, Tx)

6.   Group photo at a local brewery (your choice)

 **Sound Booth**

When I write, I often listen to music. Austin has an eclectic music scene featuring live music. The city hosts a mixture of folk, blues, jazz, bluegrass, Tejano, zydeco, new wave, punk, and indie music scenes. I also think of country with the old honky-tonk bars like Giddy Ups. I played a lot of 1990s and prior country music like George Strait, Toby Keith, and Waylon & Willie while writing those scenes. You can get into the mood behind the story by listening to the playlist I put together.

Chupacabra Spotify Playlist